After the Rain

ANGELA HARTLEY

After The Rain

Edn. 3: September 2023

ISBN   9798387032950

Cover design by Aubrey Labitigan Jai Design
Original Photography by Tim Whiteley

Angela Hartley

After the Rain

By the Author of Finding Home & Forever Home

Acknowledgements

Special thanks to all those people who have supported me throughout the process of writing and publishing After the Rain.

To Sue Vendy, Melanie Sibborn Kay, Carol Marriott-Clayton and Roisin Robertson for their invaluable support in the editing process, searching out all the errors and typos I missed.

To Barry, my husband and number one supporter and critic.

To Andy and Sarah Molloy for all their support at Carleton News, and especially to Sarah for the inspiration for the title of this book.

Finally, to Tim Whiteley for the photography for the cover. If you are unfamiliar with Tim's work, then check out his Website at   timwhiteleyartphoto.co.uk or his Instagram at whiteley516

After The Rain

Chapter 1

New York State - 2022

It was mid-July, and the rain was pelting down as Trudie cycled the last half mile towards St. Bart's hospital, pedalling as fast as her legs could take her on her trusty, if not ancient bicycle. She lived in the quaint picturesque town of Wellstone, situated in the state of New York, far from the hustle and bustle of the larger cities America was famed for. With a population of under a hundred thousand people, it was an easy place to navigate, and a safe one to get around on a bicycle. In truth though, it was her aunt's bike and one that had been designed for shopping rather than racing, so no matter how hard Trudie pedalled, speed was not something she would ever achieve. The bike was sturdy and reliable, and above all a cheap option for getting from A to B. One day she promised herself she would invest in a car and driving lessons, or at least a bike of her own that did not look like it had come out of the last century. At the moment that was not top of her priorities.

Today's summer storm had arrived suddenly, and in Trudie's case unexpectedly. This was so unlike her, given she normally prided herself on not getting caught unawares by the elements. She routinely tuned into the local radio station for the morning news and weather updates as she was getting herself ready, but must have completely missed today's forecast. Josh had phoned, which in itself was unusual, given he was normally too busy out jogging, or at the gym to talk to anyone, let alone his fiancée!

His call had started as a pleasant surprise, but had soon gone downhill, leaving her distracted and confused as she pondered what he had been rabbiting on about. Something to do with traffic, an accident and it all being a bit of a mess; nothing was clear, and then all of a sudden, he hung up and said he'd speak to her later. Very odd, even by his standards.

The knock-on effects were that she not only missed the weather warnings on the radio, but left the house later than planned, thereby catching the heavy rain, the lunch time rush, and the inevitable traffic that brought, making her journey even longer. Today had not started out well.

Arriving at the hospital shortly before noon, Trudie noticed people looking at her, some even pointing, no doubt sniggering to themselves, seeing the state she was in. Thankfully her hair was tied back in a simple band, and dressed in denim shorts, a cropped vest and running pumps, other than looking like she had entered the Miss Wet T-Shirt competition, fingers crossed there was not too much harm done by the downpour. Provided her mascara had not run that is, but looking at some of the stares she was getting, she doubted she had got off that easily.

A quick comb through her hair, a dry off with the sports towel she had pinched from Josh and kept in her locker when she got to the staff room, plus a glance in the mirror and she should be good to go. Glamourous was not a word anyone would associate with Trudie, although anyone seeing her for the first time would instantly see her natural beauty, with her long legs, her ash-brown hair usually worn loose half-way down her back and those innocent blue eyes that had the power to mesmerise anyone who was caught off guard.

After hastily securing the bike in the rack when she arrived, she grabbed her tote bag from the wicker basket and raced towards the staff room in a final attempt to avoid being late. Punctuality was one of her watch words, and being late would not bode well for the rest of the day. This morning had really put her routine out of kilter and she needed to get herself back on track and start concentrating. Josh, and whatever his latest drama was, would need to be parked for a while; she would deal with that when she got home.

"Good afternoon, Trudie," smiled Cynthia, as she entered the locker room. "How are you doing today? You look like that rain caught you good and proper. Come here, let's get you dried off before you create a puddle on the floor," she laughed.

"Thanks. I've got a towel and some spare clothes in the locker, so just give me five minutes and I should be fine," replied Trudie not wanting to cause any fuss.

"Okay, I'll leave you to it. Come through when you're ready, and we can have a catch up, and I'll run through what I'd like you to do today," replied Cynthia, before adding "Don't hurry, it's not too busy at the moment, so take your time."

Trudie liked Cynthia a lot and in the few short months in which she had been volunteering at the hospital Cynthia had taken her under her wing and helped her build-up her confidence. Sister Cynthia Cooper was the type of woman who mothered everyone, always having time to listen and never making you feel like anything was too much trouble. As the lead practitioner on the ward, she made Trudie feel really at home and welcomed within the team. Above all, she made Trudie feel that what she was doing was of value and appreciated; principles that were of real importance to Trudie.

Trudie was a true academic who loved studying and researching anything that piqued her interests, which by anyone's standards was a list not only long, but wide and varied. She had recently graduated with a first in physiotherapy, top of her class; although like all academics, that did not guarantee success in the outside world. She had applied for several positions but soon found her CV was woefully lacking in any practical hands-on experience, and her confidence in dealing with patients limited. On paper, she knew the theory, and could comfortably recite the textbooks if asked. Having the confidence to apply that to a real live scenario was a whole new ball game. Unfortunately, this had not played out too well at interview, on the odd occasions her applications had progressed to that stage, with each successive rejection knocking her confidence further.

When a random conversation with a customer over a cappuccino at the local coffee shop alerted Trudie to opportunities to volunteer at the local hospital, she seized on the idea. Any work experience would be invaluable, so, when she enquired and discovered there were roles in the physiotherapy department, it seemed to suit her down to the ground. It was only a couple of times a week, or the occasional shift at the weekends, and that would easily fit around her part-time job at the café. Any hours would be better than nothing, and she hoped if she was lucky enough to get her foot in the door, so to speak, other opportunities could potentially open up. Most of her contemporaries had now got full-time positions, if Facebook was to be believed, so Trudie was anxious not to be left behind.

A quick call to the hospital later that morning, followed by a chat with one of their business managers, and two weeks later she was contacted to say the Physiotherapy department would welcome her support. They had apparently been impressed by her qualifications and CV, and coupled with the fact it was a voluntary role, they jumped at the chance to welcome her as part of their team. They regularly took on students doing work-based placements, so Trudie was assured that anything she did would not only be of value, but provided everything worked out well, they would even be able to offer her a reference once she moved on to a more permanent and paid position.

Now, just three months in, her nervousness and apprehension when approaching patients and talking to them about their conditions was receding, with her overall confidence steadily growing day-by-day. Trudie was relatively shy and knew her bedside manner still needed quite an amount of work for it to feel fully natural, but she no longer felt uncomfortable asking probing questions about a patient's health or wellbeing, or felt it was intrusive to delve into their personal circumstances in an attempt to deal with the wider problems, or contributing factors that so often affected the patient's recovery. Text books were well and good in providing general guidance, however no two cases were ever the same when you peeled off the layers to get to the underlying issues that might be impacting the patient's recovery, she had gleaned in her short experience from the much more experienced members of the team around her.

Trudie was still far from able to practice on a one-to-one basis, but enjoyed helping out alongside Cynthia, or one of her other team members, who were patiently teaching her; helping her to develop a love for the practical side of nursing, a feeling that had previously eluded her as she had concentrated on the theoretical side. If she was going to be successful in this particular career choice, it was obvious that 'slowly, slowly' were the watchwords, knowing there were no quick fixes on offer.

Learning to deal with people, in whatever guises they presented themselves, was always going to be a challenge, though once Trudie realised that the bedside-manner she needed at the hospital was not too dissimilar from the approach she used when she spoke to customers at the café, regularly offering a shoulder to cry on, or a ready ear for anyone who needed to offload over a coffee, the proverbial light had come on. She had a natural caring nature and, in the café, loved being able to help and support, regardless of the fact she had so little experience of life or the myriad of problems it created. So, how much more difficult could it be, when at the hospital the problems were related to a subject that she had not only studied, but had excelled at academically? Now it was just a case of working on identifying her transferable skills, and fingers crossed the rest should follow naturally.

Trudie finished drying herself off, returned the now soggy towel to her locker, and braced herself for her shift on the ward. "What delights would today bring?" she mused to herself, as she left the staff room and made her way towards Cynthia, who was attending to an elderly gentleman, who Trudie recognised from one of her previous shifts. She remembered he'd had quite a twinkle in his eye, making her laugh with some of his anecdotes about his adventures over the years. As she approached him, and he winked at her, she realised the afternoon shift was going to be much more fun than she had imagined.

Chapter 2

Betty cradled her coffee as she sat gazing out at the expanse of deep blue ocean ahead of her. Relaxing in the lounge at the bow of the ship, she could feel the sheer force of the vessel as it ploughed its way through the seas, with steely determination to get them to their next port of call. Unfortunately, today was the last day of their cruise, and tomorrow it would be time to disembark and fly home; back to normality. No more relaxing, or being pampered at every turn; no more being waited on hand and foot, thought Betty ruefully.

The cruise had been Richard's idea, but deep down she knew it was for her benefit, as he had never been one for water, or moving far from the sight of land, if she was honest. In this instance though, Richard had parked his fears, and booked what he knew his wife would enjoy, even if it had the potential to make him more than a little uncomfortable.

Cruising was something Betty had heard a lot about over the years from colleagues and friends, and the concept really excited her; travelling between iconic places of interest, in pure luxury, without the hassle of having to carry your own luggage, or do the cooking or washing up after all the fine dining that was on offer. However, whenever she had tried to engage Richard in a conversation, suggesting they might want to book a trip, he always managed to evade the subject, or in turn suggest one of their trustier holiday destinations.

Angela Hartley

Richard loved his history and visiting places of architectural or historical significance, but he did not much enjoy flying, having once had a bad experience as a young man that he had never really recovered from. He did not talk much about the detail of what had happened, other than to constantly recall the event whenever flying was discussed, in a way that suggested 'never again'. This limited their options somewhat.

Unlike Betty, wanderlust was not something he suffered from. He would quite happily relax in his armchair and view the world through the pages of a book; or latterly on his computer, where he loved to search the internet to unearth wild and wacky minutiae, about anything that had caught his attention. The weirder the facts, the more he was interested in exploring further, to the extent that by the time he had delved into whatever he had been researching, he had generally lost the thread of his original thought. History and historical architecture to him was one of those subjects that he could never exhaust, nor lose interest in, although sadly not a passion shared by the rest of the family.

Betty had reluctantly, with time, accepted the situation; so, never wanted to push too hard, always happy to go with the flow. Consequently, over the years, most of their holidays had been road trips within North America or Canada, meaning Europe, and all the history and architecture it had to offer, was perversely off limits. Betty, Annie, their daughter, when she was still at home and occasionally Rufus, their Labrador, or Lottie their previous dog, were simply packed into the car and off they set; conscripted passengers on Richard's latest adventure.

So, when their travel tickets arrived a few months ago, for a two-week cruise through the Baltics, it was not only a massive surprise, but a dream come true for Betty. The fact that Richard had planned and researched it, without her knowledge, was not altogether too surprising, as he regularly went off into his own world. The fact he had kept it a secret from not just her, but the rest of their family, was harder to believe.

The itinerary looked amazing; sailing out from the south coast of England, through the English Channel, across the North Sea, heading up through Scandinavia, visiting Copenhagen and a host of interesting European countries on route. It made Betty dizzy with excitement at the thought of seeing sites she had only ever dreamt of visiting; places she had often read about, or heard others describe; locations she had seen on television, or in the movies, or those British period dramas she loved to watch.

Richard had even tagged some extra days onto their trip to visit London for a touch of sightseeing, and perhaps a little shopping before they set sail, although she doubted their budget would allow for a splurge in Harrods. Visiting London and seeing Buckingham Palace was something else Betty had only ever dreamed of. She loved the Queen and the British royal family, and all the pageantry the country was famous for; so, the thought of witnessing the Changing of the Guard, or seeing a parade, just added to her growing excitement. Overall, it promised to be more than she could ever have imagined: a holiday of a lifetime.

As the weeks ticked by and their departure date neared, her level of anticipation grew, almost like a child waiting for Christmas morning, counting the number of sleeps until the big day arrived. It consumed her completely, to the extent that it was all she ever thought of, or talked about; providing a welcome distraction from anything else that was happening around her.

Thankfully their holiday had turned out to be a great success, with in her view, cruising to be the way forward. The countries they had visited, and the sights they had experienced, had been truly awesome. Cruising through the Stockholm archipelago was sublime, perhaps topping Betty's long list of highlights, and some of the towns they explored were so quaint and picturesque, it made her cry with pleasure; but the Belgian chocolate in Bruges was to die for! As a continent, Europe had been a pure delight, and already Betty was planning where their next adventure could be. Italy was supposed to be stunning, and the Mediterranean was also somewhere she had dreamt of visiting. All of a sudden, the world and all the amazing opportunities it had to offer had opened up before her.

Richard had in turn marvelled at the architecture, the royal palaces, the never-ending churches and cathedrals, snapping his camera at anything and everything he saw, whether it moved or not. As a history buff, exploring some of the medieval towns, understanding their cultures and visiting the museums had left him spellbound; astonished at the scope and breadth of historical events he had discovered, some that had previously eluded him, or others that he had experienced only through the pages of a book or its illustrations. Sorting through the hundreds of photos when they returned would be a project in its own right, but one Betty knew he could not wait to get stuck into.

Betty even sensed Richard had reluctantly found his sea legs, and would not be so averse to booking a future cruise, should the opportunity present itself; even allowing himself to relax on the ship and enjoy the entertainment on offer. They had danced after dinner, drank cocktails watching the sun-set, or sat holding hands through shows they would never have considered of interest, or had the opportunity to see had they taken their traditional road trip; and in so doing, it had reawakened a side to their relationship that had been dormant for some time.

The flight had also been uneventful, with Richard even commenting how much things had improved since his 'last flight!', still never confessing what had been so awful, or upsetting previously. So, whilst this holiday was coming to an end and home beckoned, Betty consoled herself with the thought that there were many more adventures ahead.

As she now sat, cradling her coffee and reflecting over these last few months, she finally acknowledged the range of feelings that had been coursing through her; feelings that until this moment she had been unable to fully articulate. At the one extreme there was the pure happiness and euphoria from planning, and eventually enjoying this holiday of a lifetime. Though that was balanced with the apprehensions and concerns, bordering on trepidations, about returning to a life completely unfamiliar to them. Home beckoned, and that meant starting the next chapter of their time together. Retirement and all that brought.

Betty knew planning the holiday had provided the perfect distraction from thinking too hard about what, in reality, life after retirement would mean for both her and Richard. She now recognised she could no longer park these thoughts, and would have to face the reality head-on as soon as they got home. They would need to establish new routines, find new challenges, even make new friends, and explore new interests to spend their time on. Above all, they would need to develop a level of tolerance for each other; something that had never really been tested before.

Theirs was generally a happy marriage, with a comfortable relationship that had matured over the years, and weathered the inevitable challenges life had thrown at them. Nearly forty years of being together, living and working and bringing their family up – where had that time gone, and what did they have to show for it? Betty realised that throughout their marriage they had both always been busy doing their own thing; following their own careers, whilst valuing their own space and independence. Each had carried out the traditional roles of husband and wife, or parents. Neither had veered too much out of their traditional boxes, with each heavily reliant on the other to make the synergy work. She would be as lost in the garage, or changing a lightbulb as Richard would be in the supermarket, or doing the laundry. Their routines had been partly what had kept them sane and together for so long.

Spending time just 'being alone together', without the distraction of a formal occupation, or the routine that provided, was going to be a whole new ball game; one Betty reflected wistfully, would be a learning opportunity for them both.

She and Richard had retired the month immediately before their holiday. Richard having reached sixty, although not entitled to a full retirement package from the bank where he had worked for nearly forty years, was awarded a healthy pension. He had risen from a lowly bank clerk, to a senior branch manager during that time. However, in recent years, he had become increasingly disillusioned with his role, and more so the direction the industry was taking, leaving him in no doubt it was time to hand the reins over to the younger generation. The financial sector was not what it had been, and some of the changes in technology, governance and the whole approach to money and investments, he felt had not only left him behind, but had left him feeling disengaged from it all.

Betty was still in her late fifties, so retirement had not been on the horizon for her. However, the thought of working, whilst Richard was at home enjoying himself, had really not appealed to her, so after seeking some financial advice, and carefully doing their sums, they agreed they could afford to both jump off the hamster wheel; meaning her fate was sealed too. She could become a lady of leisure if that was what she desired, although she could not imagine that in all honesty.

Betty had enjoyed several careers throughout her working life, whilst balancing running the home with bringing up their daughter Annie. For the last ten years she had worked with a property company 'staging homes' at the more prestigious end of the market; preparing them for sale or corporate rentals. It was a role she had not realised she would love as much as she did, discovering a creative side to her personality that she had not known existed. Having to keep abreast of fashions and designs had the added benefit of keeping her mind fresh; with travelling around the region, meeting suppliers and clients, getting her out and about, giving her the level of independence that she craved.

The property company she had worked for had been a little taken aback when she announced she was planning on retiring, but supported her decision, even offering her the opportunity to do freelance work for them, on an ad-hoc basis should retirement not suit her or fully occupy her time. The property market was booming, and Betty was good at her job; and although she had really appreciated being thought of in that way, and knew the importance of keeping her options open, she did not intend taking them up on their offer. No, on balance spending more time with Richard was her preferred option. She had so many plans for them, she had mentally written a retirement bucket-list. Top of which was spending more time travelling, and looking after their grandson Jack. The cruise had just helped put a massive tick against that first one.

Now weighing up all these feelings, Betty smiled to herself as she drained the last of her coffee. "Retirement seems to suit me more than I ever imagined it would, and with a bit more practice, I could get quite good at it!" she laughed to herself.

Picking up her bag, she headed back to their stateroom, where she expected by now Richard would have finalised their packing. He was fastidious about packing, adopting his own peculiar process, which no one, other than himself, understood. Over the years, Betty had accepted that the best action for keeping the peace, and keeping their collective blood pressures down, was just to leave him to it. She would sort it all out when they got home, after all, laundry was her department.

Chapter 3

Annie was quietly sitting in the kitchen relaxing over her morning coffee, enjoying a few moments peace, before she threw herself into what promised to be a hectic morning, when her phone beeped, alerting her to the message she had been waiting for.

> *"Hi Annie, we're arriving at 09.50. Are you still able to pick us up? Message back, if there's a problem, if not see you at the meeting point. Mom xx"*

Realising it was already nine o'clock, and even though it was at most a twenty-minute drive to the railway station, at this time of day the traffic could be unpredictable. Annie placed her coffee mug by the sink and started to get herself ready. She was someone who always liked to be prepared and in control, often getting anxious if she was on the last minute or ever unsure what was happening. She guessed she had inherited her dad's genes when it came to organisation, perhaps even bordering on OCD, if she was honest. Why could she not be more laid back like her mom, she thought to herself? Her mom never got fussed, simply took everything in her stride. Years of her dad taking charge had obviously taken their toll on her mom she presumed, and rather than letting it get her annoyed, Annie realised she must have simply got into the habit of standing back, and letting him take the lead.

As it was Saturday, there was no danger of school runs, or the morning rush into the city delaying her, but with the heavy rain, and the endless road works seeming to be at every corner these days, there was no guarantee the drive would be plain sailing either. No, she would leave in good time, and just sit in the car to wait if she got there early. Better safe than sorry was her motto.

"Please Mommy, why can't I come with you to pick Grammy and Grandad up? I haven't seen them in ages," pleaded Jack, as Annie picked up her car keys from the bowl on the unit in the hallway to drive to the railway station. He had asked the previous evening, and been told no then; he had lived in hope, even getting up early just in case his mom relented and agreed to take him.

"No Jack, you wait here with Dad and I'll be back in time for lunch. It's forecast to be wet all day today, so you'd only get soaked when we got out of the car. Also, Grammy and Grandad will be tired after their journey, so I'll just drop them off and we'll go to see them tomorrow, when they can tell you all about it. I'm sure they'll have brought you a present too, so tomorrow will give them time to unpack and find it." It was roughly a twenty-minute drive to her parents' house, so a couple of hours max round trip would see her home in time to sort lunch, and then crack on with the rest of her chores.

Jack eventually relented and sulked off to find his dad, who would no doubt be on his computer, or in his study 'doing work'. Jack loved his dad, but he was always busy, and never had time to play with him as much as his best friend Zach's dad did. Whenever Jack went around to play at Zach's house, Zach's dad was always playing football in the yard with him and his brothers, or taking them to the park for a kick around and buying them an ice-cream. Jack wished his dad was more like Zach's, or that he had someone else to play with. He would love a brother, or even a sister would be okay he presumed, or better still a dog.

Jack was five and had started school the previous autumn. Although he was young for his age, his teachers believed he had settled down well. Annie was not convinced. According to his teachers, he had apparently made a couple of friends, and was displaying good social skills for his age group; although Annie had recently noticed that Jack took any opportunity to get out of going to school, preferring to stay at home to be with her. He never moaned about anything specific, but when she prised him away from her at the school gates, she had a niggling feeling that all was not as well with her son as the teachers suggested.

Whilst Annie loved Jack to bits, and resisted keeping him off school more than was necessary, she recognised it was largely her own fault that he was so clingy, and chided herself for being too protective of him when he had been younger. Jack had been a much-longed for baby, and as their first-born child was doted on by parents and grandparents alike. His early months had been fraught though with complications, partly caused by his premature and difficult birth. It resulted in the family, particularly Annie, remaining anxious as Jack grew and developed, often at a pace she feared was slower than his peers. This anxiety had obviously transferred to Jack, who was now very insecure, and became nervous and shy around others; frequently getting fretful when left with anyone other than his parents or grandparents.

The only exception so far was with Zach, his new best friend. The two of them seemed to have bonded well, and from what Annie had seen of Zach, he seemed to be a good influence on her son; helping him to develop confidence and become a little more independent. Jack loved being around him and visiting his house, occasionally sleeping over, which Annie had to admit, was usually more traumatic for her than Jack.

Zach had come back to their house after school, but Annie recalled only the once, and had never stayed for a sleepover. For some reason, the boys preferred to be at Zach's house, and whilst Annie did not have an issue with that, perhaps it would be nice to balance it up a bit, she thought. She resolved to spend more time trying to get close to what was going on with the boys, what interests they had together, and would even try to get to know Zach's parents more; even engaging with some of the other parents, if that would help Jack settle.

Easier said than done though as the whole 'school-mom' protocol was something that, if Annie was honest, she struggled with a little. Chatting in the playground, comparing what their children were achieving and organising charity events was something that did not come naturally to her. She was quite a private person, and generally liked to keep herself to herself. Arranging play dates, or after-school activities also left her bemused. Kids these days seemed to have more social events and commitments than she could get her head around. Starting school had definitely been an education, not only for Jack, but for her too.

As she manoeuvred her way carefully through the traffic towards the railway station to meet her parents,

Annie resolved she would give this some serious thought over the next couple of days. After all, her son's happiness was far too important for her to get this wrong.

Chapter 4

Shortly before her shift was due to end, and as Trudie was finishing writing-up her notes from the last patient she and Cynthia had attended to, she stared out of the window. She saw the rain as it beat against the glass panes, bouncing off the roof below her, puddles all over the car park. Watching it now, she wished she had taken the bus instead of riding her bike into the hospital that lunchtime. The cycle ride home was going to be even worse than the journey in, she thought to herself; the idea of getting drenched again, something she was not looking forward to. The rain had taken a breather for a couple of hours mid-afternoon, and had now come back with a vengeance. She could see that the sidewalks and gutters were swamped, as the rain gushed down the drainpipes, the clouds looking ominously dark and heavy. Normally at this time of year showers were short and sharp. Today was the exception, with the storm looking like it was in for the night.

Trudie reached for her phone and dialled her fiancé, Josh. It not unexpectedly, went to voicemail. She decided to leave a message anyway on the remote chance he would pick it up in the next few minutes.

> *"Josh, is there any chance of a lift home? I'm just finishing my shift and will be done in about 15 minutes. Can you meet me and put the bike in the back of the truck? Ring me back please."*

Trudie knew Josh was not working until later that evening, so would be either at the gym, or watching sport somewhere. The chances of him picking up the message and getting back to her in the next few minutes were slim at best, but she lived in hope.

Josh was not the most reliable of people, and although she believed she loved him, she often wondered what it was about him that she actually liked, other than the fact that he was drop-dead gorgeous; tall, slim with curly blond hair, worn fashionably long, just tickling the tops of his shoulders. When they were together, they usually had fun.

They had met at university a couple of years previously; both being dragged unwillingly along to a charity ball by their respective friend groups. It was a formal black-tie affair, and both felt out of place; Trudie in her taffeta ballgown, that made her feel like a prize meringue, and Josh in his hired tux, that although it looked amazing on him, made him feel uncomfortable and conspicuous.

At one particularly awkward moment, during the seemingly vacuous speeches that dragged on for over half an hour, they noticed each other across the room; at the precise moment when Josh's eyes rolled and Trudie was struggling to hide a yawn. They had never formally met, but the look they exchanged spoke volumes, leaving them both smiling, if not a little embarrassed for being caught-out.

For the remainder of the speeches, they kept glancing over at each other, each conscious of not wanting to be accused of staring, but unable to do otherwise. As soon as the final round of applause had ended, they both rose from their chairs, and magnetically were pulled towards each other.

"Do you fancy getting out of here, and catching a beer somewhere?" was all it took for Trudie to grab her bag, tell her friends not to wait up for her, and follow him out of the room, hand-in-hand, completely oblivious to the others, or the stares they were receiving. That had been two years ago, and their relationship had developed quickly. Now it appeared to have plateaued.

Their interests were so varied, and on paper their compatibility was questionable. Josh was an all-round sportsman, having just graduated in Sports Science with a second-class degree. He enjoyed playing, watching, supporting and discussing almost any and every sport imaginable. His passion was basketball, which he played to a good standard, but he also loved soccer and played in a Sunday league team, with some of the mates he had met at the bar where he worked. Sport, in whatever guise, absorbed the majority of his time, with what little he had left being shared between Trudie and his work; although if she was honest, her share seemed to be getting smaller and smaller by the day.

Josh worked in the local sports bar four nights a week, to fill his time whilst waiting for his dream job to come along. He loved the banter with the customers, working hours that left his mornings free to go running, or off to the gym, with the continual sports coverage on multiple screens around the bar, ensuring he never missed a big fixture.

Trudie knew Josh wanted to go into professional coaching eventually and recognised he needed to build up both his experience and his client base first. He had applied to several of the larger gyms for possible opportunities, plus some of the sport federations for openings on their coaching staffs; so far nothing had materialised. For an area where there was supposed to be so many vacancies, he appeared to be struggling. Trudie felt that might have more to do with his approach, and the lack of oomph he seemed to be applying to the process, rather than his CV. On most things, Josh was laid back to the point of being almost horizontal, and launching his career definitely fell into that category.

Eventually, realising Josh was not going to pick up the message in time, Trudie resorted to calling her uncle to collect her. The rain did not look to be abating, and she really did not want to chance cycling home.

Uncle Scott was reliable, available and closer to the hospital, so just ten minutes after calling him, he had arrived, hauled her bike into the back of the car; no questions asked, and headed home.

"I think we timed that perfectly," he said, as he pulled off the parking lot; a sudden bolt of lightning striking in the distance, and the storm getting heavier.

Chapter 5

Annie arrived early at the railway station and sat in the parking lot, patiently awaiting her parents' arrival, allowing the soothing music of the radio to work its magic and relax her, after what had been a stressful journey. The roads were unusually busy, with the rain forcing more people into their cars to do even the shortest journeys; everyone seemingly in a rush to get to where they were going. The weather report had just been broadcast, confirming on and off downpours were set for the remainder of the day, something Annie was not too happy about. It was the weekend, so she had a lot of things planned once she got home, and knowing that a lot of those jobs were outside, the weather would not make her work any easier.

Although it had only been three weeks since her parents had left for their holidays, to Annie it felt much longer. The days had dragged the more they were away, and being on a ship in the middle of the Baltic Sea for most of that time, coupled with the different time zones, had meant keeping in touch had proved almost impossible. Annie loved her parents equally, with her and her mom having a particularly strong bond. She missed her dreadfully whenever she was not around, missing the closeness and the security blanket her mom unconsciously provided.

Annie had not made many friends since she had graduated from university and returned back home to Wellstone, with a lot of the school friends she had made as a teenager no longer in the area, or having drifted away, leaving her feeling pretty isolated. She relied on Betty more than was probably healthy, not only for all the practical help she provided with Jack and the house, but all the emotional support she craved. With everything that was going on in her life, this emotional crutch was a godsend.

Annie and her husband Matt had been going through a difficult couple of years since Jack's arrival. Normal communications had become a little strained, meaning it was good to have her mom around. She not only provided a listening ear, but also sage advice whenever Annie needed to bounce ideas around, or dispel those worrying theories that raged around her head whenever Jack was unwell, or something just did not feel quite right.

Annie recognised her tendency towards 'worrying issues to death', and coupled with her natural need to organise and plan everything to the nth degree, this often left her panicky and stressed on the occasions Jack did not respond, or react in a way the endless text books she studied suggested was normal. Annie often phoned Betty late into the evening if Jack would not settle, with her mom reliably there to answer; with her uncanny knack of calming whatever situation had arisen. She had missed that.

Annie also worried Matt had not bonded as well with Jack as she had, often sensing he felt the baby had not only come between them, but left him unsure what support role he was expected to play in their changing family dynamic. Although she tried to encourage him to get more actively involved in raising their child, she often did not get the support or reaction she expected.

Looking back, it probably had not helped that in the early days, Annie automatically took the leading role as the baby's main caregiver, rushing to Jack's side whenever he cried out for attention; never considering that Matt could equally have soothed him, if only she had given him the time, or opportunity to react. She had unwittingly pushed him into a role that he was neither prepared for, nor apparently felt comfortable with.

Now it was dawning on her that the effect of not encouraging Matt more in those early days, the time when he was most besotted by their new son, was that any fatherhood skills he should have developed had just not been allowed to mature. Motherhood had come naturally for Annie, but she now feared, rather than continue to work at becoming a hands-on dad, Matt had retreated; taking the easy option and simply leaving her to it.

A pattern soon started to develop. As she continued to attend to their growing toddler, and his ever-changing needs, Matt, rather than trying to muscle in, would simply take himself off to his office, or to his computer, and leave them to it. In so doing he would avoid any potential hurt or rejection. Unfortunately, although Annie had never consciously wanted this to be the case, that pattern was now well established. Matt's sense of rejection, although never voiced, was palpable Annie now recognised.

In hindsight, and perhaps being completely honest, it had been more her dream than Matt's to become parents. He had appeared really excited and supportive when she became pregnant, once he had overcome the initial shock. Having a baby so soon into their marriage was unplanned, and not something they had really discussed or thought through. Nevertheless, after they got their heads around it and started to plan, reading whatever books they could find by way of preparation for their changing circumstances, their intentions had always been to co-parent, sharing both the good and less good elements of raising their children, or so Annie had thought.

Something must have gone sorely wrong along the way, with the unfortunate effect that now the father and son bond, which everyone knew was so important in any child's development, was far from established, or evident to anyone who took the time to look closely. They lived in the same household, but were like ships that passed in the night; enjoying a relationship that had an unhealthy formality about it, each struggling to engage the other in the way that should have come naturally. Matt and Jack were not doing the usual fun things that they should be doing together; trips to the park to feed the ducks, playing together in the playroom, bedtime stories, even bath-time was avoided and left for her to sort. Annie, always trying to fix everything, was at a loss to understand how to address this particular conundrum; before the relationship became irrevocably broken.

The more worrying consequence was the state of their marriage, or more precisely their sex life, with Annie having to acknowledge her share of the blame here too. The close and loving relationship they had enjoyed pre-Jack's arrival was now tense and strained, with intimacy between them a rare commodity. She still loved her husband, but struggled to show it in the way that previously had come naturally to her. Having been married for a few years, that first flush of romance when they could not avoid ripping each other's clothes off at every available opportunity was now past. She believed they still enjoyed a healthy sex life, although thinking back now, Annie realised it was several weeks since they had last attempted to make love, with even that being scuppered as the child monitor had gone off at an inopportune time, forcing her to automatically go to Jack's room to check up on him. It had ruined the moment, and by the time she had returned to their bed, Matt was sound asleep.

At five, Jack should have been sleeping through the night, but he still struggled. Several times a week their evenings or nights would be interrupted by cries as he woke or called out, or they would be awakened by the sound of his little feet padding across their room in search of his mom. For ease, Annie generally lifted him into their bed rather than returning him to his own, which had set another dangerous pattern, often leading Matt to take himself off to Jack's bed to get some sleep. Matt did not complain per se, but she knew he was far from happy with the current arrangements, or the trajectory they seemed to be taking. Overall, it did not do a lot for marital relations, and at this rate, Jack was destined to be an only child.

Annie was lost in her thoughts, when she heard the gentle tapping at the car window. Her parents were standing there, like a couple of drowned rats, probably wondering why she had not met them at the meeting point as agreed.

"Hi, Mom, Dad, sorry I was miles away," said Annie, as she got out of the car and helped her parents with their luggage.

"Our train got in five minutes early, and we were starting to get a bit worried when you weren't at the meeting point," Richard said, with a gentle rebuke. "You're normally so punctual!"

"Is everything alright, dear?" Betty enquired, sensing her daughter was not her usual self. "Are Matt and Jack both okay?"

"Yes, everything's fine. I was just mulling a few things over," replied Annie, knowing she needed to pull herself together as she switched on the engine and joined the traffic for their journey home. "Nothing that can't wait until we get back and have a good cup of tea and a proper catch up. So, tell me Dad, how was the holiday?"

Betty, sitting in the back seat glanced at her daughter's reflection in the driver's mirror as she listened to Annie and Richard chatting away. She sensed all was not well; but perhaps Annie was right, it was a discussion better had when they got home, got out of their wet clothes and had a nice glass of wine to hand. Betty wanted the holiday feeling to last a little longer, so was not sure she was ready for just a cup of tea yet, regardless of the hour!

Chapter 6

Josh was nearing the halfway point of his morning run, following a regular route that took him largely along the streets of the town. He had started road-running as a teenager and was now part of the running club at his local gym, regularly competing in full and half marathons during the running season. He had already completed around four kilometres of today's run, and would generally do an average of ten kilometres each morning before work. The weather today was making him wonder whether to call it a day and take the short cut home. He was normally an all-weather sort of guy, not fazed by a bit of rain, but this morning the rain was heavier than usual, and no matter how much motivational encouragement he was getting from the fitness app he had streaming through his earplugs, he did not feel his normal focused self.

He'd had a late night the previous evening, drinking with a few mates from the bar after his shift had finished. They had then gone and ordered tacos from the Mexican, resulting in him not getting back home until after midnight, feeling a bit worse for wear from both the alcohol and the spicy food. As an athlete, Josh was not a heavy drinker, and was generally careful with what he ate, but he did enjoy the occasional beer with the lads and was partial to the odd take-away. Everything in moderation was his motto. Perhaps last night he had pushed it a little too far.

Deciding he would cut his run short, at the next junction, across the road from the new superstore that had recently opened, Josh turned right towards the park. He would take the scenic route around the lake, and be home in fifteen minutes. With the heavy rain, the traffic and his head thumping more than he liked, it would be good to get out of the noise and car fumes and get dry.

As Josh turned the corner, he was forced to quickly dart to his left to avoid running into an oncoming cyclist, who had mounted the sidewalk to dodge the traffic. Although the cyclist wobbled, he just about managed to stay upright, but Josh lost his balance. He caught his foot on the edge of the roadside, before landing flat on his backside in the road, nursing a twisted ankle, ripped running pants, and above all, hurt pride.

As Josh stumbled into the road, the truck driver fortunately saw him, and anticipating what was about to happen, braked furiously; managing to halt his vehicle within a couple of meters of where Josh lay. The noise of the truck's screeching brakes was loud, but unfortunately not loud enough to alert the drivers of the vehicles that were following the truck, or the vehicle that was just exiting the supermarket's parking lot; or even the shoppers and people doing their normal errands, heads down against the weather. Until then, everyone had simply been battling their way through the rain and poor visibility, unaware of the unfolding incident, simply focussed on getting to their destination.

The sound of the screeching brakes was immediately followed by the noise of vehicles crashing into the back of the truck, small family sedans and SUVs, standing little if any chance, against the immovable object of a stationary ten ton truck.

As Josh moved to the side, nursing his twisted ankle, other than feeling a little dazed, he was otherwise okay. He remembered the driver coming out of his cab to check on him, before rushing off to talk to a passer-by, and then another lady telling him to stay still until the ambulance arrived. In reality, other than being a little embarrassed by having tripped, he could not see what all the fuss was about.

He sensed he had probably had a close shave, and that the driver had done well to brake in these conditions, but nothing surely to deserve the fuss and commotion that appeared to be building around him; people shouting and screaming, even the sound of approaching sirens in the distance.

Josh sat there, completely oblivious to the havoc his simple stumble had created.

Chapter 7

Sunday morning arrived and it was a beautiful bright day, with all the clouds of the previous twenty-four hours blown away. Being Sunday, Trudie, expecting Josh to be playing football with his mates, was surprised when her phone rang, the display showing it was her errant fiancé returning her call. She had rung him as soon as she got home the previous evening, and again when she had finished her dinner, but had failed to get hold of him on either occasion. Knowing his shift was due to start at seven o'clock, she had eventually given up and had a long soak in the bath and an early night instead.

"Hi there. Sorry I missed your calls yesterday," he started, "I was at the hospital, so didn't have my phone switched on …"

"Oh, no problem, Uncle Scott picked me up and drove me home. Is everything okay? I wasn't supposed to be meeting you there, was I?" enquired Trudie, wondering what on earth Josh would be doing at the hospital otherwise. He knew she was volunteering there, and occasionally called in for a coffee if he was in the area, but she did not believe they had made any arrangements for yesterday.

"No, I was having my ankle strapped. I must have landed badly on it yesterday when I fell because it started swelling up in the afternoon, and I was worried I might have chipped a bone or something. They x-rayed it and thankfully it just needs resting. The nurses strapped me up and gave me some painkillers. Means I can't work for a few days, which is a bit of a bummer," replied Josh, feeling more than a little sorry for himself.

"Rewind. What's happened, have I missed something?" asked Trudie, suddenly aware that Josh had been ranting about an accident yesterday and said something about traffic, but she had not really understood what he had been going on about.

"I told you yesterday. I tripped into the road whilst out jogging, near the new supermarket. It was all a bit crazy; a truck braked hard, apparently to avoid me. Then some other cars careered into the back of it, causing an almighty pile-up. The ambulances eventually arrived and the paramedics checked me over. I haven't got a clue what happened after that. The police took my details, and said they may be in touch, before saying I was free to go. It was only later that my ankle started to feel sore, so I rang Robby and he gave me a lift to the Emergency Department. It was a nightmare, as I was there for three hours before they eventually manged to see me! Thankfully though nothing's broken, just a bad sprain," Josh recounted, with a mix of relief and theatre in his voice.

"Sorry, I hadn't realised yesterday. I was rushing to get to work when you rang and the line wasn't too clear, and then your call ended abruptly, so I thought nothing more of it. I was in a hurry and didn't want to be late."

"Yeah, I had to hang up when the police were taking my details. All's good though now, so no damage done. Just a few days of resting and I'll be back at the gym in no time," said Josh confidently. "Anyway, do you fancy coming over later and playing nursemaid for me? Mom and Dad are away for the weekend. I could do with the company, and you could collect some pizza and beers for lunch on the way?"

Josh still lived at home with his parents, but so did Trudie, so she could not complain about that. But whereas Trudie helped around the house and was perfectly capable of living independently if she chose, her fiancé would struggle to function without his support network around him. Trudie had come to realise that there was definitely a selfish streak to Josh, almost a sense of entitlement. She had increasingly noticed he loved to be the centre of attention, happy for others to wait on him hand and foot; and in his parents' case, fund the lifestyle to which he had become accustomed.

They had been engaged now for just under twelve months, and whilst neither had any desire to rush into getting married, they had spoken of getting their own place; just a small apartment perhaps, so they could spend more time together, and have somewhere to invite their friends over. Trudie had started looking on-line at properties, even making appointments to view the odd one. On each occasion though, Josh had been called away, or had other more pressing plans, so the viewings had been cancelled.

The more this went on, the more concerned Trudie became about the seriousness of Josh's intentions, or his level of commitment to their future. She knew that university and subsequently starting work had matured her, but she was not sure she could say the same about Josh. He did not seem to want to grow up, or take on more responsibility than he was comfortable with. His parents did nothing to discourage his lifestyle, or to encourage his moving out, so Trudie often wondered why she was pushing. Also, as she was putting up most of the financing, she was mindful that she was the one who had the most to lose if, or more likely, when anything went wrong. Perhaps it was time for a serious talk, or at least some honesty about where their relationship was going, she wondered to herself. Trudie was no pushover and was not going to become anyone's fool.

"Okay, I'll see you later," she replied. "However, if you want pizza, I'd suggest you ring for a take-away when you're hungry. I'll cycle over after lunch, but I don't intend lugging beer and food too." "And what's more, I don't intend paying for it either," thought Trudie to herself, as she hung up, knowing the odds of her getting any money out of Josh would be lower than winning the lottery, and she didn't even play the lottery.

Chapter 8

The next couple of weeks passed pretty uneventfully for Josh and Trudie, as the long summer days rolled on and the daytime temperatures soared, with the humidity in the evenings making sleeping uncomfortable. Trudie had taken a few days off work to enjoy the weather and to keep her eye on Josh as he continued to rest his ankle in line with the doctor's orders. He was trying to keep his weight off it as best he could, but he was not a particularly good patient; always fractious at not being able to get out, or move around too easily. He missed his daily runs and trips to the gym, even his shifts at the bar, which had needed to be cancelled as he could not stand for too long. Balancing, with drinks in his hand, would have proved impossible. Thankfully, a couple of his mates had taken his hours on, meaning at least he had not lost his job.

He was due back at the hospital the following day for a follow-up examination, and fingers crossed he would get the all clear to be allowed to get back to work, or at least be allowed to do some light exercises. The damage to his ankle, and the surrounding muscles had been a little more serious than he had initially thought, but other than a bit of pain the doctor said he had been lucky, getting off quite lightly all things considered.

Although Trudie loved the summer and could happily lose herself in a good book for a couple of hours whilst working on her tan, resorting to going under Josh's umbrella if it got too hot, Josh found no fun in sitting in the garden or relaxing in the sun. His fair skin freckled easily, resulting in a look that did not particularly suit him. Also, as he did not have the patience to put sun cream on, he had a tendency to burn very easily. Coupled with a pretty low boredom threshold, and an inability to amuse himself, overall, this left him completely disgruntled. If Trudie was honest, Josh had not been much fun to be around for the last few days.

"What are you doing for dinner tonight?" Josh asked absentmindedly, conscious that once again no plans had been made, and they had just drifted their way aimlessly through another day. "Mom's cooking if you want to stay. Dad should be home in a couple of hours or so, so we'll probably be eating shortly after then."

They were at Josh's house, or more accurately Josh's parent's house, lounging in the garden; simply relaxing by the pool and listening to music. Josh lived in one of the more affluent areas of the town, a short fifteen-minute cycle ride from her aunt and uncle's house on the other side of the park. It was an imposing six bedroomed detached property, standing in over an acre of well-tended gardens; with not only a swimming pool, but a private tennis court, that was the pride and joy of his parents, both keen tennis players.

Josh's mom, Marcia, had been a committed amateur sportswoman in her day, often saying that was where Josh had got his prowess. Now she was largely a lady of leisure and a bit of a social butterfly; quite happy to run around after her only son, and be on hand for her husband, should he need her to host an event, or accompany him to one of his many business or charity functions. Nothing was too much trouble for

43

her son and heir, and if ever there was a reason for Josh's feeling of entitlement, then Trudie did not need to look much further than Marcia for that.

Trudie was always polite and respectful to both Josh's parents, with there never being a cross word spoken between them, even if she had been required to bite her tongue on more than a couple of occasions. In truth, she did not feel too comfortable around Marcia, sensing she was constantly being judged, and always coming up short as a potential partner, or worse still fiancée, for her son. Marcia had set her sights high for Josh and, more importantly, her daughter-in-law. She also felt uncomfortable with the way Josh allowed his mom to pander to him, waiting on him constantly. Trudie certainly did not want Marcia to feel obliged to do that for her too, or worse still, for Josh to think that she would similarly act like his mother once they were married; fetching and carrying to satisfy his every whim.

She had warmed though to Blake, Josh's dad. Blake Townsend was a respected and self-made businessman, establishing his own legal and consultancy practice by the age of thirty, which had grown steadily over the last twenty-five years and now employed over fifty people, with several partners covering the whole gamut of legal specialities. Blake had had a very different upbringing to Marcia's rarefied and privileged childhood; funding himself through college, with a series of jobs that had shown him life in all its varied hues. Consequently, he was down to earth, and on their occasional meetings, Trudie had found him very welcoming towards her, relaxed, sociable and good company. Unlike Josh's mom, who she found pretentious and a little overbearing.

"I'm not sure yet, I'll probably head home if you don't mind," replied Trudie. "I'm working at the café early tomorrow morning, so could do with getting a few things sorted before then. I've got a couple of shifts there this week, then I'm back at the hospital both Thursday and Friday afternoons. I've missed it the last couple of weeks, so it will be great to find out what everyone's been up to."

Josh selfishly showed no interest in her work or plans for the week, and sensing his obvious indifference to whether she stayed or not, Trudie stood up, using this as her opportunity to leave. She looked at her watch before continuing, "In fact, looking at the time I'll probably get going now so that I can help Aunt Caroline get dinner ready before it's too late."

"Okay if that's what you want, you go, I'll be alright here," replied Josh, shifting slightly on his sun-lounger, but not making any demonstrable effort to either disturb himself or encourage Trudie to stay.

Her growing anger at Josh always putting himself and his feelings first, had increasingly started to grate on Trudie over recent weeks, and this just made her question more and more where she fitted into his world. Biting back her annoyance at her fiancé's attitude, and not wanting to create a conflict over something and nothing, she quickly pulled her shorts and T-shirt on over her bikini, packed away her book into her tote bag, and fastened on her cycle helmet, before bending over and giving him a quick peck on the cheek.

"Right then, I'll see you later," she said, as she walked across the lawn towards where she had left her bike, leaning against the garage wall. As she was cycling off, she heard Josh call out, "give me a ring when you get home after work and I'll let you know what they said at the hospital. With a bit of luck, I'll be back at the bar doing my shift tomorrow evening, and everything will be back to normal."

Quietly seething to herself Trudie thought, "I might, but then again, I might not!" Her pent-up tension transferred itself to the pedals of the bike as she cycled home, realising not for the first time that she had done enough running around after him. Things were going to have to change if their relationship stood any chance of moving forward. No way was she his mother, and it was time for her to put her foot down!

Chapter 9

As Betty sat all alone in the Outpatients' reception area waiting to be called, she found her mind could not focus on anything. Matt, her son-in-law, had dropped her off at the hospital ten minutes earlier, leaving her to make her own way into the reception, but now as she sat in the sterile surroundings, she could not quite remember why she had come, or who she was due to see. Everything was hazy and confused; nothing seemed to make any sense anymore. Nothing seemed to have any purpose.

Only four weeks ago, or thirty-two days and three hours to be more precise, Betty had been sitting in the back of her daughter's car, being driven home from the railway station, happily listening to Annie and Richard chatting away about their holiday. Annie was eager to hear all about their trip, questioning her dad on all the places they had visited, and sites they had seen. Annie had appeared quite animated as they spoke, but Betty knew her daughter well, and sensed it was all a bit of an act. Her last clear memory was thinking her daughter seemed a little troubled and distracted, when all of a sudden, her world literally stopped.

Trying to recall now what had happened was proving not only emotionally painful, but physically and mentally difficult. Small snippets of her memory were there, floating around like pieces of a 1000-piece jigsaw puzzle, with occasionally the odd couple of pieces joining up. Largely though, the pieces were not making any sense. It was like trying to construct the jigsaw without the help of the picture on the box.

The doctors had indicated that with all the trauma and upheaval Betty had experienced, it would take time for her memory to recover; but they were hopeful that with the right help and therapy she would make a full recovery. Physically, Betty had got off remarkably lightly, according to the doctors. As she sat here now, all alone, that proved to be little consolation.

Betty had not heard her name being called, so was jolted when the receptionist approached her and gently touched her shoulder. "Mrs Elizabeth Newman?" she enquired. "The doctor is ready for you now, if you would like to make your way to Room 3, just down the corridor."

"Sorry. I was miles away. Thank you," said Betty, as she got up from her chair and made her way towards the room indicated. Her back ached a little from sitting, and her neck was still uncomfortable, even though she wore a brace to give her support; but her legs were strong and carried her safely to the room the receptionist had directed her towards. As she reached for the door handle, another piece of the jigsaw floated into place, reminding Betty why she was at the hospital today, and as it did, it took all of her composure to open the door and walk towards the therapist.

"Mrs Newman, please take a seat," the doctor said, as Betty made her way to the chair opposite the padded examination table, that resembled one in an operating theatre, and appeared to take up the majority of the space in the small room. "My name is Doctor Francis, and today I'm going to assess you to determine what support we can provide to assist your recovery," she said, smiling reassuringly at her patient; at the same time, noting she demonstrated all the signs of tension and discomfort one would expect after the trauma she had experienced. "I've had a read of your notes," Doctor Francis continued, "so I'm aware of what you have been through. May I begin by offering you my deepest condolences on your loss," but sensing Betty was understandably still in shock added, "if at any stage things get too difficult for you, then please let me know and we can have a break. I'm hopeful though, following our discussion and a brief examination, I will be able to devise a schedule, that over the coming months will treat your physical condition. With the right exercises and work on your mobility, I am confident that you will make a full recovery."

Betty smiled kindly at the doctor, aware she was trying her best to deal with a difficult situation, but in truth how could she even start to recover the situation? The pain in her heart far outweighed the pain in her neck or her back, and no number of exercises or amount of physiotherapy would address that. Betty wondered whether it was even worth the effort of trying, such was her desire to just give up; or give-in to the demons that kept surfacing whenever she was asleep, and increasingly as she was awake.

Annie and Richard had been her world, and losing both of them, so tragically in the car crash was beyond imaginable. One moment, one split second that changed her life, her future, her everything. Robbing her of her husband, her daughter, her grandson's mother, her reason to go on.

Betty still struggled to remember exactly what had happened. Flashing images and snatches of memory kept coming back to her; images of being lifted into an ambulance, then waking up the following morning, alone in what looked like a hospital room, with no other patients around. A kindly nurse appeared to be watching over her, and even though Betty searched the room with her eyes, she could not see Richard anywhere, and could not understand where he was.

The concept of time meant nothing to Betty, and although she stayed conscious, over the following couple of days she remained heavily sedated. The nurses monitored her carefully so they could manage any pain she may be experiencing; a series of machines and equipment constantly bleeping in the background. A stream of faces appeared at her bedside maintaining a silent vigil over her, but none of the faces meant anything to her. Betty called out for Richard repeatedly, both in her waking and sleeping hours. He never appeared.

On the third day, the nurses started to bring Betty around, gradually weaning her off the sedatives and encouraging her to eat and drink a little to build up her strength. X-rays and MRI scans had confirmed there were no broken bones or head injuries to be concerned with, just bruising and discomfort, so transferring her out of the bed into a chair, and encouraging a little exercise to and from the bathroom, in their view was in order.

Betty was a compliant patient who succumbed to the nurses' attention, and although she had no appetite, with gentle coaxing she started to eat and drink a little, even sitting by the bed for a few minutes at a time each day, staring into space. She was starting to feel a little more alert to her surroundings, picking up on the occasional word the doctors or nursing team were saying, but all that seemed to do was generate greater confusion. Betty still had no real understanding of where she was, or why she was there; at the same time failing to find the words to articulate the questions that started to form in her head. Yes or no, seemed to be the limit to her vocabulary whenever she was asked a question.

On the fourth day, a lady approached the bed, alongside a doctor Betty now vaguely recognised, and introduced herself as Police Sergeant Gill Dreyfuss. She sat down next to Betty and began asking what she could recall of the incident.

"I'm sorry, I don't recall anything. The last thing I remember clearly is Annie picking Richard and me up from the train station to drive us home. We had been on our holiday. Perhaps if you speak to one of them, they may be able to recall more. I don't know where Richard is, I presume he's busy as he's not been in to see me yet, which is a bit surprising knowing Richard. Annie will be at home, with our grandson, Jack."

The doctor and the police sergeant exchanged a glance between them. Betty noticed the look on both their faces, immediately sensing there was something she was missing "Is there something wrong?" she asked.

Sergeant Dreyfuss gently took hold of Betty's hand. "I'm sorry to have to break this to you. Sadly, you have been involved in an accident." The police lady then glanced at the doctor to get his agreement before she continued. "There is an investigation underway, so I can't say too much at the moment. From the witness statements, we believe the car you were travelling in was forced to brake suddenly, and due to the wet weather conditions, it appears the car skidded into the back of another vehicle. Several emergency teams responded very quickly, as apart from yourself, there were multiple casualties. I understand from the reports I have seen that the paramedics did all they could to treat both the driver and the passenger of the car you were in, both at the scene and later in hospital. Unfortunately, they or the doctors were unable to save them."

Sensing Mrs Newman had not taken in what she was saying, Sergeant Dreyfuss continued, "I'm sorry, I have to inform you that both your husband and your daughter died here at St Bart's a couple of days ago, resulting from the multiple injuries they sustained in the accident."

Betty listened, but did not really hear, or comprehend what was being said to her. As the nice lady spoke, she vaguely recalled a jolt, could even hear sirens in her head, people shouting and screaming, probably her own voice among those crying out, whilst the concept of Annie and Richard having been killed seemed to wash over her. How could that happen? Annie had her whole life ahead of her, and she and Richard were just setting out on their retirement. No, the nice lady must have got that wrong.

Now, sitting in the physiotherapist's room, a month after being discharged from hospital and the concept still did not sit well with her. She knew shock and denial were among the first steps of the grieving process, and in time she would eventually adjust to life after Richard, life after Annie; although at this stage, no matter how hard she imagined, or how kindly people spoke to her, she could never envisage reaching the stage where anything would ever remotely feel like normal again.

Chapter 10

Matt was sitting in his car waiting to pick Betty up from the hospital, still nursing the cold coffee he had picked up from the drive-through on his way there half an hour earlier. The radio was on, tuned to one of the local stations. He was not really listening to it. The presenter was talking to a guest about global warming or something, but in truth he was not following the discussion. It was just background noise; a bit of company for the journey, the music or topic of discussion completely irrelevant.

After dropping Betty off, he had driven to collect a few groceries, and had even run the car through the car wash, such was his need to keep busy and act as normally as he could; maintaining this bravado was not something he was finding easy. Everyone was saying how well he was doing; how strong he was being. In reality, he did not feel strong. In fact, he did not feel much at all.

He accepted he was grieving as much as his mother-in-law was, but did not know how to handle or even articulate his feelings. He felt numb. Like most men, he bottled up his emotions, always trying to put a brave face on for the sake of Jack, or anyone else around him; afraid of breaking down or appearing weak. Deep down though, he was seriously struggling, not only to come to terms with losing Annie, but facing the prospect of being the only parent left to bring up their son. Life had somehow become hard all of a sudden, and Matt was not sure how he would cope, and at his darker moments whether he could even be bothered to go on.

Matt believed that he and Annie had had a close and loving relationship, happy for most of their marriage, driving along life's metaphorical highway together. He knew the last few years had seen a few bends in the road, even the odd pothole, but they had always navigated their way around them.

Annie, unlike him, could talk openly about anything that worried her, with the luxury of having her parents to turn to whenever she needed to download, or get advice on anything Matt could not help with. Matt did not have that same luxury. His parents were no longer alive and Simon, his only brother, ten years his senior, was not someone he was particularly close to anymore. Growing up they had been close, and after their parents died, they had supported each other, but after Simon married and moved to London to live closer to his wife Sara's family, they drifted apart. The brothers rarely saw each other nowadays, with the occasional email or Christmas card being the extent of their contact. Sara and Annie had not really hit it off, so other than a polite acknowledgement of each other, there remained little in common between the two sisters-in-law.

Matt also recognised he was a bit of a loner. He was someone uncomfortable with building or maintaining relationships, happy to let them drift if they did not come easy to him. Having worked from home for the last few years, he had never cultivated a wide set of work colleagues; just those contacts he needed to talk to, or the odd one he would occasionally meet for a beer, but all-in-all, his support network was limited.

As he waited, he had hazy recollections of the morning Annie had left to collect her parents from the railway station. The visions, or more importantly the lack of visions, kept replaying in his mind. They'd had a bit of a heated debate the previous evening, about what he could not recall, so had been giving each other a wide berth that morning. He had not even said goodbye to her; too busy on his computer, or doing something that he had no memory of in his office, probably keeping out of her way for fear of saying the wrong thing.

He remembered Jack sulking in, asking for him to play ball, but fobbed him off, using some lame excuse about being busy. Whereas, in reality it was Saturday morning, so work should not have been troubling him. Engaging with Jack was something he really struggled with, something now he realised guiltily he had always left to Annie. She was so much better at it than him; so much better at most things, if he was honest.

The car door opened, bringing Matt abruptly out of his reverie.

"Thank you for waiting. Please can we go home now," Betty added quickly, and a bit out of breath; obviously flustered after her ordeal with the doctor.

As she sank into the front seat, with the ease of movement of a woman much older than her years would suggest, Matt was reminded again how hard the last few weeks had been for her. Betty had always been a fit and active woman; young both in mind and spirit. She was renowned for never leaving the house without her lipstick on, always well-groomed and stylish in the latest fashions. She was forever on the go, moving from one project to the next, with the agility of someone twenty years her junior.

Today though, sitting beside him, with her mismatched bag and shoes, her jacket not quite buttoned up correctly, and her hair wispy around her face, with no attempt to hide the grey roots, she looked bewildered and frankly like the proverbial stuffing had been well and truly knocked out of her.

"No problem. How did everything go with the doctor? What did they suggest?" he enquired.

"She's apparently making an appointment for some physiotherapy, something to do with the whiplash I suffered, and has suggested some exercises to help my back and neck in the meantime. Plus, I've got some tablets to help me sleep," Betty replied, showing a complete lack of enthusiasm and indifference to the hospital's proposed treatment.

Betty had been relatively lucky in the accident; a touch of whiplash, mild concussion and a few bumps and bruises, thankfully nothing broken. The hospital had kept her in for a few days of observation; thereafter content there was nothing more serious, so discharged her with an exercise plan to help her regain her full movement.

Betty's frame of mind however, had not been conducive to 'doing exercises' or looking after herself in any shape or form. As a result, instead of her neck pains abating, they had started to move further down her back, thereby causing greater distress. Coupled with the fact she was not sleeping, eating or had any desire to go out for fresh air, even for a simple walk around the park, her mood and her health had steadily worsened.

Matt, since the accident, had taken to popping around to Betty's house to check up on his mother-in-law a couple of times a week, usually with Jack in tow, in the hope that her grandson would be able to chivvy her along, or brighten up her mood. He knew grief affected everyone personally and on so many different levels. For himself, he needed to keep active and divert his attentions away from becoming maudlin, keeping himself strong for his son. Betty was different and needed to deal with her grief in her own way, and importantly in her own time. Her grief was just as deep as his own, but her usual coping mechanisms had simply abandoned her, and Matt could not stand back any longer, simply watching without trying to intervene.

Betty's decline was palpable; not just in her demeanour, but in the general state of her home. There were dirty pots abandoned everywhere, cleaning to be done, and by the looks of the contents of her fridge, nothing remotely within its sell-by date. Being normally a houseproud woman, who prided herself on her standards both inside and outside of the front door, well, to see the combined impact of everything was simply heart-breaking. Matt strongly requested, no insisted, Betty seek help from the doctor, even standing by the phone when she had made today's appointment; and looking at her now, he was glad he had. He could see a bit of physio would be a great help to get her body moving again, although sadly he realised it would take more than a few exercises to kickstart the rest of her into recovery.

Baby steps perhaps was what was needed for him too.

Chapter 11

"Good morning, Trudie. How are you feeling today?" smiled Sister Cynthia Cooper as Trudie arrived on the ward just before noon, obviously full of the joys of spring, and clearly ready for her afternoon of volunteering.

"I feel great today, thank you for asking," replied Trudie, with a smile on her face, before adding, "Josh has been out of town with some friends for the last couple of days, watching the New York Yankees play I think, although to be honest, I'm not too sure. I just know it's got something to do with baseball. I probably wasn't listening too closely!" she rambled. "The peace and quiet has been great – it's so relaxing when he's not around." Now, listening to herself admit this, she again wondered why she continued to put up with what was increasingly becoming a one-sided relationship. Josh always put himself and his wishes first, selfishly following his own agenda, regardless of the impact on his fiancée, or anyone else for that matter. Initially his behaviour had niggled her, particularly as he sidestepped anything that smelled of work or commitment. Over time she realised she had become attuned to it, noticing the triggers early, even accepting of it. If she was honest, she looked forward to their time apart, which frankly, she recognised, did not bode well for any long-term relationship.

Trudie had tried to have a discussion with Josh about where their relationship was heading, particularly over the last few weeks since his accident.

Being pampered at home by his mother had made him even more self-obsessed than usual; and although they had managed a few hours alone, the timing had never been right. The prospect of them ever buying a house together or getting married, as had been their intention, in Trudie's view was now so far off the mark, it was almost laughable.

Since leaving university, Trudie seemed to be the only one in their relationship that had matured in her attitude towards life. Josh was the eternal student, happy to meander through aimlessly, without a care in the world, his parents unashamedly funding that lifestyle, never encouraging him to grow up or assume responsibility of any kind. Something needed to change, but not today, thought Trudie, bringing her mind back to her work.

"What would you like me to do today, Sister?" Trudie politely enquired, after realising she had been rambling on for a while whilst Cynthia had patiently waited for her to finish.

"We have a new patient today. A lady called Mrs Newman, Elizabeth. I believe she prefers to be called Betty, reading her notes. She was involved in a road collision just under two months ago and has suffered whiplash, which has left her with back and neck pains. However, she also tragically lost her husband and daughter in the crash, so unfortunately her pain goes much deeper than purely physical. We're going to have to tread very carefully with her, and let her open up in her own time. Would you like to assist me when she arrives in about forty minutes?"

"Yes please," replied Trudie, always anxious to help and gain experience. "What would you like me to do?"

"I'd suggest you sit in, listen carefully, and take notes; not just on what she says, but more importantly on her reactions to what I do, or what I ask her. From her notes it's obvious that she's blanked out a lot of what's happened, and is finding it understandably difficult to move on, or help herself in some of the more basic tasks. Doctor Francis has referred her for treatment, with her comments suggesting she is worried about her on multiple levels. So, we're going to have to work hard to get to the bottom of this one, especially if we're to help this lady get her mobility, and equally important, her life back."

So far, Trudie had mainly assisted with patients who had impaired movement due to perhaps a trapped nerve or a twisted muscle, brought on by either an accident or a sporting injury. In each case the patient had been able to clearly articulate where their pain was, what they believed had caused it, and importantly were grateful for any treatment the team could offer to help regain their strength. By the sound of this patient, that would not be the case. Trudie knew from her case studies at university, that situations like this presented a real challenge, not only in getting the patient to open up to the nature of their injury, but more crucially for them to have the desire to engage in any treatment plan for moving forward.

"This is going to need physiotherapy at its holistic best," thought Trudie to herself as she prepared to meet their next patient.

Chapter 12

Later that afternoon, just before one o'clock, Betty arrived promptly for her appointment, having travelled to the hospital by taxi. Matt was unavailable to drive her due to a work commitment that he had been unable to get out of, so had booked the taxi to ensure Betty was there on time. The taxi company was given clear instructions for ensuring their passenger not only got to her destination on time, but was not abandoned once they arrived at the hospital.

The journey itself was uneventful, nonetheless Betty was relieved when the driver pulled into the parking lot and opened the door for her, helping her towards the hospital's entrance as Matt had instructed. Anxiety around car journeys was something Betty would have to either get used to, or stop venturing out, because there was no way she could ever see herself driving again; and as kind as Matt was being, she could not rely on him being her chauffeur on demand.

"Good afternoon, Mrs Newman," the receptionist greeted her on arrival. "Someone will be with you shortly. Please take a seat and I'll let them know you're here," she said, indicating the waiting area.

Betty ambled across to the six or so vacant blue vinyl chairs that were placed along the wall opposite the reception desk, lowering herself carefully down onto the middle chair. It felt hard and cold, and with her back, it was not the most comfortable of seats. There was no one to talk to, which suited her perfectly.

She just sat, and watched the receptionist as she continued to answer the phone and deal with other patients as they arrived, subsequently directing them to where they needed to be just as she had with her.

Betty noticed the stack of magazines on the small table at the end of her row of chairs, spotting one on interior design that she had regularly subscribed to; but today made no attempt to move or pick it up. Even flicking through the pages, and seeing the glossy pictures that over the years had inspired her, was too much. Throughout her career in the real estate market, magazines such as these had been her bread and butter; religiously devouring them the moment they dropped through the door; eager to understand the latest designs, colours and trends, to ensure that when she created the settings and atmospheres of the houses she staged, these were presented in the best possible light. She had been good at her job, with a real eye for detail, knowing what looked attractive, and more importantly what look would attract their clients. That seemed so long ago now, she mused.

"Mrs Newman, please follow me. Sister Cooper is ready to see you now." Betty had not noticed the receptionist walking over towards her, although her voice soon brought Betty out of her reverie as she stood in front of her smiling.

She followed the receptionist across the corridor to a door that was marked 'Treatment Room', where a middle-aged, well-built woman was awaiting her, wearing what she presumed was her uniform of blue trousers, with a crisp white jacket and a badge on the lapel. Betty could not quite focus on what it said, but presumed it was her name.

"Hello, please come on through Mrs Newman. We're ready to see you now, have a seat," said

Cynthia, inviting her into the room and directing her to one of the three chairs that had been arranged around a low table, on which Betty noticed some glasses of water and a box of tissues. Trudie was already in the room, smiling and standing behind one of the chairs waiting to meet their new patient.

Once Betty was seated, Cynthia continued. "My name is Cynthia Cooper, and I'm the lead physiotherapist at St. Bart's hospital, and this is my colleague, Trudie Lewis, who will be joining me today while we carry out your assessment. Before I continue, may I call you Betty?" Betty smiled as she gave a small nod of her head.

"Now, today all we'll be doing is carrying out a short physical assessment, and asking you a few questions. Is that okay with you?" Cynthia asked. "Based on that, we will then develop a plan for your treatment, and book you a series of further sessions over the next month or so. Without wanting to anticipate the outcome too much, we would normally expect treatment to take about three to four weeks to get the movement fully restored, but let's see how we get on, shall we?" explained Cynthia reassuringly.

Betty continued to watch the two women, her eyes darting between them as the older one spoke whilst the younger one sat scribbling in her notebook. So far, she had not spoken, but Betty thought she had a pretty face, a nice smile and lovely brown hair.

"Right, I'm going to ask you to take your jacket off in a moment, and move to the examination table if that's okay with you? Whilst you're doing that, would you like Trudie to make us all a nice cup of tea?" enquired Cynthia, with a smile on her face, conscious of needing to be especially patient with Betty.

Over the next fifteen minutes, Cynthia carried out a thorough physical examination of the neck and back areas, to establish the full extent of the damage, and in so doing determine her plan for treatment. Betty just sat placidly and allowed her to get on with it; never opening up or saying a word, just occasionally wincing whenever Cynthia touched a sensitive area.

Trudie soon returned to the room, placing the cups of tea on the table and continued to observe Cynthia as she skilfully used her hands to assess Betty's condition. She noticed how considerate Cynthia was being towards Betty today, her usual jolly banter with patients toned down, replaced by a sensitivity prompted no doubt by her understanding of the deeper pain Betty was experiencing.

"Thank you," smiled Cynthia, indicating the first part of the process was over. "Would you like to take a seat again, and we will continue our chat over a nice cup of tea?"

During the examination, Cynthia had observed all the typical whiplash symptoms she would expect resulting from injuries sustained in a car accident. She had also detected some early, more worrying signs of probable muscle atrophy; muscle loss due in Betty's case she feared to her current poor diet and lack of mobility: with her age also a factor worthy of consideration. As a woman who was only in her late-fifties, she needed to keep active, but through gentle probing, the answers to those questions confirmed Betty was neither looking after her diet, nor taking any exercise; frankly appearing to have given up completely on managing her overall wellbeing.

From the notes Trudie had made, even she realised that the treatment plan would need to involve a lot more than a few exercises and a weekly visit to the clinic; and as she watched Cynthia wrapping the examination up, she wondered to herself what she would advise in a case like this? What tools would she look to employ if Betty was her patient?

Chapter 13

Two weeks later Betty arrived for the third of the eight appointments that had been scheduled and waited to be called, in what was now becoming quite a familiar setting. The chairs were not getting any more comfortable, although the receptionist now passed the time of day with her, and chatted a little as she waited. At first Betty had been reluctant to engage in any discussions, contented to wait in silence with her own thoughts, but as the receptionist spoke directly to her, it seemed rude to ignore her, and anyway she seemed friendly enough, so what harm could there be in exchanging a few pleasantries? In fact, she had even spoken to the taxi driver on the journey over, assuring him she could make her own way into the hospital now. Without realising it, the routine seemed to be helping a little; baby steps as Matt kept reminding her.

The previous two appointments had largely concentrated on her neck and back, with gentle massage and manipulation administered by one of the physiotherapists to ease the discomfort, plus a dose of heat treatment on some of the more tender, or difficult to reach areas. If Betty was honest, it did seem to be working, and in an effort to try to engage more with the process, she had even managed to do some of the exercises she had been sent home with, gentle stretching and twisting as directed in the privacy of her bedroom, nothing too strenuous though.

One of the nurses had also measured Betty's weight, and noticing she had lost over five kilos since her last check-up, advised her as sympathetically as she could, of the risks she was putting her body through; the potential harm she could inflict on herself should the situation be allowed to continue. The nurse knew loss of appetite was understandable after what her patient had gone through. She had read Betty's notes and had real sympathy for her situation; the loneliness of eating alone, or simply not being bothered to eat, or not caring about buying fresh or nutritious food were all factors the nurse could easily identify with, and had seen so often with other patients. Grief was a difficult condition to control, as each person managed it in their own way and in their own time. And unless they had the desire or motivation to do anything about it, well, who knew what the outcome would be?

Matt had also noticed his mother-in-law's gradual weight loss, and commented as subtly as he could when he had called around to the house on the contents, or more pointedly the lack of contents in Betty's fridge. He had even started to take Betty to the supermarket every week, rather than just dropping groceries off for her; in the hope that by shopping for her own meals, it might help kick-start the process of eating more healthily, enjoying food again and building back her appetite, but he had to admit it was a bit of an uphill struggle.

"Hello Betty, good to see you again. Do you want to come through and I'll see if the physio is ready for you?" smiled Trudie, as she escorted Betty into the treatment room, opening the door to allow her to enter first. "I'll go and get you a cup of tea whilst you take off your coat and get comfortable, if you like."

"Thank you, dear'" replied Betty automatically, unable to remember the young lady's name. She did recall seeing her before though, so perhaps it might come to her later.

Trudie had been on duty for all of Betty's previous appointments, so by now had got to know her a little, but equally knew how difficult the nursing staff were finding it to get her to open up. Today was no different. As Trudie sat in and assisted, taking notes as Sister Cooper had previously asked her to do, she observed how much Betty seemed to have cocooned herself, almost building a protective shell around her; presumably in an attempt to prevent any further breakages to either her delicate body, or her spirit. Trudie knew that some patients felt that by ignoring the subject it might eventually go away. Somehow she did not think that was the case here.

Betty was always polite, listened to what was being said, never challenging or grumbling about the treatment being administered, although equally never opening up to what the real problem was that was ailing her. The physical damage was healing, but the psychological damage was far from healed.

None of the physios had directly spoken to, or questioned Betty about the loss of her husband or her daughter, believing it not to be within their remit. They were fully aware of the nature of the car crash, but they were there to treat the physical injury, not to provide counselling per se. However, the more Trudie observed Betty, the more she saw a lost and lonely woman, damaged by factors outside her control, in need of someone to talk to, someone to help her to deal with the obvious distress she was suffering, and hopefully help her to put some order around it. Someone above all who could help her to climb out of the circle of depression she was obviously falling into.

Trudie felt if only she could identify the right trigger or strategy to help Betty open up, then perhaps she could be the one to help her to move on. She knew that there were a lot more qualified and experienced people around her; and as such, she needed to tread very carefully and not overstep the mark. After all, she was only a volunteer at the hospital, not a respected medical professional, nevertheless something told her that she might just be the one to help. Trudie might be young and inexperienced. Grief though was something she was no stranger to.

Chapter 14

"I'd like a pot of tea please, for one," asked the lady, as the young waitress approached the table near the window to take her order; the quiet table away from the door, nestled behind a post and furthest away from the toilets. It was probably the most private table in the whole café, and where many a young couple had met if they did not want to be overheard by passing customers.

"Certainly madam, would you like a scone or some cake to accompany that? Or we have some lovely fresh pastries if you fancy one of those today," she replied, pointing over to the refrigerated cabinet near the counter, where another assistant was busy preparing hot drinks, standing with her back to Betty.

Betty stared over to where the waitress was pointing. She liked the look of the cakes, and realising that other than a small piece of toast that morning, had not eaten anything else all day, decided to order something.

"Thank you, yes that would be nice. Can I please have a slice of that carrot cake?" Her stomach had started to rumble at the sights and aromas in the café, making her realise how hungry she actually was. Noticing the time, it dawned on her she had somehow missed lunch. After the lectures she had received from both the nurses and Matt, all well intentioned of course, she was trying really hard to remember to eat something, no matter how meagre an amount at each meal time. Her appetite was still very poor, with the simple joy of eating and sharing a meal long gone, but she now accepted she needed to at least try.

She had been busy all morning dealing with paperwork at the solicitor's office, tidying up some affairs of Richard's that she could not put off any longer. The solicitor had been very patient and had not hurried her, although his call last week had made it obvious that she could not postpone for much longer. As such, she had booked the appointment, made the journey into town and dealt with it: relieved at least that it was now sorted, and something else she did not need to worry about. Being a bank manager, Richard had always been meticulous in his paperwork, always with an eye to detail and being prepared for any eventuality, so it had not surprised Betty that his affairs were in order, making the whole process she'd had to go through as painless as possible, under the circumstances. Financially she had no worries as Richard's pension had left her well provided for, although no amount of money could compensate for the loss she still felt. No, it was one worry less, but there were plenty of other things still to fret about. For now, though, all she needed was a quiet cup of tea before she arranged her taxi home.

Recognising her voice, Trudie turned from where she was making the coffee and smiled over at Betty. "I'll take that lady's order over if you don't mind holding the fort for a few minutes," said Trudie to Wendy, the young waitress who was working today, after she had placed the cup and saucer, tea pot, small milk jug and generous slice of carrot cake onto the tray. "I might have a chat with her and take my break, if you could manage the hot drinks for a while? It's not too busy, just give me a shout if you're struggling."

Trudie had been working since ten o'clock that morning and was not due to finish for another couple more hours, so five minutes off her feet would be welcomed, provided Betty was happy to have a chat with her. Trudie had spoken with Cynthia at work about talking to Betty, outlining some of her own story, and Cynthia had been cautiously supportive, provided it was managed sensitively. Trudie had reassured her on that front, and privately had given some thought to what to say; so now, as Betty sat there, it seemed a perfect opportunity to at least try to break the ice.

"Hello Betty, it's Trudie from the hospital, how are you feeling today?" started Trudie, as she placed the tray on the table. "Are you meeting someone, or would you welcome some company? I could do with a sit down if you fancy a chat. Equally, if you'd prefer being left alone, then that's fine too," she smiled, not wanting to impose.

Placing Trudie's face from the hospital, Betty felt more relaxed. "That would be lovely dear, please join me," replied Betty, before adding, "I've had some business in town, so have just come in for a rest before I head home."

"Well, you've chosen a good place to stop, and that carrot cake is delicious, one of my favourites too! I need to be careful though, as working here I could eat cake all day. I have to be very disciplined and limit myself to the odd slice each week," laughed Trudie, conscious she was starting to babble.

"So, do you not work at the hospital?" enquired Betty, now a little confused who this lady was. She thought she had recognised her from her physio appointments, but had obviously been mistaken.

"Oh, yes, sorry to confuse you. No, I work here a couple of days a week, and volunteer at the hospital a couple of days too. It's a little unorthodox, and a bit of a long story. The short version is that I have graduated as a physiotherapist, just haven't got a proper job yet. The hospital is giving me some work experience whilst I find something more permanent, and the café is giving me a bit of spending money. Thankfully, I live with my aunt and uncle, so don't have any bills to pay, but I don't like to ask them for anything else; and I don't want to dip into my savings every time I need anything new, as no doubt I'll need that money when I eventually buy a house of my own, although there's no rush," rattled Trudie, almost managing to lay out her whole life story in a single breath.

"Well, that does sound very sensible," replied Betty, with a smile on her face, suddenly warming to the young lady in front of her. She seemed an interesting mix of scatty and level-headedness all at the same time; in fact, quite pretty in a very natural way, Betty observed. She now recalled seeing her in the hospital on several occasions, but had to admit to never really noticing her properly, or taking the time to engage at any level, and for the life of her, had no idea what her name was.

Something about what she said though, made Betty ask "why do you live with your aunt and uncle then, where are your parents, if that's not too personal a question?"

"Well, that is a longer story. My parents both died when I was only five years old. We lived in Canada, just outside Vancouver, and they'd gone skiing with a group of friends for the weekend. I was staying over with my grandparents at the time. The small aircraft they were travelling in got into trouble, and crashed in the mountains. Apparently, there was a problem with visibility coming into land. The weather was so bad, the plane didn't stand a chance. There were four couples on the flight, all friends, including my godparents. None of them, including the pilot, survived. My grandparents, my dad's Mom and Dad, were unable to look after me long-term, so my mom's sister, and her husband took me in. Hence, I moved down here to live with them. They have both been great and I love them to bits, and I also have a cousin, who is more like my big brother."

Listening and watching the pain on the young girl's face as she recalled the events, Betty's eyes started to well up. The similarities and parallels to her own situation were obvious. Fatal accidents, nobody's fault, grieving relatives and children left without parents. Betty thought how similar in age she would have been to how old Jack is now; still a baby really. At five, what life did she have with her parents, what memories would she have been able to hold onto?

"I'm so sorry to hear that, dear. You must have been devastated," replied Betty, feeling a real empathy towards this young lady.

"I suppose I was. In reality though, I was so young I was protected from so much of it. I can't really remember feeling very upset. I can remember snippets, although nothing that really makes any sense. I do remember missing my mom especially, as she was the one who probably had the most to do with me, and she was the one I remember having fun with. Apparently, my dad worked away a lot, he was a pilot ironically! So, mainly it was me and Mom at home. After the accident, I can remember feeling unhappy that I wasn't going to school with the rest of my friends. I suppose that was the point I moved down here, with my aunt and uncle and Marcus, my cousin. Without them I don't know what would have happened to me, or who would have taken me on. Growing up with Marcus as a big brother soon felt natural, and in time, I suppose, the other memories just faded."

"How sad to hear that," Betty replied, gently placing her hand over Trudie's, at the same time recognising that she was not the only one in the world to have suffered tragedy. For some reason she could not explain, she continued "I've just suffered a serious loss myself. Two months ago, as you know, I was in a car accident. What you probably don't know is that my daughter was driving the car, and my husband was in the passenger side. The police say Annie drove into the back of a truck, which had braked suddenly when somebody had fallen into the road. She skidded, and as the roads were wet, the brakes just didn't react soon enough. Both she and Richard were killed. The ambulance got them both to hospital, but their injuries were so bad that neither survived the night, I'm told."

That was the first time Betty had uttered a single word about the accident to anyone, and God only knew why this young lady was the one she had opened up to, but it had felt right. She had bottled up her feelings for over two months now, never wanting to have to admit her beloved husband and daughter were gone, a real sense of denial driving her actions. In her mind, if she did not admit it, perhaps it had not really happened, and they would both walk back through the door, laughing and joking as normal.

However, no matter how many nights she waited for the door to open, or for the phone to ring, it had not happened. She was all alone, and not just that, she felt guilty that she was the one to survive. Why had she not sat in the front of the car, why had they not arranged a taxi, why had they not all died, why, why, why? All those questions continued to go through her head, with the only saving grace being that Annie had not brought Jack to the railway station with her. The thought of her grandson, either being involved in the crash, or worse still, killed as a result of it, sent shudders down her spine. Having him and Matt were the only comfort she now had. Betty had no-one else in the world.

"I'm so sorry to hear that," continued Trudie. "I can only imagine how difficult it must be. As I said, I was so young that I can't really recall everything. I don't know what I would have done if my aunt and uncle hadn't been there for me."

"Yes dear, I can see in some ways you were very lucky to have such a loving family around you. Unfortunately, I don't really have anyone left. My grandson and my widowed son-in-law are my only family in the whole world; and what comfort can that be to anyone now?" sighed Betty.

The two women sat for a few minutes holding hands, each finding a degree of solace from the other, both feeling complete empathy for the other's suffering. Two women that on paper had nothing in common, but at the same time had everything in common.

Chapter 15

Later that evening Trudie was at home with Aunt Caroline. They had just finished dinner and were tidying the dishes away and getting the breakfast things ready for the following morning. Her aunt had a nightly routine that involved laying the table, getting the bowls, spoons and cereal boxes out, and setting the cups ready for their early morning cups of tea. This was a tradition Trudie never questioned, she just went along with. Over recent years she had noticed the increasing number of times the breakfast things were simply and quietly put straight back into the cupboard untouched; her aunt disappointed another meal had passed without them sitting down as a family. Guiltily, Trudie realised both she and Marcus were the worst offenders, often either out too early for work, or lazing in bed if it was their days off. For whatever reason, both having long since outgrown the need for family breakfasts.

Uncle Scott worked at one of the local main car dealerships as a regional sales manager, so kept regular office hours; setting his watch by the time of his breakfast, lunch and dinner that Aunt Caroline adhered to with even greater punctuality. He left the house at eight fifteen sharp, in his smart, if dated suit, for his ten-minute drive to the garage; thereby ensuring he was at his desk promptly by eight thirty when the showroom doors opened, and the first customers started to filter in. Recently trade had been brisk and commissions had been healthy, but it was definitely an industry that had its ups and downs.

Aunt Caroline was a stay-at-home wife who kept house and ably managed the family finances, alongside all the shopping and domestic chores. After leaving school she had worked as a typist in a local office for a couple of years, before meeting Scott on a work's night out one Christmas time. Caroline was not someone who really enjoyed socialising, so tended to sit quietly in a corner, people watching; patiently waiting until it was time to go home. She rarely engaged in the chatter that was going on around her, happy to be left with her own company.

That evening, she had been casually staring around the bar, when she unwittingly made eye contact with Scott, before quickly looking away with embarrassment after being spotted. When Scott approached her five minutes later, and started to talk to her, even offering to buy her a drink, she relaxed a little. Dating was not something she had any experience of, but he seemed to be quite harmless, and as most of her colleagues appeared to have moved on, it passed the time before her dad was due to pick her up outside the bar at eleven o'clock.

They were soon dating and married within the year, finding there was a certain affinity between them. Neither would say it was the big romance, and Caroline assured herself that was not what everyone wanted. Sometimes a person's values and principles were equally, if not more important; someone you could trust and rely on, no matter what. Scott was plain speaking, plain dressing, and was not someone who attempted to stand out in any shape or form. He was not unattractive, and at six foot tall was quite striking, but made no attempt to enhance his looks. Similarly,

Caroline was what some would describe as 'wholesome'. She saw no value in wasting money on fancy hair dos or fashionable clothes; happy to leave her hair its natural colour, now grey, and recycle her clothes from one season to the next. She had maintained her figure over the years, so the clothes she wore in her twenties still fitted her now that she was in her fifties.

After they had married and moved into their first home, Caroline soon realised that office work was not for her. She had no career aspirations; she simply yearned for a large family, always imagining herself surrounded by a brood of children that would keep her fulfilled. Scott was more than happy to go along with this idea. He had been an only child and had always wanted siblings, so having a big family was something of which he was more than supportive.

Marcus arrived within the first eighteen months of being married, their eagerly anticipated firstborn. Sadly, he turned out to be their only child, as shortly after his birth, Caroline learned that she would be unable to have further children due to complications with Marcus' delivery. Although devastated, Caroline and Scott resigned themselves to their fate. So, when Trudie arrived almost ten years later, although the circumstances were tragic, it was a blessing in disguise, finally giving Caroline someone else to shower all her maternal love on. At ten and five years old, the two children proved more than a handful, but you would never have thought that, noticing the smiles it brought to both Caroline and Scott's faces on a daily basis.

Theirs was a traditional marriage, harking back to older times. They muddled along well enough together; both clear in their individual roles as

79

breadwinner and homemaker. It would not have suited everyone, but it suited them. Trudie recognised her aunt and uncle were quirky to say the least. They were her family though, and she would not hear a bad word said against them. Over the years, they had been so kind to her and accepted her almost as if she was their daughter; never once making her feel unwelcomed or unloved in their home.

Her aunt had once opened up to how disappointed they had been when they found out they could not have more children, so to have the opportunity to bring Trudie up as their own, to them was like winning first prize in the national lottery. They had built a tight family and God help anyone who tried to unsettle that. Aunt Caroline was more fiercely protective than any lioness could ever be, and Trudie felt secure in that love.

"When I was five and I first came to live with you, can you remember how long it took me to stop talking about Mom and Dad as if they were still here?" asked Trudie, a little unsure herself where her questioning was going, or what she was really asking.

"That's a funny question, where on earth did that come from? Are you worried about something love?" her aunt asked, a little surprised by what Trudie had said. It was just the two of them in the kitchen, and not unusual for them to have a heart-to-heart at this time of day, but that particular question was completely left field. Normally it was a 'what's Josh done now,' type of discussion, with Caroline sensing more recently that all was not as settled there as it had been. It was a long time since Trudie had brought her parents up in any discussion.

"No, it's just I've met a lady who's recently had the most horrific loss, and I really want to try to help her if I can. I'm trying to remember how I dealt with it, and I'm struggling, which makes me feel awful, as I don't ever want to forget them," she said, a slight quiver in her voice and tears not far off.

"You'll never forget them. I won't let you, even if you struggled to remember, I'll always be here to remind you. Nancy was a beautiful sister, and an even better mom, and your dad was so handsome; perhaps too handsome for his own good! That's probably where you get your looks from." Caroline dried her hands on the apron around her waist and walked over to Trudie, embracing her as she added, "You were so loved by both your parents, and by all your grandparents. You know that all your Canadian family have a special place in their heart for you too, and probably wish they saw more of you."

Trudie's maternal grandparents had lived close to where she had been brought up, Caroline never having left the area where she had been born. They had both died three years ago, just two months apart; her grandma believed to have died of a broken heart, after losing her husband and soul mate of sixty years, to cancer. Trudie had lots of happy memories of them when she had been growing up, memories that she shared with Marcus, but not so many memories of her Canadian family.

Trudie's dad, Martin, had an older brother Duncan, who still lived in Canada with his wife and their two sons, Darren and David, her cousins. They had each married now, with children of their own. Her paternal grandparents, although now quite elderly and living in residential care, were also still around. It was a while though since Trudie had last visited any of them.

"You're right. I should make more of an effort to go and see them. Uncle Duncan was lovely to me last time I went up. That was probably about five years ago, and other than in photos, I've not seen my cousins' children. Did David have a boy, and Darren a girl or have I got that muddled – there's so many 'Ds' that I get confused?" questioned Trudie, suddenly ashamed of the fact that she could not remember.

"I think you're right, but please don't quote me," laughed Caroline. "Don't you remember you once mapped all your Canadian relatives out on that genealogy site, and researched into where your dad's parents had originated from. I remember you being absorbed for ages, locked upstairs in your room. And how amazed you were by some of the things you discovered. You took it up to show your grandparents last time you visited, if I recall correctly."

"Gosh, You're right. I'd forgotten about that. That was years ago. In fact, it was the summer before I went off to university. I remember, it was a great distraction while I waited for my exam results. I've probably still got it somewhere – I'll have to dig it out and update it now David and Darren's children have arrived!"

As Trudie recalled all the research she had done, exploring into distant ancestors and their backgrounds, even going to the library to follow up on some of the weirder things she had discovered, events she had never heard of, she remembered how close it had made her feel to her parents, particularly her dad's family. It gave her the sense that she was intrinsically part of something bigger; not just 'Trudie the orphan', no longer so alone.

It started to trigger a thought in her mind, that perhaps there may be a nugget in what she had done to deal with her sense of loneliness or separation, or whatever it was she had been feeling at the time, to help Betty in some way deal with hers. Betty had said she was all alone in the world, so maybe helping her to capture and document what she knew about those she had lost, might help her too. It could also give her grandson something to cling onto when his memories of his mom eventually started to fade, and potentially Betty was not around to help him, as Aunt Caroline had helped her. This was definitely something to think about.

Realising it might be risky to just dive in, Trudie thought she should probably run her idea passed Cynthia first. The last thing she wanted to do was interfere, or worse still, risk putting the fragile progress Betty was making, back in any way.

Chapter 16

Two days later, Trudie arrived at the hospital, earlier than usual for her afternoon volunteering session, anxious to catch Cynthia. She wanted to discuss her ideas about helping Betty before her shift started. She had caught the earlier bus, the weather in October being too unreliable to risk cycling, thereby allowing herself that extra bit of time; knowing if she had caught her normal bus, she would be on the last minute.

She had checked the previous day and knew Betty's appointment was at two o'clock, and had even checked Cynthia's rota, reassuring herself she was on duty. Now, as she hung her coat up and changed into her uniform, she was pleased to see she had a good hour before Betty's arrival to outline her plan.

After speaking with Aunt Caroline, Trudie had wracked her brains for inspiration, eventually coming up with the idea of talking to Betty about collating a 'story book'; one that was all about Annie, containing all those special moments in her life. A book that in time, she could share with Jack; full of the pictures and precious memories a mother would normally share with their child as they grew up, just Annie was no longer able to do so. Memories perhaps of Annie's first days at school, of her playing sports, perhaps winning medals for her swimming or gymnastics, photos of her getting married, giving them their first grandchild – all those treasured milestones that a parent proudly keeps locked away in their heart, always ready to share and rekindle when the time comes. Perhaps those 'fashion faux pas' photos, wearing home knitted jumpers, or sporting the latest hairstyles; even the baby photos, splashing around naked in the bath. All the embarrassing photos that only come out when a prospective boyfriend or girlfriend is introduced, and somehow needs to be impressed. She could also add some funny stories. Trudie recalled the time her aunt had told her of the full-scale manhunt that was narrowly avoided in a particular store after she had wandered off, whilst her parents was momentarily distracted; later to be found hiding behind a clothes rail, unaware of the chaos that she was creating, or her parents' state of mind while all this was unfolding. Memories that later you can laugh about, but at the time caused many an anxious moment.

Trudie knew nothing about Annie or her life, although the more she thought about it, the more cathartic she felt it might be for Betty; sadly, wishing she'd had something similar for herself of her own parents' lives. Memories were sometimes painful to recall, but hopefully happy memories, of a time when she and Richard had been quietly raising their daughter, oblivious to the tragedies that would later unfold, might help Betty move on. What was equally important, these memories might provide a legacy for Jack to fall back on when times became difficult in his own life, and where he, like Trudie, struggled to remember, or worse still had no knowledge of his past.

After Trudie had recounted for Cynthia her discussion with Betty in the café, and how this had made her feel, she outlined her idea about the memory book, sharing with Cynthia a little of her own background to add context to why she thought it might be helpful.

"So, what do you think? Is it something you think could work? I know how powerful memories can be, and providing a framework for recalling these might be really helpful. I wouldn't want to suggest it though if you thought it would do any harm."

"'No, I actually really like your idea, Trudie. I think it's something that potentially could work; I'm just so sorry to hear that you went through something similar. How do you feel now?" asked Cynthia, concerned that although Trudie had come up with a great suggestion, following through on it might stir unpleasant memories for her too.

"I was lucky, as I had my family to fall-back on. They supported me through everything, and they have been amazing. I couldn't have wished for better parents, and a brother thrown in for free, although technically he's only my cousin! Aunt Caroline and Uncle Scott have always been there for me. By the sounds of it though, other than her son-in-law, who is himself grieving, Betty only has her grandson Jack left. He's her only bloodline. To not have anyone else to turn to must be really scary."

"Yes, I see what you mean. Why don't we see what today's session brings, and then take it from there? Betty's responding well to the physiotherapy, and should, I believe, be discharged in a week or so; so, physically there's a great improvement, but your idea might just be what's needed to help her emotional recovery. How about I sit in on today's session with you and Nurse Taylor and we can test the water?" encouraged Cynthia.

A couple of hours later, as Betty was quietly sitting alone in the Patients' lounge, enjoying what had become her customary cup of tea after her physio session had finished, Cynthia and Trudie approached her and asked if they could join her for a moment. Betty smiled at them.

"Please do," she replied. "Is everything alright? Have I forgotten something?" she asked, unsure why they wanted to join her. Usually, she sat for around ten minutes enjoying her drink, before the receptionist came through to let her know her taxi was waiting outside. Sometimes there were others in the lounge, and occasionally she had nodded to them, although never had cause to speak to anyone.

"Everything's fine," smiled Cynthia, unsure suddenly where to begin. "As you know, next week will be your last physio session, and as we said earlier, everyone is really pleased with the progress you've been making, particularly with your exercises at home. We've been thinking about whether there's anything else we could do to help you in another way, perhaps with your wider recuperation." Betty looked at the two women, unsure what they were talking about. The older lady seemed to be stumbling around for her words.

"You're very kind. I'm sure I'll be fine. Thank you." She finished off her drink, looked at her watch and added, a little dismissively, "now, my taxi will be here any minute. I think I should go and find my coat. I'm not sure where I left it."

"Betty, before you go, can I just tell you about an idea we've had?" Trudie said cautiously, unsure whether Betty had already pulled up the drawbridge, meaning it was too late. However, as she remained in her seat, continuing to keep eye contact, Trudie persisted. "I wanted to tell you a little about how I dealt with the loss of my parents, to see if there's a way I could help you in a similar manner," she began, before taking a deep breath and outlining her idea in more detail.

As Betty listened, she vaguely recalled the young lady telling her about her parents and the plane crash they'd had. In fact, it brought back a clear memory of her sitting in the café the previous week, talking about Richard and Annie's death for the first time, a conversation until then she had forgotten had taken place. The young lady spoke with such calm and reassurance, that for the first time Betty started to engage with what she was saying, even smiling at some of the suggestions she was making. It was as if she actually understood how Betty felt; showing real empathy towards her, not just offering platitudes to make her feel better, as most people did.

As Trudie was finishing speaking, the door opened and the receptionist entered, announcing the arrival of Betty's taxi, her coat draped over her arms, ready to present to Betty after she had abandoned it in the reception area earlier. "Ah, thank you dear" she said, taking the coat from the receptionist. Then turning back to Trudie, she added, "I have to go now, but I like the idea of what you're saying. Let me have a chat with my son-in-law, and I'll let you know next week what he thinks."

And with that, she picked up her bag and walked to the door, with more purpose in her step than she had displayed in weeks. The idea of doing something both positive and creative appealed to Betty, and if it helped her process what was happening in her head, then even better.

All she needed to do now was remember the nice lady's name.

Chapter 17

"What do you mean? Why on earth does the hospital want to see pictures of Annie, or want to know about her life? What's that got to do with your physio treatment?" enquired Matt, completely baffled when Betty had spoken to him the following day. He had called round to her house to collect her and take her to buy some groceries, pleased when she opened the door, already in her coat, her hair tidy and clearly awaiting his arrival. She certainly seemed more perky and upbeat than she had been on his previous visits. It was clear the physiotherapy was working, as she did not appear to be in anywhere near as much pain or discomfort when she walked. Obviously though, the confusion was getting worse, so he needed to keep his eye on that.

"I'll come into the hospital with you for your next visit, and I'll sort it out. I'm sure there's been a misunderstanding, or there's a simple explanation," he added, without wanting to go as far as directly implying she was wrong.

Betty had reflected on what Trudie had said all the way home, even late into the evening, after she'd had her dinner. She had gone as far as searching out some of the old photos that were kept in boxes under the stairs, along with the numerous other keepsakes that had been accumulated over the years. The photos had been meticulously stored in albums, in date order, just the way Richard liked it. They were mainly of Annie growing up, probably up to the point she went away to university, Betty thought, noticing the dates on the top of one of the boxes. There were few, if any, of Matt in what she could see, although there was the odd one or two of Annie with other boyfriends, even some of the less savoury characters she had brought home in her late teens.

Annie had been a bit of a rebel growing up, as some of the outfits in these photos attested to. She had always been confident, outspoken and never short of friends, and being tall and good looking, she seemed to attract boys without any effort, often losing them with the same ease, thought Betty, recalling many an occasion when her daughter simply discarded a boy for no apparent reason, other than she'd had enough of him, or just lost interest. Some of the girls she hung around with were also an 'acquired taste'; perhaps the politest way Betty could think of describing many of the friends that had passed through their lives over the years.

Matt had been different. She recalled the first time Annie had brought him home and introduced him to her and Richard as 'The One', and them both being pleasantly surprised as he was not her usual type. For one, he was clean, tidy with a smart haircut, his body devoid of any obvious tattoos or piercings. Dressed in his blue jeans and a plain tee shirt, he just looked 'normal'. And two, he came across as polite, well-spoken and with good manners, shaking hands with them both when he came into the house, even bringing her a bunch of flowers, which would have been unthinkable from any of her previous boyfriends.

Annie and Matt had met at the student bar, where the beers were cheap and there was always someone around to talk to if you'd had a tough day, which on that particular day, Annie had. She saw Matt sitting alone at the bar, and feeling a bit down herself, sat and asked if she could join him. She had seen him around, and thought he was quite attractive, but other than that they had never spoken. They were both in their final year, doing completely different degree courses; his in accountancy, hers in geography, so academically their paths had never crossed, and as far as Annie knew, they had no mutual friends.

Matt, surprised to be approached by one of the hotter, more vivacious girls on campus, the ones who normally did not pay him much attention, nodded and pointed to the stool next to him; after all, he had nothing else he needed to do or rush back to his rooms for. He had seen her around, often at the centre of a crowd. Believing she was well out of his league, had never paid her much attention.

He bought Annie a drink, listened to her woes, and surprised himself by making her laugh with his parody of what he had heard he say. It was what Annie needed. Someone who did not take her too seriously, or hang on her every word; someone completely different from the usual cronies she hung around with. They struck it off instantly, and after that first drink, regularly met up as friends for a chat after lectures, even occasionally sharing a pizza, or going out for a burger. Any ideas of romance were far from the horizon, but over time their friendship developed, into something much deeper.

Matt was very focussed, with his head screwed on; both serious and more mature than his years would suggest. He had a clarity on his future direction, namely to set up his own accountancy firm within five years of graduating. Annie still had no idea what she wanted to do, other than enjoy life, and perhaps throw in a bit of travelling; after all a geography degree had to count for something, didn't it? On the surface, it was difficult to see the two together, or how their relationship would work, but somehow it did, with each of their personalities rubbing off on the other. Annie became a little more focussed, and Matt loosened up a little.

As she sifted through the albums, some of the memories they evoked brought a small tear to Betty's eyes, whereas others a little laugh; a sensation she realised she had not experienced for a while. There had been many good days, she thought, as she gently touched the photos, outlining the faces with her finger. Nowadays, they were all digital, with no one bothering to print them out anymore, but Betty still loved the feel of old photos.

Now, listening to Matt as he drove to the grocery store, his tone still implying she had got herself confused, Betty hoped he was wrong, and that she had not daydreamed or misinterpreted what the hospital had suggested. The idea of making something constructive and positive out of what could only be described as a horrendous situation, sounded a lovely thing to do. It would never replace either her loving husband Richard, or her darling daughter Annie, but it might help to celebrate their lives, and importantly show Jack what a lovely Mom and Grandad he'd had.

If it helped keep those memories alive, then what harm could it do?

Chapter 18

"Well, that was a strange session," observed Cynthia, as she watched Betty and her son-in-law walking arm-in-arm out of the building.

"Yes. I think I got there in the end, thankfully! He took some convincing though, didn't he?" replied Trudie, relieved that not only had Matt agreed with her, that helping Betty create a memory book for Jack might be therapeutic, but he had even conceded in the end, that he might be prepared to get involved too.

"Yes. I'm not sure what magic you worked, because his mood when he arrived was certainly not there. I shouldn't laugh, but I think he was seriously suggesting Betty had lost her marbles, or was I imagining things?" Cynthia chuckled. "So, to turn him around a full one hundred and eighty degrees is credit to how good your idea is. Having met him, it will probably help him too. I get the impression he's trying to be strong for everyone else's sake. I'm not sure if there's anyone there for him though."

"No, I agree. Something didn't seem quite right, did it? He's very much on the defensive, is my take. Whenever anything was mentioned, it was almost as if he only wanted to see the negatives, not the positives. I fear he's grieving more than he's prepared to let on."

"I agree. Betty can be quite a character when she wants, can't she?" laughed Cynthia again. "She really surprised me the way she spoke to him - not the shy and retiring violet we were introduced to only a couple of months ago! No, she's certainly come out of her shell, and good for her. Now she's got her strength back, I'm not sure I'd want to take her on."

Matt and Betty had arrived early for her final physiotherapy appointment, with Matt offering to stay and then drive her home, cancelling her usual taxi. Betty, although pleased for the company, knew Matt had an ulterior motive; wanting to check with the nurses she was not going senile. Since their discussion about creating a memory book, and particularly Matt's response, she had even been questioning herself whether she was losing her mind. The conversation at the hospital had seemed real, she could even recall the earlier conversation in the café, although it may all have been an illusion, a daydream.

It was well known, the memory can play tricks on you, especially when you are grieving, but day-by-day, Betty sensed her thoughts were getting clearer; as if the fog was finally starting to lift. She was more conscious of her surroundings, her wellbeing, even her appearance. So, if Matt was right and she was to be told she was losing it, it would be hard to bear, particularly on top of everything else she was having to deal with.

When Betty was called into the treatment room, Matt went too, which although a little unorthodox, Betty was happy for his company. If her memory was going, or worse still she was starting to show signs of early-onset dementia, then having Matt around to take on board what was being said to her was important. Although she was still a couple of years off sixty, she knew age was no barrier to that illness; and without her son-in-law, then who else would support her once her memory, or the rest of her faculties had left her?

"As I mentioned to Betty, Mr Lacey," Trudie said once they were all seated comfortably. "From personal experience, I know how hard it is to lose a close relative, a parent, a child, a partner, but also, how hard it is to keep your memories alive, particularly when the people you most want to share them with have gone. Betty may have told you, my parents both died when I was the same age as Jack. I've been very lucky to have my aunt and uncle around to keep reminding me about them. Creating my own memory book though, and looking into my own family tree, was so therapeutic for me. It helped me to feel less isolated and part of something much bigger. It was for that reason I suggested Betty might want to consider something similar for Jack, to keep Annie's memory alive for him; well, for all of you really."

"Thank you for sharing that with me, Miss Lewis," Matt began, reading Trudie's name badge on her jacket. "And thank you for thinking of ways to help Betty. I know how much she appreciated your suggestion," he added, not wanting to let on how much he had doubted his mother-in-law. "I can see the value of this, and it may be something for us to think about in the future perhaps, once all the dust has settled."

"Oh Matt, I don't want to put this off. I want to start straight away," chirped in Betty, more forcefully than Cynthia or Trudie had ever heard her speak before. "I'm just not sure what to do first, or how to structure my thoughts," she added, looking at Trudie. She was now certain she was far from losing her mind, and having been given a relatively clean bill of health physically, had to start thinking about what to do next with her life. Staying at home, simply moping around was not an option for her. Richard would certainly not have approved of that, she thought to herself, and neither was the option of going back to work something she'd relish. "I just may need a bit of help. So, what do you think?" she added, now directing her question squarely at Matt.

Seeing Matt was struggling to be as positive as Betty, and clearly not fully bought into the idea; happier presumably to put it off until Betty had forgotten all about it, Trudie stepped in.

"I'd be happy to help you, if you'd like me to, Betty? I could pop round to your house and we could talk through some ideas, which might help you get started...."

"No, I'll help," replied Matt, obviously uncomfortable with the idea of someone muscling in on their lives, no matter how well intentioned they were. He did not know this young woman from Adam, and did not feel happy to just let her waltz into their lives and have access to their memories. "Thank you, but I think we can manage without you."

"Nonsense," Betty said, equally spirited, looking directly at her son-in-law. "I would love to have Trudie's help, and get her involved in some way. It's something we can all work on together. How soon can we get started?"

Betty felt enthused all of a sudden. Trudie's idea would give her a project, something to focus both her mind and her time on; a channel into which to funnel all her energies. However, although she was taken by the idea, it was disappointing that Matt could not see it in quite the same way. Delaying it for another time, as he suggested, would help nobody in her view, because if nothing else, what these last few months had taught Betty was that tomorrow doesn't always come.

Chapter 19

Trudie was in the kitchen the following morning, rushing around, after having overslept for the first time she could remember. For some reason, she had forgotten to set her alarm, and had only woken when a noise in the garden startled her; bringing her out of a deep sleep and firmly back into reality.

Seeing it was almost nine o'clock, she had quickly pulled on her dressing gown and darted downstairs; a note on the table from Caroline saying she had popped out, and would be back shortly. Trudie quickly put the kettle on to boil, the toast into the toaster; leaving her just under thirty minutes to have a quick breakfast and get showered, before cycling over to the café for her lunchtime shift.

As she waited for the kettle to boil, she looked out of the window to see a beautiful autumnal morning and smiled. She was in great spirits remembering the previous day, when her talk with Betty, and her son-in-law Matt, had gone so well. She was excited to get started, and had even suggested she call round to Betty's house over the weekend to help start the planning. Matt had reluctantly stood by whilst Betty provided Trudie with her address, still unsure about what was being proposed, and still a little suspicious of Trudie's intentions.

Her mobile started to ring. "Oh, you're finally home, are you? I've been trying to contact you for days. Why've you not been answering your phone?" moaned Josh when Trudie eventually answered the call. It was obvious from the disgruntled tone of his voice, that he was in a bad mood. "I needed to speak to you. Why've you not been returning any of my messages?" he asked.

"I've been busy, with work and one thing or another," she replied, unsure how much she wanted to tell him about what she had been planning with Betty and Matt over the last week. "Anyway, what's the urgency? I'm in a bit of a hurry this morning. Has someone died?"

"Well, yes, but that's not why I phoned you," answered Josh, nonchalantly.

"What do you mean?" Trudie questioned, unsure what he was going on about.

"Oh yeah. Well, the police finally came around to follow up on that accident I had a couple of months ago, d'you remember when I tripped into the road? I don't know what's been keeping them so long. Anyway, it's all sorted now. They had a couple of things they needed to clarify before they closed down their files, something to do with questions on an insurance form. Apparently, a couple of people died, and their claims are being processed. A man and his daughter, I think the police said, but no one I know," he added, quite dismissively.

"Right," said Trudie, a frightening thought forming in her mind, one she could not ignore, and certainly did not want to entertain.

"Anyway, that's not why I was phoning," he continued. "The reason I needed to get hold of you, was that some of the lads are going away for a few days to Las Vegas; a bit of gambling, a lot of drinking, you know the sort of trip I mean? I'd called to see if you wanted to come too. Some of them are taking their girlfriends, and a few other girls from the bar are tagging along, so I thought you might enjoy it. A bit of shopping, some sight-seeing, the odd cocktail; you know, all that girly stuff. Anyway, it's too late now as all the bookings have been finalised."

"Sounds like fun. Never mind, we can go another time," she replied, a little absentmindedly, thinking a trip to Las Vegas, spending time and getting drunk with a group of girls she did not particularly like, or get on with, was the furthest from fun she could imagine. She was also mulling over what Josh had said about the fatalities; could what she was thinking be true?

"Sorry if I spoilt it for you though," she added, a bit of an afterthought.

"Don't worry, you haven't. I'm going anyway," he advised. "We fly out on Sunday afternoon. One of the other lads isn't taking his girlfriend either, so we've decided to share. It's going to be great. Five days and nights of partying. Shame you can't drive though, otherwise you could've given us a lift to the airport."

Trudie half-listened, as Josh got more excited about his trip; not only insensitive to her feelings at having been left out, but completely oblivious to the damage he might have caused if she was right about the accident. As he spoke, all that went through her mind was how much the whole conversation summed him up. Always out for himself, the eternal playboy, who never really considered her or anyone else, unless it suited him to do so. Also, to think he had no idea of what she really wanted from a holiday, let alone life, did not bode well for their future together.

The idea of her fiancé in Las Vegas, getting drunk and no doubt testing his luck without her in tow, did absolutely nothing for her; other than reinforce her feelings that their relationship had run its course. He had just unwittingly managed to drive the final nail into the coffin that represented their future. Whether he had accidently been responsible for Richard and Annie's deaths, or not, was one thing, but regardless, she realised now she'd had enough.

"Well, have a great time. And when you get back, I think it's time for us to have a talk about our future," replied Trudie, in a tone of voice that supported the importance of what she was saying. She needed to have a serious think while he was away about how she brought this relationship to an end, because one thing was certain, it was going nowhere, and they had no future together.

"Right babe, see you soon. Love ya!" laughed Josh. In reply, all Trudie could do was maintain her composure as she shook her head and hung up the phone. He just did not get it at all.

"Is everything okay?" enquired Caroline, who had been standing behind Trudie, having just returned from the stores, careful not to eavesdrop as she had been speaking to Josh. She could tell from her niece's tone of voice that all was not well. Knowing it was her fiancé on the other end of the line probably explained it. Recently, Trudie rarely seemed to be happy after either speaking to him or meeting up with him. Caroline, not Josh's greatest fan, would continue to tolerate him for as long as necessary, although if what she suspected was true, hopefully that would not be for too much longer.

"Yes, everything'll be fine," replied Trudie, unsure she wanted to say much more to her aunt until she had thought it through herself. "It's just that I've got a bit of thinking to do about me and Josh over the next couple of days, whilst he's swanning off to Las

Vegas with his mates. Nothing to worry about, I'll tell you later. Now, unless I get my skates on, I'm going to be late."

Remembering the kettle and the toast, now sitting burned in the toaster, she sighed, "I think I'll get my breakfast at the café."

Chapter 20

On Sunday morning, Trudie knocked on the door of Betty's house at eleven o'clock as previously arranged. It was only a couple of miles away from where she lived, so would have been an easy cycle ride, however Uncle Scott had insisted on driving her over, even offering to come and collect her later, arguing the weather could be quite changeable as the nights were drawing in, stressing "I don't want you walking home alone in the dark." You would think she was a child the way they occasionally treated her, not a twenty-three-year-old woman. Rather than cause a fuss, or have Aunt Caroline worrying more than she was anyway, she had graciously accepted.

The house was a neat, detached, double-fronted, two-storey property, with a small garden to the front and a paved drive way, with a double garage. A dark blue SUV stood on the drive, next to a small Ford sedan, boasting a sticker in the rear window advising 'Drive Carefully, Grandson on board'. There were lights on in one of the downstairs windows, and as Trudie rang the bell, from the corner of her eye, she noticed the curtains twitch before Betty arrived to open it.

Scott waved, then as instructed waited until Trudie had gone into the house before driving away. He memorised the details to provide Caroline with a full debrief of what he had seen. They were both a little nervous of her going into a stranger's house, even though Trudie had assured them she would be fine.

"Come in dear, we're in the lounge, come on through. Here, give me your coat and I'll hang it up for you," Betty said, smiling at Trudie as she entered the small hallway. There were several doors leading off it, but only one was opened, so Trudie made her way in to find a small boy sitting on the carpet, his eyes locked onto the television that was playing some adventure movie that was absorbing him, with Matt perched on the end of the settee, nursing a cup of tea.

"Hello Matt, lovely to see you again," said Trudie, unsurprised that he was there to keep a watchful eye over his mother-in-law, and the family silver no doubt. "And I presume this is Jack?" she enquired, when the little boy briefly turned his head as she entered the room.

"Yes, hello again." Matt replied, seemingly not in the mood for small talk, deduced Trudie.

"Well, we've made a start by sorting out some of the old photos," Betty began, a mix of excitement and nostalgia evident in her voice. "That was the easy bit, as Richard was very methodical about his photos, well most things really. Everything was catalogued, in date order mainly, with some sorted by occasion; there's a pile of baby snaps, a lot of birthday celebrations, holidays, school photos, you know the type I mean?" she asked, smiling at Trudie. "We're not sure what to do next. There's so many to choose from, and each brings back its own memory. Some I haven't thought about for a long time," Betty sighed. "It seems ages since we last got these boxes out, and going by the dates, we've probably not added to them for years. Like I was saying to Matt earlier, most of the recent ones are on Richard's laptop, and I haven't got to that yet," before adding to no one in particular, with more than a heavy heart, "heaven knows what I'm going to do with all the photos of our cruise."

"Well, you've certainly got a lot to choose from," remarked Trudie, looking at the pile Betty had amassed. "More than I ever had when my parents died. I don't think they, or for that matter any of my dad's side of the family, were keen photographers, so other than a handful of baby snaps, there were few of me in their things when I eventually got around to sorting through them. There were a few dodgy videos though, which I did laugh at, of me taking my first steps and learning to ride a bike, but they were mainly out of focus, so could have been anyone," laughed Trudie. "Thankfully Caroline, my aunt, had lots of photos from my maternal grandparents, so we delved into them and found loads of my mom when she was growing up. It's surprising how similar we looked, and seeing her as a teenager was a bit like looking in the mirror for me, apart from the outfits and hairdos. I'm not sure I'd have the nerve to wear some of the clothes or hairstyles she got away with. I suppose it was the eighties and nineties, so that probably explains a lot."

Matt sat quietly and listened as the two women chatted, not wanting to get drawn into what he thought was a fruitless exercise, and frankly a waste of his and Betty's time. However, the more he watched and saw the reaction his mother-in-law was having to Trudie, and the way she opened up about her own childhood, talking about things he had never heard before, it made him smile. It was the first time Betty had seemed 'alive' for weeks, and as they sorted through the piles of photos, there was a level of energy about her actions that he would not have thought possible only a week or two ago. It made him wonder whether there might be more to Trudie's idea than he had previously given credit, especially when he noticed that in the course of their discussions, Jack had stealthily moved away from his movie and towards his grandma, now sitting almost on her lap, absorbed by what the adults were talking about. He occasionally asked her a question about some of the photos she held, interested to learn who the people in them were.

"Is that one me, Grammy, when I was little?" he asked, as Betty held a small black and white photograph of a baby, swaddled in a crocheted blanket, being nursed by a pretty young woman, probably no more than fourteen or fifteen years old.

"No Jack, that's actually me when I was a baby," Betty replied, a small tear in her eyes as she gently caressed the photo, smiling. "I thought I'd misplaced this and it's the only one I have of my mother, so I'm delighted to have found it again," she added, no doubt for Trudie and Matt's benefit.

"Oh, please can I take a look?" asked Trudie, sensing a depth of feeling in Betty's voice that she had not heard before. Taking the photo she remarked, "What a pretty young girl your mother was. You have a look of her, I think. Do you know when and where was this taken?"

"No, I'm not sure. I think it was Ireland in the early sixties, but she died shortly after I was born, so I never got to know her. Apparently, there was no family to take me in, so I was put up for adoption and sent over to America before I was a month old, to live with my adoptive parents. That must have been taken some time back in 1964, the year I was born, as I'm fifty-eight now."

"That's sad, to have never known her or your dad," said Trudie. "And you say you've no family at all over in Ireland? Have you never thought to look into your adoption, particularly with the internet and all the resources around these days to help you?"

"No, not really. Mother never spoke of her, nor on the odd occasion I asked about my background, encouraged me to look for any wider family. So, I suppose over time I didn't think to either. My parents were very kind to me, and in their own way I'm sure they loved me, but they were not what you would call loving parents. They were in their early forties when they took me in. Mother once told me they could never have children of their own, so I was probably their last hope; they were staunch church goers, very upright citizens, and I got the impression the adoption was arranged through there. I don't know for sure as Mother never talked about it and Father certainly didn't."

Turning the photo over, Trudie could just make out some handwriting on the back, it seemed to read 'Brigid and Maeve – 1964'.

"Have you ever noticed this, Betty?"

"Oh yes, I do remember that now. I did notice it once and mentioned it to Mother. She couldn't shed any light on it. I'm not sure if one of those was the name I was given or not, but it's not my adopted name. I was always known as Elizabeth growing up, and only began to call myself Betty when I started work and met Richard. Elizabeth seemed too formal in the office, and Betty made me fit in easier."

The more Trudie listened, the more she got drawn in. Betty's life, growing up in the sixties and seventies, had been very strict and disciplined; not at all the bohemian lifestyle Trudie had come to associate with that generation. There was no talk of hippies, drugs or rock and roll, just a bland upbringing, with adoptive parents who appeared to spend their time reinforcing the strict doctrines they had been raised on through the church Betty repeatedly mentioned she had been taken to, right up to the point at which she and Richard married.

Betty spoke warmly about meeting Richard at a house party organised by one of her colleagues in the office, Mandy she recalled, where she had worked as a clerk typist in her early twenties. A mixed group of both men and women were going to the party, so Betty had tagged along for the sake of it. She was not used to parties, or alcohol or socialising in any shape or form for that matter, so had no expectations of the evening; but something told her she should go, even if it meant telling her parents a little white lie about her whereabouts, or why she would be late home.

Richard had been dragged unwillingly to the party by a friend of a friend; the same friend who abandoned him as soon as they walked into the room, and noticed the girl he had obviously had his eyes on, talking to another man. Richard, sensing he had been set up, was biding his time, quietly sitting in a corner nursing a can of beer, before making his excuses to leave, when he noticed Betty walk in. Something about her instantly drew his attention, leaving him mesmerised. His eyes followed her, watching as she uncomfortably walked around the room, not talking to anyone, or having anyone come up to talk to her either. Betty laughed as she recalled how far out of her depth she had felt that evening, even saying how Richard had rescued her from social embarrassment when he had brought her a drink over, and sensing her discomfort, started to chat to her.

After the party, they started meeting up for an occasional drink, a meal, or even a trip to the cinema to see a movie, something Betty knew her parents would not have approved of. Whilst they owned a television, it was heavily censored in terms of what they, or Betty was encouraged to watch. As such, she had to be careful to slip away without sparking her parents' curiosity, because even though she was of an age where this should not have been an issue, she knew her parents would think otherwise.

Richard made her laugh and actually showed an interest in her and her opinions. He even complimented her on the way she looked, the way she wore her hair, occasionally suggesting styles that he thought might suit her, or fashions that she would look good in. This was not something Betty was used to, having always been encouraged to live in the shadows; keeping quiet unless spoken to, and never under any circumstances drawing attention to herself, or her body in any way. It felt nice to be appreciated for who she was, and not just seen as her parents' daughter, the product of the drab existence in which they had imprisoned her.

Conversation with Richard was easy in those early days, with Betty like a sponge, eager to learn everything she could about a world from which she had been shielded. They chatted about subjects she'd previously had no concept of, or opinions on. Richard talked warmly about interests or hobbies he had developed over the years, either growing up at home, or when he had gone away to university to study mathematics. He, like Betty, was an only child, although it was obvious from the way he spoke, that not only had he been doted on by both his parents, he had been brought up in a much different way than she had. His parents had shown him unconditional love and support, which Betty found both endearing and comforting.

The more they met up, the more she looked forward to their next meeting, and over time she started to develop feelings for him. Betty had never been in love, and frankly had no experience in that department, but there was definitely a warmth in her stomach whenever she thought about Richard, or mentioned him to her colleagues at work. Although he was not the most exciting of men, nor had the Hollywood good-looks of some of the screen-idols she was starting to develop an interest in, he cared for her and valued her in a way she was completely unused to, and there was something very attractive about that. Richard was solid, had a steady job in banking and knew what he wanted from life; and after six months of old-fashioned courting, he made it clear that he saw Betty as part of that future, proposing and presenting her with a simple solitaire diamond ring; one he had chosen himself, assuring her the store would change it if she preferred a different design.

Betty had met Richard's parents relatively early on in their friendship, and saw first-hand the loving, caring and welcoming people he had talked so affectionately about, and the type of happy marriage people in love could lead. The more Richard hinted at the future they could have, the more Betty realised that any doubts she might have had about wanting to be part of that life were quickly extinguished, even if it went against her parents' wishes.

When she eventually brought Richard home to meet her parents, whilst they had not openly objected to him, he had not been made to feel especially welcomed. To their knowledge he was the first boyfriend she'd had, and certainly the first she had introduced to them. Her parents had always hoped she would marry someone from within their church community, someone who they knew had the same values as they had, and could look after their daughter in the way they felt appropriate. They had even suggested on a number of occasions, sons of fellow parishioners, who they felt were more appropriate matches for her, even arranging for Elizabeth to walk out with them, or meet up at church socials, where they would not get into any harm and remain under the watchful gaze of others.

Betty did not agree with either her parents' choices, or the direction she knew they wanted her to take for the remainder of her life; no doubt, staying ostensibly under the church's control, with an equally devout husband calling the tune. No, she had enough spirit to know that was not what she wanted, and although she hated to go against her parents' wishes, or defy them openly, she refused to be paired-up for their convenience. So, by accepting Richard's proposal of marriage, she saw a sure way out of her dilemma.

Trudie was fascinated as Betty described her life; her strict upbringing and education in the sixties and seventies, followed by her starting work in the eighties, even her early years of marriage, before Annie arrived two years later. After that, the unending run of baby stories had come, followed by stories of a much-loved daughter as she grew up.

Each story had a set of photos to accompany the events she retold, and the people contained in them. Trudie noticed those people were always the same; a limited set of close family, with fewer photos of Betty's parents with Annie, either as a baby or a child as the years passed. It was almost as if they distanced themselves from each other after her marriage to Richard; though it was difficult to say who was the catalyst for that, or in fact, if that was actually the case. It was possible there was some other explanation which Betty did not want to discuss, so Trudie did not pry beyond what she was told.

Betty had mentioned her parents were both only children, so it was understandable there was no mention of any siblings, aunts, uncles or cousins, but equally there was no mention of grandparents, or even close family friends of her parents. It was almost as if Betty had been raised in a vacuum, with any interactions limited simply to people from the church her parents attended, and that sounded very sad indeed.

After several hours of sorting and sifting through the various piles of photos Trudie, realising what time it was, declared, "I think I'd better be going. It's nearly dinner time, and I hadn't realised how late it had become. It's getting quite dark outside and my aunt will be wondering where I am."

"Oh dear, thank you for all your help, and I'm sorry for taking up all your time. You've been very kind," smiled Betty, herself now realising how late it was.

"No, it's been my pleasure and I've loved hearing your stories. I think you've loads of material here to create a fabulous memory book for Jack, if you still want to do one that is?"

"Oh yes. The more I've thought about it, and talked it through with you today, the more I know how positive an experience it will be for Jack to understand his mom and what she meant to us," said Betty, looking over for Matt's endorsement. Without waiting for his reply, she sighed as she once again picked up the photo of her as a baby. "I just wish I'd had more than this to understand my heritage, or the family I was born into. Oh well, there's nothing I can do about that now, is there?"

"Yes, I know what you mean. If you want me to help any further, then I'm more than happy to do so. You have my number, so please call me anytime," she added, noting an odd look on Matt's face; one she could not quite fathom the meaning of. Was he suspicious of her motives still, or just not sold on the idea? Either way, there was certainly a level of concern there that Trudie could not deduce.

As she drove home with Uncle Scott, her mind would not stop whirling following the time she'd spent with Betty and the numerous stories they had shared. But there was something about what she had said at the end of the day that was not quite ringing true. Trudie was at a loss to put her finger on exactly what it was, leaving a niggling feeling that would not go away.

Chapter 21

Aunt Caroline was, as usual, pottering around the kitchen when Trudie walked back into the house a short time later, her apron wrapped proudly around her waist like a badge of honour, with aromas that suggested she had been baking whilst Trudie had been out. The smell made Trudie realise how hungry she was, having only had a quick sandwich before she had left home, and just a cup of tea at Betty's.

Uncle Scott had kept his own counsel driving home, neither asking too much about her afternoon, nor offering any insight into his own thoughts on the subject. He was a quiet man, not one for getting too involved in other people's business, unlike his wife who would happily try to solve the world's problems singlehandedly given the chance.

Caroline was not a gossip by any stretch of the imagination, but she did like to offer an opinion on most things, and if there was ever an opportunity to offer advice, then she was certainly never shy in coming forward.

"So have you had a fruitful afternoon?" she enquired as soon as Trudie entered the kitchen, making her way directly to the red and white gingham cloth, from where the aromas were coming to investigate what was hiding underneath it. Seeing there were chocolate muffins, along with oat biscuits and shortbreads, she was spoilt for choice in terms of which to have first.

"Yes, it's been very interesting listening to Betty tell her story. By the sounds of it, her daughter Annie was a character in her youth," she laughed, careful not to splutter crumbs as she did so, or speak with her mouth full. "Betty got a bit sad though, as it brought back memories of her youth, and specifically her own birth, which she doesn't know much about."

"What do you mean?" enquired Caroline, putting down her cloth as she sat at the table alongside Trudie, her interest now piqued. "Did her adoptive parents not tell her anything about her birth mother?"

"Not really. She was told she was adopted and brought over to America from Ireland in the early sixties, and that her mother died shortly after giving birth to her, due to complications. All she has is one photo of her mother holding her as a new-born, with a couple of scrawled names on the reverse of the photo, which she presumes were hers and her mom's names, but she's not sure. It just says 'Brigid and Maeve – 1964'. It was sad, because the girl nursing her only looked about fourteen or fifteen, so a child herself."

"That is sad. Unfortunately, death in or around childbirth was not unheard of in those days; in fact, it was more common than you'd think," said Caroline. Although, as she listened to Trudie, something just did not quite feel right, particularly if her limited knowledge of Irish history was anything to go by. Ireland was renowned as one of those countries, specifically in the last century, where large families were the norm. Child mortality rates were high, with contraception and abortion certainly frowned upon by the church and state.

"What about her maternal grandparents, or another family member? Surely if her mother was only a teenager when she gave birth, there would have been someone with her who could have taken the baby in, I'd have thought. It seems strange she was put up for adoption."

"I'm not sure. Betty believes there's no one. Her adoptive parents never mentioned anyone else and rarely spoke of it. In fact, I don't think Betty knew she was adopted until she was much older. Her parents were very strict apparently, and their lives revolved around their church. Betty believes now that they may have arranged her adoption through there, as she has vague recollections of other families mentioning something similar, but she's not sure."

"And has she never looked into it? Surely, as an adult she would be curious, especially once her adoptive parents died?"

"Apparently not. I suppose if she knew her mother was dead, then she probably didn't feel there was anyone to go looking for. I'm not sure she'd know where to start anyway, given the limited information she has. It's sad, especially now that her daughter and husband are gone too. She feels so alone."

As Caroline continued to listen, she recalled a news article she had read a couple of months previously about changes in Ireland, specifically relating to the legislation around adoption. She explained to Trudie that it had interested her because she had gone to senior school with a girl called Bernadette, whose older sister Jean had been adopted from Ireland back in the late 1950s. It was the first time Caroline had ever really heard about adoption or Ireland, so she had lapped up what Bernadette told her, fascinated. When Jean turned eighteen, she had wanted to research her background, but according to Bernadette had struggled to find out anything about her birth parents. At that time, there was no internet or infrastructure in place to support searches, so nothing had come of it. A complete dead-end.

Caroline had mused at the time of reading the article, whether it would help Jean, presumably if she was still around and interested in searching. Now, as she recalled it to Trudie, she wondered if it might help Betty too. Today there were so many ways of finding things out, not just with the technology, but the agencies around to help. So, perhaps it might not be the lost cause it had once been.

"Why don't you suggest you do some digging, and see if it's worth looking into for her?" suggested Caroline, always looking to solve a problem. "What harm can it do? And you love to do that sort of thing, don't you?"

As Trudie shoved the final bit of her second muffin into her mouth, she pondered the idea. Researching anything was a passion of hers, and this could be an interesting little project for her.

Chapter 22

Later that evening, Trudie was sitting on her bed, her laptop on her knee, scouring the internet for any information she could find to support what her aunt had suggested. As a true academic, anytime research was suggested, Trudie lapped it up like a drug. She loved nothing better than to lose herself in information; the more complex or challenging the better.

When she had been at university, whilst others had loathed studying the prescribed text books, or wasting their time in the library doing research, she had thrived on it. Never happier than when her head was buried in a book, or she was using whatever search engines she could find to mine the internet. Nothing normally fazed her, although this time she knew it would be a long-shot to find answers to questions Betty might not even want to consider; recognising not only the scant information she understood Betty had, but also some of the ramifications the search might involve. No search could be guaranteed to find just the good stuff; with many a family skeleton being best left in the cupboard.

Trudie soon discovered that what her aunt had said about the changing law, was in fact true. A very recent change, following the introduction of the Birth Information and Tracing Act, now provided people who had been adopted with a legal right to discover their true identities. Apparently, birth parents had previously been able to block children seeking them out, no doubt afraid of what a child landing on their doorstep would mean to them many years down the line, when their lives had moved on and new ones built. However, the change in law now meant children were entitled to see their own birth documents, with agencies even springing up to help support those searches.

Trudie had seen many a movie portraying stories of unmarried, or occasionally married women being sent away from society to have their illegitimate babies in secret. In most cases it was to avoid bringing shame on their families. Some of their stories were based in Ireland, though not exclusively, and some were linked to religious beliefs, but again not all. Frequently, babies conceived as the result of an affair, or an underage pregnancy, needed to be hidden away in some way; resulting in many babies being put up for adoption, or even being passed off as belonging to another family member. Trudie read examples of stories coming to light where women had passed off their daughters' babies as their own; bringing up their grandchild, arguing he or she was a menopause baby to anyone who dared to ask. There appeared to be a myriad of reasons for what happened, and presumably in some cultures similar practices still existed.

Trudie could also remember seeing coverage of orphanages and children's homes, many run by nuns; stories that on occasion left your blood cold with the cruelty of how both mothers and babies were treated, or the state of the facilities in which they were housed. The church had often played a shameful part in these historic acts, often by turning a blind eye to what was going on, other times directly facilitating it.

Trudie read more recent articles containing apologies for some of the atrocities that had been caused, knowing no apology would ever make it right to those who were impacted by the scandals at the time, she thought sadly.

The news and films reflected different times for sure, and how much of it was true or edited for effect was another question. The deeper she read the more concerning it became. It was not isolated incidents that were being described in the pages of the articles or links she clicked on, more a culture that had been allowed to persist for decades. In some cases, it was condoned by some of the highest offices in the land; not only the church, but political and authoritative figures alike.

Some of the articles spoke of the unknown number of children who were adopted and shipped around the world for new lives. America appeared to be one of the main countries that engaged in the process of taking children from Ireland, often with money or incentives thrown in. Some articles spoke of the Black Market that sprung up for babies back in the 1950s and 1960s, addressing the legalities, or more often the illegalities of it all, even talking of forged paperwork where formal documents were unavailable, or parental consent had not been given. It was frightening to think how widespread this practice had been, or from a humanitarian perspective how desperate the young girls were; raised in a culture where having children out of wedlock was frowned upon, to the extent that they themselves would be abandoned by their families if they persisted in keeping their child.

The more Trudie read, the more similarities she saw in what Betty had hinted at, raising a strong possibility a similar tale might lie behind her own adoption. Although she was certain she could find something out if she started to look, this was not her story to uncover. She could not undertake any research on Betty's behalf without her full knowledge and consent; and was that something Betty would want after all these years, or equally something she would feel happy Trudie getting involved in? After all, they hardly knew each other; just casual acquaintances through the hospital, not someone you would want delving into your most personal information.

Trudie sensed Matt would certainly not want her involved, given he was already suspicious of her motives for befriending his mother-in-law. He would argue they were alright as they were, and best to leave these things alone. After all, with Betty's mother dead, what would she hope to achieve by going on a fool's errand?

Trudie switched off her laptop and decided she had done enough thinking for one day. Her eyes were tired and staring at the screen was not helping. Reflecting on everything she had done over the last couple of days she realised if nothing else, it had provided a great distraction from having to think about Josh and what he was no doubt up to in Las Vegas. He would be home in a couple of days, so switching off the bedside light, she decided she had better get some sleep. She would need all her energies for dealing with his return. The fallout was unlikely to be pleasant.

Chapter 23

Later that week, Trudie was once again sitting in the kitchen with Aunt Caroline, this time nursing a very large glass of red wine. She had called in at the liquor store on the way home to buy a bottle, knowing alcohol was not something that was usually kept in the house. Caroline occasionally had a drink, but it was a treat normally reserved for special occasions, and usually then limited to the odd glass of sherry or port.

After the day Trudie had experienced, wine was the least she needed to calm herself down if she was to unwind before bed. As she sat, staring at the new batch of cakes sitting on the table in front of her, screaming out to be eaten, she said to her aunt, "perhaps some cake would go well with the wine," unable to resist it any longer.

"So, he's not taken it too well then, has he?" enquired Caroline, handing Trudie a large slice of the lemon drizzle cake. She knew she had called around earlier in the day to Josh's house to break off their engagement, and as far as Caroline was concerned, it was not a moment too soon. She just hoped Trudie had the strength of her convictions, and had not given in to his pleas for yet another chance.

He had apparently returned from Las Vegas the previous evening, messaging Trudie as soon as he had landed to invite her out for a drink. Given the way she had left it, she was reluctant to have their next round of discussions in a bar, so had said no, telling him she would come round to the house the following morning before her shift at the café started. If nothing else that would mean he would have to get out of bed early, she smiled to herself, knowing how much he hated early mornings.

"Ha, that's a bit of an understatement," she laughed. "He was convinced I was only finishing with him because of Vegas, and as he maintained he hadn't slept with anyone whilst he was there, he couldn't see what I was being so childish over. I would have hoped not sleeping with anyone else was a given, and not something I needed reassurance over, but obviously not!"

"So how have you left it?" she asked. "Is he likely to come crawling back?"

"I bloody hope not, but even if he does, he can get lost. I'm sick and tired of running around after him, being at his beck and call just like his bloody mother!"

"Trudie, there's no need for that language, dear," giving her a look that said, "I know you're upset, but resorting to swearing is never the answer."

"I'm sorry, I'm just annoyed with myself that I've let it get to me so much. I don't know why I didn't finish it sooner. I naively kept hoping he'd grow up. I think his accident, and his response to it, was the final straw."

"What do you mean?" questioned Caroline, a puzzled look on her face. "What's his accident got to do with anything? That was months ago, wasn't it?"

Realising she had probably said too much, Trudie topped up her wine whilst she gathered her thoughts. The look on her face had not go unnoticed by Caroline.

"Are you going to tell me what's going on, or not? Because I can see there's more to it than you're letting on and it's obviously bothering you."

Her aunt had always had the knack of being able to read her like a book; it was almost as if she had a sixth sense wherever Trudie was concerned. Trudie sighed, realising she was not going to be able to avoid telling her, and anyway it wasn't a secret, was it?

"Well, it's quite simple really," Trudie began, very matter-of-factly. "When Josh tripped into the road, it caused a truck to break suddenly to avoid him, which then caused a car to smash into the back of it. That car unfortunately was being driven by Betty's daughter, Annie, meaning Josh was responsible for killing both her and Richard."

"Oh dear, that's awful," Caroline replied, shocked. "Surely Josh can't be held responsible for that, can he? You said it was an accident, that he tripped when someone ran into him, didn't you? You can't call your engagement off just because of that." Whilst she had never been Josh's number one fan, she equally felt a need to defend him on this one.

"I know it wasn't his fault directly, but what's really been bugging me is his whole attitude. There's neither remorse nor compassion; all he felt was annoyed that he was out of action for a few days with a sprained ankle. He's never given a second thought to the wider picture, or the consequences."

"So, have you spoken to him about this?" continued Caroline, keen now to hear the full story.

"Yes, earlier today. I don't think he'd even realised himself before I mentioned it. He'd never thought to ask any questions of the police, just accepted what they told him at face value. He was not really interested in anything else, only bothered about himself as always. Typical Josh behaviour," Trudie concluded.

"So how did you find out, has Betty said something to you?" enquired Caroline, suddenly fascinated by the unfolding story.

"Heavens, no. Betty just knows it was an accident. I don't think I could look her in the eye if she knew my fiancé was responsible for their deaths!" reacted Trudie. "I only worked it out when I put some of the pieces together, and went back through my diary and the news articles for that day. Josh was never named in any of the papers, but everything else was exactly as both had described the event, so there's no doubt."

"Well, that is truly awful." Caroline, for once appeared lost for words.

"What I need to work out now, is whether I have the nerve to tell Betty, or do I keep quiet and continue to help her, or should I just walk away? I'm really confused and haven't got a clue what to do for the best. If I don't say anything, I'll feel like I'm lying to her, and if I do say something, I risk losing her as a friend, which in a way is what she's become to me these last few weeks. And above all else, I want to help her to try to find some family, because in my heart I sense there must be someone out there for her," sighed Trudie suddenly feeling mentally drained by it all and at a complete loss to find a way out of her dilemma.

Having now drained her glass of wine, and eaten two pieces of cake, she decided it was time for bed, so kissed her aunt good night and headed upstairs to her room. She was hoping a good night's sleep might bring some clarity to the situation, but when she got under the covers and snuggled down, her mind continued to whirl.

Tossing and turning in an attempt to get comfortable, Trudie soon realised sleep was a long way off for her.

Chapter 24

The following afternoon, Josh was sitting in the snug at his parents' home, watching the sports channel with the highlights of one of the football games that had been on over the weekend. It was a mindless distraction from thinking about anything else; the bowl of popcorn and bottle of beer remaining untouched in front of him.

His parents were expected home shortly, and no doubt his mom would make him something to eat as soon as she got in, he thought to himself, feeling too idle to sort out his own food, or even leave the settee for any length of time. They had been away for a couple of nights to celebrate their wedding anniversary, staying at some plush lodge somewhere upstate, he seemed to recall. Josh was not sure exactly where, and to be honest, was not too bothered. He rarely paid much attention to his parents or their comings and goings these days. He missed his mom's cooking though, and as he would not know one end of a saucepan from the other, had been living on take-aways, or whatever junk food he could find lying around since they had left.

The upshot though, was they were not yet aware of his break-up with Trudie, or more correctly her break-up from him, or about the accusations she was making about the accident itself – which frankly was the first he had heard about it as well. He was feeling particularly sorry for himself, and just needed them to come home and let him know everything would be okay.

"Hello, Josh. Are you home?'' he heard his mom shouting from the hallway sometime later, waking him from the doze he had obviously fallen into. The television was still on, the coverage having moved onto tennis in the meantime.

"In here," he moaned, half asleep as his mom opened the door to the snug.

"What's wrong with you, are you ill?" was her immediate question, seeing him stretched out, crumpled tissues strewn all around him, and empty plates, bowls and glasses littering the floor and the side tables.

"Trudie's finished with me," he replied dramatically, without further explanation and obviously looking for the sympathy vote.

"Why, what have you done this time? What did you get up to in Vegas that you've not told us about?" Although Marcia was not a particular fan of Trudie, or too enamoured about their engagement, she knew her son, with all her maternal instincts sensing he would not be without blame in some shape or form with whatever had gone on.

"That had nothing to do with it, and for your information Mother I didn't get up to anything in Vegas, thank you very much!" he replied, disgruntled that his mom had not immediately jumped to his defence.

"Well, something must have happened, because everything was fine a couple of days ago when we left," she replied, harsher than usual.

"What's happening?" asked Blake on entering the room, sensing from the tone of his wife's voice that something was wrong. Marcia rarely raised her voice, or spoke without affection when addressing her golden child.

"I'm not sure, other than Josh is feeling very sorry for himself," she replied provocatively. "It would appear Trudie has ended their engagement without any good reason."

"I didn't say without any reason, I just said it had nothing to do with Vegas," he replied sighing. "If you must know, her reason was related to the accident I had a few months ago."

Blake and Marcia exchanged a glance, obviously confused. "What's that got to do with anything?"

"Well, apparently my accident killed two people, leaving a women Trudie knows without her husband and daughter. I wouldn't mind, but I knew nothing about any of it! She called me insensitive, without compassion, lacking in any remorse, plus rattled off an even longer list of my shortcomings, which basically summed up to me being a completely selfish bastard."

"Right. I suggest you start at the beginning, and you tell us all about what's happened," proposed Blake, in an attempt to get to the bottom of what Josh had said.

"Well, I'm in need of a strong G&T before we start!" announced Marcia, as she made her way to the drinks cabinet.

For the next hour or so, Josh talked his parents through what had happened; detailing the accident itself, the commotion at the time, the police taking a statement at the scene, his visit to the hospital to be checked out, and the subsequent visit from the police to let him know the outcome of their enquiry, informing him that there had been fatalities, and that no further action would be taken.

"So, where does Trudie fit into all this?" enquired Marcia, still confused as to why this had a bearing on her son's relationship.

"Well, it would appear that the lady who lost her husband and her daughter is a patient Trudie sees at the hospital. She sustained some minor injuries and whiplash that required physio. They've apparently become quite close, so when Trudie joined up the dots and realised my involvement, it's left her in a difficult position, she says." Seeing his mom was still confused he added, "I think she's really cross that I showed, in her view, no compassion, or even said I was sorry. I was just my usual selfish self apparently!"

Blake loved his son, and was not blind to his shortcomings, so could sympathise completely with Trudie's assessment of him. He knew how much his wife spoiled him, even recognised how selfish Josh had become over recent years, and for that, knew he needed to shoulder some of the blame. He should not have allowed it to continue, and should have encouraged his son to be more independent and more accountable long before now.

"Right, I think we need to get this sorted. Firstly, I'd like to understand whether what Trudie's saying is correct, which I don't doubt, but I'd prefer to hear the official line. And secondly, if she is correct, and your accident was to blame, then I believe an apology, at the least, is in order to the lady concerned. What you and Trudie do once that's sorted is up to you. For now, we'll address the accident and you can then deal with the fallout. I must say though that if you want to win her back, then working on that list she gave you will be a good start," he said, reaching for his phone and searching for the mobile number for Greg Darcy, Chief of Police, and one of his golfing buddies. "I'll make a call straight away and arrange a meeting at the police station first thing tomorrow morning."

Marcia and Josh exchanged a glance as he left the room. They both knew that once Blake's mind was made up, there was no shifting it.

Chapter 25

Two weeks later, Betty was putting her hat and coat on, ready to go to the stores to run a few errands and collect some fresh fruit and groceries. It was a crisp autumnal morning; the sun was bright in the cloudless sky and there appeared to be a bit of a nip in the air. It was the type of morning when provided you wrapped up well, a walk in the park was in order, or perhaps a ride out into the countryside to see the changing leaves.

Today though for Betty, it was just a quick trip into town, with perhaps a stop off at the café for some lunch if she had time, and a bit of company. Betty missed having people around the house, people to fuss over and care for. It was all a bit lonely, but she was determined not to let it get her down, especially on a day like today, when the good weather beckoned. No, she would not sit in and wallow. It was time to start getting her life back in order. Richard would have had no time for her malingering, or feeling sorry for herself.

As Betty picked up her keys and shopping bag, she noticed an envelope had been posted through the door. It lay on the mat all alone, looking quite lost. Betty rarely received mail these days, most formal correspondence seemed to be done online, and although she was getting used to dealing with all the bills and utilities now Richard had gone, it was not something she enjoyed or looked forward to. Matt had kindly set up her online accounts and her standing orders at the bank, transferring everything into her name, which she had been so grateful for, but it was all still a bit of a minefield to her. She had established herself a morning routine for checking what had come in, making notes in her diary of dates she needed to remember. With most transactions automatic now she rarely had anything to worry about. Everything seemed so impersonal.

Bending down to pick the envelope up, she noticed it was handwritten, and had been hand delivered as there was no stamp on it, nor any indication of where it may have come from. Intrigued by it, she considered reading it when she got back, but curiosity got the better of her, so she opened the envelope. Inside was a single sheet of old-fashioned, quality writing paper, the type people seldom used these days, with a handwritten letter in a script that indicated a well-educated person. It looked and felt comforting.

As Betty read the short message, tears started to well up in her eyes. The message was a relatively simple one, although at the same time quite complex, leaving her with a mix of emotions she could not fathom, or in fact know how to respond to. When she had finished reading it for the second time, she wiped her eyes, before carefully putting the sheet of paper back into the envelope, and placing it on the console table in the hallway. She would deal with it when she got back, whatever that meant, she had no idea.

Wellstone town centre was relatively busy. Young moms were pushing prams and strollers around the park, people were cycling along the high street, opting to leave their cars at home, and dog walkers were out exercising their pets, standing around chatting whilst their dogs politely sniffed each other. It was such a beautiful morning that most people had probably had the same idea; get out of the house for some fresh air and exercise whilst the weather holds, as it will be a long hard winter ahead. The rain and snow were never far off at this time of year.

The stores were all decorated for the season, with most store fronts and doorways either displaying pumpkins, or harvest arrangements to entice their customers in. Thanksgiving was only a week or so away, Betty realised, and for most families it was a time to celebrate, which was usually good for morale, as well as business. People would be shopping for extra food, presents and all manner of things, stocking up for the winter no doubt, or Christmas just a few weeks later.

This year, the season would feel hollow. With both Richard and Annie gone, what did she have to feel particularly thankful for? She knew Matt felt the same way, with neither of them feeling like celebrating the holiday, but for Jack's benefit they had decided to do something low key. After all, life had to go on. They had spoken about it earlier in the week, on the phone one evening, after Jack had returned home from school and started asking questions of Matt. The teachers had been talking about it in class. The school was preparing a small service, to which parents and grandparents were invited, so he had wanted to understand what it meant. He was proving to be quite an inquisitive little boy, with school bringing both structure to his day and a distraction from thinking about his mom. His class was being asked to dress up for the event, so thankfully no lines to learn, although it did mean Matt needed to find Jack a suitable outfit, he had mentioned to Betty. Annie had always handled dressing-up days; it was yet another area he had no expertise in, the list just seemed to get longer each day.

Matt had spoken at length to Betty about his concerns for Jack, opening up in a way about his feelings that had taken her a little by surprise. He had shared some of his fears for 'what happened if' scenarios; them both painfully aware of how tenuous life was, and how easy it was to lose it. He too was concerned about the lack of family. His only brother, Simon and his wife Sara, would, he imagined, take Jack in if anything happened to him and Betty was not around, but it was not something that they had ever had cause to discuss, or been forced to face before. "You always think there'll be a tomorrow," he had said to Betty, ruefully one day, during one of his darker times. He had also realised how demanding a young child could be, never fully appreciating how much Annie had done for Jack, nor how much he had sat back and let her. It was not just the feeding and clothing, or all the emotional stuff, but the unending arrangements that needed to be made to accommodate his school life, his social life – in fact, everything. It had certainly been a rude awakening for him to suddenly become the one responsible for being 'The Person' Jack turned to for almost everything.

Betty had always got on well with Matt, even if on occasion she had questioned to herself whether he was right for Annie, or whether their relationship was built to last. They had appeared to drift apart in recent years, leaving Betty to worry whether Matt would bale out at some stage if life got too difficult, leaving Annie to raise their son alone. She had noticed how the balance in their relationship had subtly changed after Jack's birth, and although Matt had never been particularly outgoing beforehand, he had certainly become more insular after his son's arrival. It was Annie who did the heavy lifting where childcare was concerned, Annie who worried about her son and constantly placed him at the forefront of everything she did, often at the expense of Matt or his feelings, Betty had noticed, on more than one occasion. In fact, she recalled how preoccupied Annie had been the day of the accident; sensing at the time all was not well, now never able to discover what had really been troubling her.

Recently there was something endearing about the rawness of Matt's feelings when he opened up to her about Annie's death; the way he was taking on his role as daddy to Jack, conscious of his every shortcoming as a father. Also, the way he continued to look out for her, ensuring she was supported, not just with her hospital appointments, but in all the small everyday things he did for her without question. Yes, his selfless behaviour had certainly endeared him to her, even more than she had previously realised. She was seeing a side to her son-in-law, a strength of character, that had been hidden for some time, only resurfacing now perhaps, out of the necessity of the situation. Betty realised they both needed to hold on to each other, almost using the other as an emotional life raft as they navigated their way through these difficult times. After all, there was no one else going to be there for either of them, was there?

Trudie turned her head slightly as she heard the tinkle of the bell ring as the café door opened, bringing in not just another customer, but an unwelcome draught of cold air into the bargain. Unfortunately, the café was on the shady side of the street, so it was not benefitting from either the warmth or the brightness of the sunshine, and although the heating was on it was difficult to keep the café warm with all the comings and goings.

Today was one of her days for working, and as they were short staffed, she had offered to do a double shift, covering for one of the ladies who had "gone away for a few days to deal with a family emergency," she had been told by Millie, the café's owner, thankfully without being furnished with any of the gory details. Trudie had arrived early for opening time and would be staying around to lock up too. It had been a busy morning, and now at one forty-five, the lunchtime rush had just finished. She was hoping for a few minutes sit down, preferably with a bite to eat, before the afternoon tea rush started, or the school run moms descended.

"Hello dear," smiled Betty, as she approached the counter to order her drink and something to eat. The young waitress was off, so the normal table service was not operating. "What a lovely surprise to see you today, I'd forgotten you worked here," she added, feeling a little taken aback for forgetting that. Her memory was recovering gradually, and day-by-day it seemed to be getting clearer, with the occasional lapses making Betty realise what a slow process her recovery was. Although the doctors were pleased with her progress, Betty still got frustrated when things she had previously been able to do without effort, were now proving to be a challenge.

"Hello Betty, lovely to see you too. What would you like to order? I'm just about to go on a break, so, would you like me to bring you something over, and perhaps join you for a few minutes? I could do with the sit down," smiled Trudie, pleased that Betty had not only recognised her, but had taken the time to make conversation. They had not been in touch since the meeting at her house a couple of weekends ago, so Trudie was unsure exactly how the land lay in respect of the memory book idea she had discussed. Trudie was not a pushy person, so although she had left her mobile number, she was not surprised Betty had not been in touch. It had been a nice idea, perhaps just not something that either Betty or her son-in-law wanted to do, or even need her help with. And from Trudie's perspective, she had no desire to push her into doing something she was not completely comfortable with.

"Oh, that would be nice, dear. I'll have a piece of that cake and a cup of tea please," she said, pointing to the chocolate fudge cake. "And if possible, I'll have two of those cranberry muffins to take-out. I think this fresh air has made me hungry. I'll have one after dinner, or perhaps save them until tomorrow when my son-in-law is coming round."

Trudie smiled as she watched Betty amble over to a small table near the window, carrying her small shopping bag full of groceries, with a bunch of cheerful flowers balanced on top. There was an obvious spring in her step and a lightness about her, one that Trudie did not recognise from the last time she had seen her, leaving her to wonder what had happened in the meantime.

"I'm glad I've seen you," Betty announced as soon as Trudie placed the tray on the table in front of them. "I wanted to tell you about all the progress we've made on the memory book. I also wanted to let you know about a letter I received this morning from a nice young man. Its contents should have made me upset and angry, but the more I've thought about it this morning, it's quite the reverse, in fact."

Intrigued to learn more, Trudie sat back and listened; for once lost for words, as Betty outlined its content, and more specifically its sender.

Chapter 26

Betty showed the letter to Matt the following afternoon when he called around to the house with Jack, after having picked him up after school. It had become a ritual that twice a week they called in, sometimes just for a catch up if they were on their way somewhere else, other times to stay longer and to share a meal with her. Betty looked forward to these occasions, as it gave her not only a reason to prepare food for someone other than herself, but also a bit of adult company, and most importantly some precious time with her grandson. He was growing up so fast, and the changes she had witnessed in the few short months since Annie had gone were incredible. Whether it was school, or having to be more independent without his mom doing everything for him was a question, or whether it was just him growing up; whatever it was, he was a delight to be around.

The school was well aware of his recent circumstances, and had even referred him for a few sessions of grief counselling to see if that would help, keeping a close eye on his behaviour in the classroom. They were looking for any triggers or signs of him getting upset. So far, everyone was pleasantly surprised with how well adjusted a little boy he was. With children, as with adults, grief can hit at any time, leaving no one complacent as far as Jack was concerned.

Matt started to read the letter Betty handed to him, having already been told roughly what it contained on the phone the previous evening. Arriving home from town, she had been quite buoyed up by the day's events, so could not wait to share it with him.

Mrs Newman,

Please allow me to introduce myself. My name is Josh Townsend and I am twenty-four years old and live at home with my parents.

You're probably wondering why I am writing to you. The reason is twofold. Firstly, it's to send you my deepest condolences for the loss of your husband and daughter. I can't begin to imagine how you must be feeling.

The second reason is harder to express, and it's the most difficult letter I have ever had to write. If you knew the number of times I have rewritten it, you would worry about the trees, but I wanted to be certain I got the tone right, as what I have to tell you is not just difficult for me to write, but will be hard for you to read.

Last July, I was out jogging one Saturday morning when the rain started. I decided to cut short my run and head home before it got too bad. Whilst I was running around a corner, an oncoming cyclist nearly crashed into me, causing me to slip on the wet ground and trip into the road. It was nothing more than a twisted ankle and hurt pride, so once the police had spoken to me, I made my way home.

What I was only made aware of quite recently, was that the truck that braked to avoid hitting me, was the same vehicle your daughter crashed into.

As such, my stupid accident caused your daughter and husband to lose their lives. I will never forgive myself for the heartless way I didn't look back to check what was going on around me, or for dealing with the consequences of my actions. I admit, I selfishly brushed myself down and simply went home. The enormity of what my actions led to is only now sinking in.

I want to offer my sincere apologies for your loss, and for the part I unwittingly played in it. I know nothing will ever replace them. I just wanted you to know how truly sorry I am.

Kindest regards
Josh Townsend

"What do you make of his letter, Matt?" she asked, once he had obviously had time to digest its contents. "I must admit, at first it upset me. Then when I read it a second time, I realised it wasn't the poor boy's fault, just an unfortunate accident. He seems really distraught, don't you think?"

"I suppose it doesn't tell us anything we didn't already know does it, other than we now have a name? The police had said the truck driver braked suddenly to avoid a collision with a pedestrian, but I presume we didn't know what the pedestrian was doing in the road until now, so perhaps that sheds some light onto it. I suppose it must have taken some guts though to write you that letter, so credit there for owning up to it."

"Yes, I agree. I may reply to him to let him know I harbour no hard feelings, if that will make him feel better. What do you think?"

"That's very magnanimous of you, Betty. I'm not sure I'd be as forgiving as that. Like you say, he is taking a degree of responsibility, which certainly has to be applauded." Matt was increasingly impressed by the way his mother-in-law was coping. In the initial days after the accident, he recalled how concerned he had been, not just about her welfare, but her general state of health, fearing this might tip her over the edge. Somehow she had pulled herself through it, and was now dealing with things in a manner that surprised him. There was a positivity in her attitude and approach to life that he thought he would never see again, which after only four months was astonishing. He wished he felt the same level of positivity. If anything, he found coping to be more of a strain each passing day.

In those early days, Matt had almost blocked out his feelings, concentrating on the practicalities to get him through, but recently those feelings were certainly making themselves more vocal, with grief hitting him at the most unexpected times. Christmas was just around the corner, Thanksgiving next week, Annie's birthday was not far off, saying nothing of their wedding anniversary, or Jack's sixth birthday early next year. All those big events in the calendar they had always marked together, that now he was left to mark by himself.

"I also meant to tell you, I bumped into Trudie in the café yesterday and we had a lovely chat over a cup of tea. She was asking how we were getting on with the memory book, so I told her. She also made a suggestion about doing some research into my Irish background and seeing if there's anything she can discover about my mother and her family. I know she's not alive, although it would be interesting to know a little more about her, and you never know, there may be some distant cousins still around. What do you think?"

"Oh, I don't know. What do you think? Is it something you'd like to do? It sounds like a potential witch-hunt to me given you've no real leads to go on," cautioned Matt. He was uncomfortable with the idea, although aware it was something Betty seemed eager to embark on.

"Well, Trudie thinks it's worth a shot, and if we don't find anything, then there's nothing lost, is there? Don't worry Matt, my expectations aren't too high, and it might be fun having a look – and that's a commodity we've all been sort on recently, isn't it?"

Feeling sufficiently rebuked, Matt thought he would leave it to 'Saint Trudie' to manage, and resolved to keep his own counsel on the matter.

Chapter 27

Later that same evening after dinner, Trudie was on her laptop in her bedroom, trying to concentrate on researching more about Irish adoptions in the 1960s, in preparation for meeting up with Betty at the weekend to formally kick off their search. They had spoken in the café the previous day, Trudie telling her what she had learned so far, and the processes that would be involved, making it clear though, that without Betty's consent and involvement, she would not be able to take it any further. It was not her story to uncover, she'd explained. Even so, she was prepared to help Betty every step of the way and had offered to do all the research for her, navigating her way around the internet, if that was what she wanted.

Betty had only taken a moment to think about it, before declaring that yes, she would love Trudie to do that, even exclaiming "it will be a bit of an adventure," as she reached over and took Trudie's hand, quietly saying "thank you, dear." The two women smiled at each other, neither appreciating that a bond had been struck between them that day, one that would have ramifications for both their futures.

Now though, as she surfed between pages of information, she struggled to focus on what she was reading; her mind continually wandering back to Josh, and what she needed to do about him. He had messaged her a couple of times since their last meeting, begging her for a second chance and saying he would change. So far, she had not replied, unsure exactly what she would say if she did respond. If she was honest, some days she missed him, other days she was glad to see the back of him. In her heart, she had even questioned what good a second chance would do for either of them. Josh's ability to change or grow up, or think about anyone other than himself and his mother, was so remote a possibility it was almost laughable.

And for herself, what did she want from life? Had the idea of getting married and settling down been a spur of the moment decision that in hindsight neither of them was really ready for? Dating had been fun, but the expectations brought about following their engagement were possibly too much for either of them to deal with.

Then completely out of the blue, Betty had told her about the letter she had received, the knowledge of which threw Trudie into a complete spin, rendering her speechless as she sat opposite her in the café drinking her tea and eating her lunch. Betty had stressed how sincere it had felt, how kind the young man had seemed, and how distraught it had made him feel to know the effects his accident had had on her life, for which he was truly sorry. Hearing this, Trudie was completely taken aback. It was exactly what she had hoped Josh's reaction would have been at the time, just something she had never imagined she would hear. It left her not only wondering what had prompted him to do that, but also at a loss to decide what to say to him in response. Technically, they had finished, broken off their engagement, so she did not need to say anything. Emotionally though it created loose ends that could just not be ignored, evoking memories of the Josh she had first started dating, the caring, sensitive person she had fallen in love with at university.

Just before eleven o'clock, her phone beeped, alerting her to an incoming message. Reading the screen, she was not surprised, particularly given the time of night, to see it was from Josh. He was a night owl, rarely going to bed before the early hours of the morning, and occasionally sleeping in until lunchtime, if his schedule at the bar allowed. Bar work did not lend itself to keeping sociable hours and his routine of finishing late and then taking in a couple of hours television before bed had become his norm.

His message was simple:

"Can we meet? I don't want to leave it like this J xx"

Perhaps he's right, she thought to herself, re-reading his brief message, assessing at the same time whether to reply or simply ignore it, as she had done with the last couple of messages he had sent earlier in the week. "Perhaps we do need to discuss it like adults," she thought to herself, recalling how angry she had become, and how petulant Josh was when they had last spoken at his house.

She recalled how his parents had been away for a few days, meaning Josh had returned home from Las Vegas to an empty house; no one to welcome him, or listen to his tales of what they had all got up to on the Strip, or how much money they had gambled away at the tables. Trudie had not been at all attentive, and Josh had become annoyed with her when she kept trying to change the subject, each of them completely uninterested in what the other was trying to say.

Both of them emotionally had been on a bit of a high, and if she was honest, when she launched into her monologue listing all his shortcomings, as well as at the same time throwing in the curved ball about his accident, and the tragic consequences it had inflicted, it had taken him a bit by surprise. He was stunned, at a complete loss for what to say in response; any of his usual bravado instantly deserting him. Although she had signposted it before his Las Vegas trip, it was fair to say he had not seen a split coming, saying nothing about being completely non-plussed by her revelation. No, she could not leave it like that.

"OK. I'm free Monday afternoon. Message me where"

"Great. Thanks. Love you xx"

Reading his final message did little to settle her thoughts. Did she still love him, or had it run its course? She had been so certain it was over, but for whatever reason doubts continued to haunt her.

As she shut down her laptop, realising how late it had become, also knowing she was wasting her time trying to concentrate any longer on the research, her mind wandered to the time they had first dated. She recalled the fun and excitement of it all, the student parties she had been dragged along to, kicking and screaming, knowing she should have been revising, and in the end had enjoyed. The carefree nature of independent living, away from the watchful gaze of their parents, providing them freedom to just be themselves. They had made love under the stars, got drunk on cheap booze, even high on the odd occasion, but Trudie would not be going there again, that was for sure, recalling the way she had felt the morning after!

They were both different characters, and although they had originated from the same town, living barely three miles apart in a relatively close-knit community, their paths had never crossed before their first meeting at university. They had enjoyed completely different upbringings, with diverse experiences of life as a consequence. Josh's, with his private education and access to all the luxuries that lifestyle provided, was the polar opposite to the homely lifestyle Trudie had been raised in. She had gone to the local high school, the same one her cousin Marcus had attended five years before her, Caroline and Scott seeing no need to look further afield. In their view, it was not only within easy walking distance, but had served Marcus well, so they had no complaints.

Their parents had never moved in the same social circles either; Marcia hosting many ladies' luncheons for the numerous charities she sponsored, whilst Caroline happily baked at home, content in her cosy kitchen, providing the anchor she believed her family needed.

On paper, their relationship should never have worked. Josh had brought out her fun side, introducing her to a new and exciting world beyond the confines of the library's walls. He had also broadened her friendship group to include his friends, all similar characters to himself, she recalled now in retrospect; none she had really gelled with, or continued to see. Following graduation and their return to Wellstone, they had tried to keep the spark going, but somehow it was never the same.

With hindsight, had her attempts to calm his boyish exuberance and get him to connect with the real world by getting a job, taking some responsibility, growing up and above all cutting his apron strings all been in vain? Their engagement, as she recalled was her suggestion, as was the idea to move in together and buy a flat, probably resulting from the fact they were both frustrated with the confines of living under their parents' roofs again. Perhaps she had overestimated his level of commitment to their relationship. Perhaps they had never really known each other at all, she admitted to herself.

Her thoughts continued to vacillate, and by the time she eventually fell asleep, no conclusion in terms of what direction she needed to take had been reached.

Chapter 28

"Good morning," Betty smiled, as she opened the door to Trudie late on Sunday morning. "You look like you've come prepared," she added, commenting not only on the laptop bag she was carrying over her shoulder, but the box of cakes she was balancing in her hands. "Here, let me take those from you," relieving Trudie of a Tupperware box that looked like it had seen a lot of service over the years. She had been sitting near the front window, watching out for her arrival, so had seen the car as it drew up.

"Thanks. Yes, my aunt was up early this morning baking. She suggested I bring some over for us in case we needed a sugar fix later. I'm not sure what's in the box, although I'll guarantee it'll be good whatever it is. I don't know what time she got up, or if she even went to bed. I swear, she seems to live in that kitchen," she laughed, as she shook off her coat and took off her shoes, leaving both by the door, before making her way into the sitting room. Betty had cream coloured carpets throughout her downstairs rooms, and the last thing Trudie wanted to do was walk dirt in, or leave soggy footprints. The rain had stopped for a brief interlude, leaving the streets wet, with puddles everywhere.

"Was that your uncle I saw dropping you off? It's just I didn't recognise the car," she enquired. She was not particularly nosy by nature, although recently she had tried to be a little more observant. Following the accident, her memory had been impaired for a while, so now she made a conscious effort to try to remember things, as well as taking more of an interest in what was going on around her.

"No, that was Marcus, my cousin, in his car. He's off meeting friends for lunch, so it was on his way. I probably should consider learning to drive and getting my own car. I usually cycle everywhere if the weather's good, so I don't really need one. It's just the winter months, you know, when it's a bit cold for cycling, and there's always the risk of rain, and the chance I'll get soaked on my return."

"Well come through, the fire's already on. Let's get you thawed out before we get started. How about I make us both a hot drink while you get your laptop set up, and we can try those cakes your aunt has sent."

Several minutes later, Betty returned with a tray of drinks, plates of cakes and a selection of small sandwiches she had prepared earlier, placing them carefully on the table next to where the laptop had been set up. She was conscious that last time Trudie had visited, when Matt and Jack had been here, other than a cup of tea, she had not offered her anything by way of refreshments. After she had left, Betty had felt embarrassed, so this time was determined to work on improving her hostess skills. After all, it was nice to have someone to prepare a meal for, and even nicer to have someone to share it with.

Eating alone was one of the things she'd struggled most with since Richard had gone. Nothing ever seemed worth the trouble when cooking for one, she thought, remembering some of the meals she had prepared, the dinner parties she had hosted over the years. Richard was not the most sociable of characters, although they did have a few close friends who he enjoyed sharing an evening with, mulling things over with a bottle or two of wine.

"Thank you." Trudie said, noticing the tray being placed down beside her. "The first thing we need to do, I think, is to register with the Adoption Authority of Ireland. I've got the link here," she said, pointing at the screen. "From what I've read, this new Law, you know the one I was telling you about in the café, well, it entitles people like yourself to have full and unrestricted access to your birth certificate, plus any information related to your early life, care or medical information they held on you before your adoption took place."

"That sounds good. So, what happens then?" enquired Betty, keen to follow up on what Trudie was suggesting, but not at all confident about how to go about it.

"Well, once you've registered, then I presume it may take a while for the records to come back. At least once they do, we'll have more information to go on. To be honest, I don't know exactly what the process is as everything is new, and no doubt they'll be inundated with hundreds of people like yourself seeking information. I presume once you've registered, we'll get access to more help, and hopefully it will become clearer," replied Trudie, with her fingers crossed. She was certainly no expert in this field, but when it came to tenacity and digging into the detail of whatever she was researching, then there were few to rival her.

"Okay," said Betty, excited to get started. "I suppose the only information I have so far is my birthdate, my adoptive parents' names and this photo to go on, which gives us a bit of a timeline I suppose. And the names 'Brigid and Maeve', although which is which I don't know," she smiled, looking at the photo once again. "Oh, I almost forgot. I managed to find my adoption papers, which may help. I'll go and fetch them. They were in a locked box with my parents' other papers, which I found when my mother died a few years ago. I'd forgotten all about it, and just put the box in the loft. Thankfully I found the key for it in Mother's jewellery box. Matt lifted it down for me the other day when he came round for dinner with Jack because it was quite heavy. They seemed to hoard everything," she rambled on to herself, as Trudie continued to flick between screens, trying to concentrate on what she was reading, as well as listening to what Betty was saying.

"That's promising. Hopefully, there'll be something in them that's useful. I've read in a few of the articles though that a lot of adoption papers back in the fifties and sixties were illegal, or forged, so we need to be careful. Let's see what yours look like."

Returning a few minutes later, Betty handed a thin folder to Trudie. She flicked through the documents it contained; a jumble of letters, scribbled notes and an official looking document that was headed 'Adoption Certificate'. "Well, this looks promising," Trudie remarked, quickly scanning through the document to see how authentic it looked. "It lists your mother as Ruby Miller, an address not far from here, and her occupation - as a store assistant. Does that sound about right?" she asked, passing the document to Betty.

"Yes, Miller was my maiden name, and that address is where I was brought up, so presumably they never moved house after they adopted me. I didn't know she worked in a store though. In fact, I don't recall her ever working. She always seemed to be at home, looking after my father and me. I know he ran an electrical business, and I think he must have been quite successful as we were never short of anything, but business, and certainly money, was never spoken of in the house."

Continuing to flick through the file, Trudie continued, "there're some letters here that suggest your parents' church was involved as we suspected, even one between them and a mother and baby home in Dublin called St Winifred's, dating back to March 1964. That tallies with the year you were born indicated on the back of your photo. The letter talks about Mr and Mrs Miller being put on a list for an adoption when a suitable baby becomes available, although there's no mention of any specific child. The way it's written, it suggests it's not the first time it's happened either. They've obviously used that home to adopt other babies, or children over the years. That looks really promising, let me google it and see what comes up," she suggested, her fingers already poised over the keyboard.

Moments later, Trudie scan read the screen; an article from one of the local Irish newspapers flashed up, recording that the home no longer existed, stating it had been closed since the mid 1960s, after a fire tragically razed the building, with the unfortunate loss of lives, as well as the loss of documents that had been housed there. The building never reopened, which according to the article was celebrated by the locals, some of whom had long feared the practices that went on behind the building's doors.

"Well, it looks like it was a mother and baby home – St Winifred's, not far from Dublin. The home's no longer in existence. Most of the records may have been lost in a fire the article suggests.

Anyway, let's put what we do have into the system and see what happens," said Trudie, some of her earlier enthusiasm now washed away. "Hopefully, your adoption certificate will be legal, meaning it should lead to you accessing your birth certificate, at least. That would then give us something to track down your mom's details, her family name and presumably help us search for her death certificate."

"Yes, that would be good. It's so sad to think she died so young and as a result of complications due to my birth. She must have only been about fifteen or sixteen, so sad."

Trudie noticed from the tone of Betty's response that she was starting to get a little maudlin, the process obviously forcing her to think about things she had never really considered before.

"Yes, it is," replied Trudie, keen not to be drawn down a path that would upset Betty further. But something continued to niggle her, as she once again looked at the photo Betty was holding. Something she had not really picked up on before now. The baby looked a couple of weeks old, obviously not a new-born; with the girl nursing her looking healthy and relatively robust, almost like a farmer's daughter. If there had been complications at the time of birth, the photo certainly gave no hint of that at all. It showed a young girl, full of sadness, who at the same time looked full of love for the little bundle she had swaddled in her arms. What was the true story here, Trudie mused to herself? Something was not quite adding up, and she just prayed she was not opening up a hornet's nest by encouraging Betty to embark on this search.

Chapter 29

"So, how did you get on with Josh last night?" enquired Caroline, as she and Trudie were clearing away the breakfast things. She knew they had met up a couple of times recently and had gone out the previous evening.

"Not too bad. We went out for a quick drink to Lowrey's. The bar was packed, with several of the regulars dressed up, some sort of stag do I imagine. There were a few bar games going on, and it all got a bit rowdy at one stage. Thankfully, for once Josh didn't try to get involved. We left around ten o'clock, before it got out of control, so nothing really exciting to report, I'm afraid." Trudie was still unsure where hers and Josh's relationship was going, and although she had agreed to meet up with him occasionally for the odd drink or a pizza, to see how things went, there were no promises, and certainly no commitments on her part. In her mind, she had resolved to give it until the new year, and then make a decision. The next few weeks were make or break, although she was not sure Josh saw it that way.

In truth, her feelings had wavered considerably since she had read the letter he had written to Betty, his words unexpectedly touching her, with the fact he had owned up for the part he had played in the sorry affair something she was grateful for. It had taken some of the discomfort out of the discussions she had with Betty. Trudie had always been fearful that she was hiding something from her, and in doing so being dishonest. Now it was in the open, and Betty appeared to be none the worse for knowing the part Josh had played, it was much better. That said though, Betty still did not know Josh was her fiancé, or anything really about her personal life, and Trudie did not feel sharing that detail would do anything to help their developing friendship.

She could also tell Josh was making a real effort, no doubt the result of the no holds barred talking to his dad had apparently given him after they had been to the police station to enquire after the accident. Blake had surprisingly come down on her side, agreeing that his son's behaviour was not acceptable. Things needed to change as far as he was concerned, and if that meant him and Marcia having to be much harder on their son, in an attempt to get him to grow up, then so be it. He for one would not be pandering to Josh anymore. "It's time to grow a pair," his father had apparently told him.

Fundamentally though, as far as Trudie was concerned, there was no discernible difference, nor any evidence that he was metamorphosising into an adult. He was obviously trying to be more considerate of her feelings, less selfish perhaps. Somehow it felt a little too contrived for her liking. Their relationship had lost the naturalness it had once had, and if she was honest, some of the trust had gone too.

"Well, just be careful young lady," warned Caroline. She was wise enough to keep her own counsel, and not offer unsolicited advice. At the same time her face could not hide the concern she felt that Trudie would get dragged back into a relationship that Caroline sensed was not right for her. "So, is it the hospital today or the café, or are you off to Betty's again? I've lost track of your movements recently. You never seem to be at home any more. All this gallivanting about!"

"Well, it's a bit of both," laughed Trudie. Whilst she loved her aunt to bits, and was well aware of how she felt about Josh, she was also conscious she did not need her controlling her life either. At twenty-three, she was old enough to make her own decisions, to know her own mind, and without wanting to hurt her aunt, did not want to give her the impression she needed her approval in terms of her life choices. "I'm off to the hospital now. I'm covering the lunchtime shift from ten until two this afternoon, then I'm going to call in at Betty's on my way home. She messaged me yesterday to say she'd received a response to that request we'd made for her birth certificate, so I'm going to check it out. I should be home between four and five o'clock. I'll help with dinner tonight, even give you a night off if you like," she added, giving her aunt a kiss as she left the room.

Thankfully it was a beautiful sunny day, with the forecast for a clear and chilly afternoon with only a light breeze. The rain was going to hold off until the weekend, according to the forecasters on the radio this morning, so Trudie felt confident cycling on her trusty bike. As she retrieved it from the garage, and wheeled it into the driveway, loading up the front basket with her laptop, a satchel with all her belongings in, and the lunch box Caroline had lovingly packed for her, it was not the first time she thought it was time to upgrade her transport. Seeing Marcus' car parked alongside the house, she recognised driving lessons and buying a car of her own was something she had put off for far too long, making a new year's resolution to sort it out as soon as Christmas was over, and the worst of the weather was behind them.

Two New Year's resolutions in one day! Not bad, Trudie thought to herself, given it was still only the first day of December.

Chapter 30

Trudie had now been volunteering at the hospital for over six months, gaining an increasing amount of experience and confidence each day with the patients she dealt with. Sister Cynthia Cooper still kept a close eye on her development, ensuring she was never left fully responsible for any patient, although increasingly allowing her to get more involved with their treatment plans and carrying out simple procedures. She saw not only how kind and considerate Trudie was with their patients, but also found her work ethic remarkable, particularly given she was only a volunteer and could walk away at any time.

"So, Trudie, do you mind me asking what your long-term plans, or your job prospects are?" Cynthia enquired that afternoon, while they were having a short break between appointments.

"If I'm honest, I haven't given it much thought recently." Trudie realised that she had been so busy focussing on everything else, that job hunting had been far from the top of her agenda. "I guess I've stopped applying for positions whilst I've been here. I suppose I should start again. I can't volunteer all my life, can I? I do need to get a proper job, and put my qualifications to some good use, and perhaps settle down one day. I can't live with my aunt all my life, can I? That would make me a sad case!" She laughed at the thought.

Living with her family was comforting, and other than her time at university it was all she had ever known. Her early memories of living just outside

Vancouver, in Canada, in the years before her parents had died, were now so distant she struggled to recall anything about them. The sudden image of a big garden and tall trees, with a swing fastened to one, her dad pushing her whilst her mom laughed in the background came to mind. Those images were few and far between and lasted only fleetingly.

Her aunt and uncle, when they had become her legal guardians, had not just taken her in, but had given her a real home and shown her a parent's love, replacing her own parents in a way that had been seamless to the young Trudie. She knew how devastated her aunt would be when she eventually did decide to leave home, accepting that perhaps subconsciously that was contributing to her reluctance to make that final move.

Marcus was technically still living at home too. Trudie knew that although her aunt was not happy with his current arrangements, she was at a loss to do anything about it. He was gradually spending less and less time at home, and more and more nights away. It was due to the fact he was dating a girl called Penny, who worked in town at the travel agents, and rented her own flat on the other side of town. Penny and Marcus had been together for nearly two years now, with Penny making it abundantly clear she would like him to move in with her, and take their relationship to the next level as far as commitment was concerned. Marcus was hedging his bets, unsure whether he was ready to commit in the way Penny wanted, happy to keep a foot in both camps, for as long as he could get away with it, Trudie suspected.

Caroline knew that at twenty-eight it was right that he should want his own space, although living as he was, in a manner that neither showed any commitment nor future for him or Penny, was not something she was pleased about. She did not dislike Penny at all, always making her welcome at their home, though staying overnight was not something she encouraged. No, as far as she was concerned, Marcus needed to make his mind up and not string Penny along any longer.

Trudie accepted it was a little frustrating, not only for Marcus, but for herself too, living by somebody else's rules, and she knew having her own space would be good. However, the concept of buying a flat with Josh no longer seemed viable, particularly given the current state of their relationship. In reality though, what was stopping her from buying her own place if that was what she really wanted? Money was certainly not the issue; the insurance pay-out she had received when her parents died, had left her more than comfortable, but without a job or somewhere to put down roots, on balance she realised she was happy enough staying put for the time being. Perhaps in the new year it was something she could give some more thought to.

"Well, if you ever do decide to stay, then I'm sure I could put a good word in for you here at the hospital," whispered Cynthia, conspiratorially. "I can't say too much for now, it's just that there may be a job coming up in this department in the New Year if you're interested, and I for one would love to see you get it."

As Trudie cycled from the hospital over to Betty's house later that afternoon, she began to realise that her list of new year's resolutions was starting to mount up. The position Cynthia had hinted at sounded tempting.

In terms of priorities, where should she start? Was sorting out her career the most important, or was perhaps getting a home of her own something she needed to focus on? Certainly, passing her driving test and buying a car was a priority, as she needed to get more independence and could not envisage another winter of relying on her aunt's old bike. But was that top of the list, or was deciding what she needed to do about her erstwhile fiancé her key challenge? She did not want to counter her aunt's wrath about stringing Josh along, in the same way Marcus was apparently guilty of.

Well, it was certainly a conundrum, and definitely something to chew over, she thought to herself, as she cycled faster towards the warmth of Betty's house, desperate to avoid the rain clouds that had made an ominous appearance, regardless of what the forecasters had predicted.

Chapter 31

"Come on in, dear. Take your coat off and warm up, you look chilled. At least you avoided the rain. Go through, the fire is on, and I'll make us both a warm drink if you like. Have you had your lunch yet?" bombarded Betty, with questions for Trudie as soon as she had walked through the door, talking to her like the old friend she had become over recent weeks.

"Oh, thank you," she replied, taking off her coat and boots in the hallway. "Yes, I've already eaten, but a warm drink would be lovely. I've come straight from the hospital, so it was quite a long cycle. I've just been thinking, it's probably time to start driving and get myself a car, then I wouldn't always be on edge worrying about the weather. I was desperate not to get my laptop wet today," she added, carrying her things through to the dining room table, which over recent weeks had almost become their office, before returning to the kitchen to give Betty a hand with their drinks.

"Yes, a car would be useful, all the flitting around you seem to do," observed Betty, before adding, "I didn't think I would ever drive again after the accident. Then I realised I couldn't cope without the car, relying on Matt all the time to take me places. And I'm sure Richard would not have wanted to see it rotting away in the garage."

They both felt so relaxed around each other these days, a naturalness having developed in the way they spoke to each other that no one would have foreseen; each obviously finding an affinity with the other, that was not only comfortable, but felt tangible. It was as if they had known each other a lifetime, not simply a matter of a few short months.

"Well, I'm so excited," started Betty, handing Trudie a steaming mug of coffee. "My birth certificate has turned up. It's only an electronic copy for now. The email says I'll receive a formal copy in the post in a few days."

"That's amazing," replied Trudie, taking a sip of her drink. "I thought it could take months, so for it to arrive in just over a couple of weeks since it was requested is fantastic. Either you landed really lucky, or they haven't had as many enquiries as they thought. Either way, that's brilliant news. What does it say?"

"Come through, I'll show you," said Betty, leading the way back into the lounge. Following closely behind her, Trudie noticed a lightness in her step, with an ease in her movements that she had never seen before, her back was ramrod straight with her neck showing no obvious signs of the injury she had suffered. As a physiotherapist, she smiled to see the improvement in her patient, and as her friend she was so relieved to see shades of the woman Betty had clearly been before the tragic accident. Something was spurring her on, giving her a reason to live again, and for that Trudie allowed herself a brief moment of pride.

"So, reading this your mom's name was Brigid O'Malley, so that probably makes you Maeve," smiled Trudie, recalling the notation on the photo. "And her date of birth was 2nd June, 1948, so her age was sixteen, which aligns to what we thought when we looked at the photo. It says she was a spinster, and according to this, her occupation was a farm hand. By the looks of her address, she was probably living on a farm. It says Hill End Farm, Dublin, I can't quite make out the name of the village, but let me enlarge it and see if I can read it better."

"Yes, that's what I thought too," said Betty, before adding, "It's funny, you mentioned she looked a bit like a farm girl didn't you, when you initially looked at the photo?"

"Yes, that's right. There was something about her ruddy complexion and her build. Even though it was a black and white photo, her rosy cheeks seemed to shine through, and she didn't look like she was a waif who hadn't had a good meal in her life. No, she looked strong, which made it even sadder to learn that childbirth was what had killed her."

Trudie enlarged the certificate so she could make out the name of the village, and straight away googled it to see where it was.

"Look here, Betty. It's showing it's just outside Dublin, about ten miles I'd guess. It doesn't look like a big place even now, so how big it was back in the sixties I don't know. Let me see what I can find."

For the next hour, Trudie searched all the records and archives her permissions would allow her, lost in a world she felt completely adept in. It always amazed and fascinated her the depth of history that could be unearthed at the touch of a button, and how easy it was to follow a chain of information when you knew what you were searching for.

She had originally enrolled with one of the genealogy search engine sites several years previously, when she had begun looking into her own background, spending many an hour at the time lost in her research. She would follow trails simply for the pleasure of seeing where they led, invariably forgetting what she had started out looking for. Although she occasionally still dabbled, nowadays she found little time to exercise her passion, so doing this for Betty was pure pleasure.

Thankfully, she had maintained her subscriptions to the genealogy sites, always with the intention of coming back to it someday, so now was able to not only access the basics, but delve deeper, allowing her into census information, births, marriages and deaths, even service records and parish records. Betty had watched, fascinated as Trudie scribbled notes into the A4 Jotter pad she had brought with her, recording bits of information as she flitted between pages on the screen, with the occasional gasp, or exclamation as she unearthed something new.

"That was a funny noise," Betty observed after a particularly loud "wow" from Trudie.

"Well, I may have found something, but I'm not sure," she said, calling Betty over. "Come and look at this and see what you think."

Betty saw Trudie had census information on her screen for 1961 and 1966.

"What am I looking at?" she enquired.

"Well, Ireland carries out a census every five years. I've found your mother was listed in the 1961 census at the address on the birth certificate," she said, pointing to the screen. "By 1966, she's not recorded as living there, which would be correct as by then she'd died. What's confusing, is there's no evidence of any death certificate. It shows she lived with her parents, Collette and Dominic O'Malley, and an older brother called Connor, who was twenty in 1965 and still living at home. He was shown as a farm labourer as well. I also can't find any death certificate for him. I have found a record of the ones for their parents though, your grandparents. It looks like they died in 1982, both on the same date. I'm not sure what happened there, as they must have only been in their late-fifties or early sixties at the time of their deaths."

Betty was absorbed by what Trudie was saying, "Well, my grandparents must have been very young when I was born then, so I wonder why they didn't take me in when my mother died?"

"Yes, your grandmother must have only been about thirty-nine or forty when you were born, which is very young to be a grandmother, I'd say. I suppose they must have married and had their children young. I've no idea why you didn't go and live with them though. That's a mystery, so we'll need to keep digging. If you're sure you still want me to do, that is?"

"Oh yes, please do. This is fascinating. I wonder what happened to Connor? He'd only be around seventy-seven or so now if he's still alive," she asked, doing a quick calculation in her head. "Is there anything else on him that you can find?"

"Well, I haven't got his actual DOB, just his age from the census information. The later one in 1971 still shows him at the same address. By then though, he'd be in his mid-twenties and possibly still unmarried. I might check what churches there are in the area, and see if I can access some of their parish records. They're normally a great source of information. I'm going to guess the family was Catholic, so I'll start with the Catholic ones." Keen to get on Trudie suggested, "why don't you make us another drink, while I do some more digging?"

An hour or so later and Trudie was still beavering away, her notebook filling as more scribbles were added the deeper she delved. As usual, she had gone a little off-piste, finding all sorts of articles, interested to read about Ireland, a country she had never really been aware of. After a while, she was starting to feel tired and glancing out of the window she could see that whilst she had been lost in her research, the afternoon had turned into evening. Outside was pitch black, with the gentle tapping against the window alerting her to the rain. Looking at her watch, she noticed the time.

"Oh, I'd not realised how late it was, and I'd completely forgotten I'm on my bike!" she said, as Betty emerged from the kitchen, having obviously been busying herself whilst Trudie worked. "I don't fancy cycling home in this, and my aunt will be wondering where I am. I've just remembered I'd promised to cook dinner too, give her a night off! I'm surprised she's not rung," she added looking at her phone for any missed calls.

'Why don't I run you, or order you a taxi and you can leave your bike here. In fact, you can stay for dinner if you want. There's plenty. I can easily ask Matt to drop it off for you tomorrow. He's calling in the morning after he's dropped Jack off at school."

"No, thank-you. That would have been lovely. I'll phone Uncle Scott as he can easily fit it in his car, save Matt or you the trouble. Also, as I'm supposed to be making dinner, I really should get home," she replied. "I'll just ring him, and then whilst I'm waiting for him to arrive, I'll let you know what I've found out, and what I intend doing when I get home, if you'd like?"

Chapter 32

Later that evening, after dinner was finished and the kitchen cleared and reset for the following morning, Caroline eventually settled down in front of the television with Scott to watch one of the documentaries they were so fond of, leaving Trudie sitting at the kitchen table, pondering the events of the day. It was only nine o'clock, so not particularly late, but she was beginning to feel weary, and rather than join them decided she would go upstairs.

She popped her head around the lounge door. "Good night, I'm going up now. I'll see you both in the morning. Thanks again for the lift tonight Uncle Scott. I really do need to start driving!"

They had spoken over dinner about Trudie wanting to start to learn to drive, and although Scott had offered to teach her, she had said she would prefer to take lessons, "if that's okay," she had said, not wanting to hurt his feelings. She added that she would appreciate him looking out for a little car for her in the New Year though; nothing too glamorous, just a little run around.

"Good night love, we'll see you tomorrow, sleep tight," replied Scott, not taking his eyes from the screen. "I'll get straight onto looking for a car for you tomorrow, and I'll also see if anyone can recommend a good instructor. We'll need to get you someone reliable," she heard him add as she climbed the stairs.

She really did not need him to do that, as there were plenty of names she could get hold of herself.

For one reason or another they both continued to assume she was still their little girl; in constant need of handholding, whatever stage of her life she was at. It was comforting in some ways to feel so loved, but at the same time could be a little claustrophobic.

It had been a long day. Volunteering at the hospital in the morning, then spending the afternoon at Betty's, concentrating in front of the computer for hours, staring at the screen, before coming home and preparing dinner as promised. In reality, her aunt had already done the majority before she'd arrived home, leaving Trudie to take over what little there was left to do, instructing her aunt to sit down whilst she finished everything off. She seemed to have been on the go all day, and if she was honest, it was not surprising she was starting to feel tired. Before she switched the lights off though, there was just one more thing whirling around her mind. She knew that unless she addressed it before she went to bed, there would be no prospect of her getting to sleep at all.

Opening her laptop, she penned an email to Father William McNally at St Magdalene's church, using the details she had found online for the small parish church in the village closest to the address of the farm Betty's mother had been brought up in, working on the assumption Google Maps was up-to-date! She had no knowledge at all of the area, so it was a real stab in the dark.

> *Father McNally,*
> *I hope you will excuse my direct approach, but I'm trying to find information relating to a gentleman called Connor O'Malley, who I*

believe may have lived in your parish. He would be in his late seventies by now, assuming he is still alive.

He lived at Hill End Farm in the 1960s, and was the son of Collette and Dominic O'Malley, who I understand are now both deceased.

Any information you have relating to this family would be of use. I am searching on behalf of a friend of mine who now lives in America. She believes she may be related in some way to Connor.

If you would prefer to speak to me directly, I can telephone you to explain more, or you can phone me. I live in Wellstone, New York State, so we are currently five hours behind you if you do want to call. My number and email are below. Thank you.

Regards

Trudie Lewis.

Re-reading the note, ensuring it carried sufficient information to solicit a response, without providing too many sensitive details, Trudie pressed the send button. She knew it was a long shot, but it was worth a try. She had searched on all the usual links and social media pages for 'Connor O'Malley' to see if there were any easier leads, discovering too many people of that name to whittle it down. Finding him may prove difficult, as apart from anything else, the chances of him having a huge social profile in his late seventies, seemed highly unlikely.

From what Trudie had read earlier that afternoon, farming in the 1960s in Ireland had been in dire straits, with many farmers protesting about the state of their industry and particularly the lack of support they were receiving financially from the government. There were accounts of protests in Dublin, with some reporting numbers of farmers being jailed back in 1966, when their grievances about receiving a fair deal led to fighting and arrests being made. In such a small rural community, times would certainly have been very difficult back then.

The more Trudie read about it, noting all the unrest and uncertainty at the time, the more she suspected as a young man he would likely have moved to Dublin to find work, potentially seeking his fortune outside of farming; even perhaps further afield, settling down and getting married, no doubt starting his own family. There was no guarantee he would have stayed in Ireland, with many articles reporting on the level of Irish emigration to countries like America or other such places. Ireland had a long history of struggles, not only with poverty, but conflicts around religion and the politics of the day. She had found it fascinating to research a little about a country she knew nothing of. The more she read, the more she realised how wide a net she needed to cast. No, it did not look promising, although nothing ventured, nothing gained was her motto. Having sent the email, she would wait to see if she got any response, and in parallel rack her brains for other ways to dig around.

She was certainly not giving up. For now, though, knowing she had done all she could for today, she logged off her laptop and got ready for bed, wrapping herself up against the cold of the night in her trusty red and white checked pyjamas, smiling to herself that as Christmas was just around the corner, she would soon be getting a new pair 'from Santa'; another of her aunt and uncle's traditions they insisted on honouring, regardless of her age!

Chapter 33

The following morning, Trudie woke around seven o'clock to the sound of her radio alarm, the usual news headlines the station broadcasted on the hour washing over her as she tried to engage her brain. Today Trudie has another busy day ahead of her, with a double shift at the café, covering for one of her ladies who had gone to visit her family upstate for a few days ahead of the Christmas holidays. As she looked at the darkness outside her bedroom window, and felt the chill in the air from the cold winter morning, she seriously considered whether to roll over and stay snug in her nice warm bed.

The sound of the alarm usually had Trudie springing out of bed, straight into the shower in preparation for the day ahead. Today she was just not feeling it. The temptation to ignore her alarm, and simply go back to sleep for a couple of hours was something she struggled to resist, as she slowly moved her legs from under the quilt. She should be feeling refreshed from her relatively early night the previous evening. Instead, she felt weary. Her head ached and her throat was a little sore, she noticed when she sat up and tried to swallow.

"Trudie, are you up yet?" shouted her aunt, as she made her way along the upstairs landing. "I'll go down and start breakfast. See you downstairs in a few minutes, dear." Caroline was always up first and liked to be on duty in the kitchen before the rest of the family turned up.

"No, not yet," she replied to her aunt. "I'm not feeling too good. I think I might be coming down with a cold or flu. My head is aching and I feel weary."

Caroline came into her bedroom, looked at the patient, and laying a hand on her forehead declared "I think you've got a temperature, young lady. I suggest you stay where you are, and I'll bring you up a hot drink with some painkillers. You need to keep your fluids up. Then I suggest you go back to sleep for a while and see if you feel any better by lunchtime. I don't think it warrants me calling the doctor by the looks of it. Just a bit of rest is my advice."

Caroline was relatively patient when it came to illness. She had little time for malingerers, or people looking for attention. Trudie was neither of these, with Caroline able to count on the fingers of one hand the number of days she had been ill, with never a cause to call the doctor, or rush her to the hospital in all the years they had looked after her. Marcus on the other hand, was a different kettle of fish. He regularly feigned illness to get out of things he did not want to do, with a tendency towards melodrama whenever he had a slight temperature, or a twisted muscle, always fearing the worst from whatever symptoms he had.

"But I've got a double shift at the café today, and I can't let Millie down," Trudie replied, moaning as she pulled herself out of bed. As she tried to put weight onto her legs, she struggled to balance, wobbling as she steadied herself on the bedpost.

"Well, you're clearly not going anywhere fast," her aunt observed, with a smile on her face. "Now, get yourself back into bed, and I'll be back up in a few minutes with a hot drink and some tablets. You've definitely caught something by the looks of it, and none of those old ladies in the café will thank you for taking it in, spreading germs so close to Christmas, will they?"

Knowing her aunt was right, Trudie reluctantly got back under the quilt, reaching for her mobile phone in the process. She would need to call Millie, the café's owner, to let her know she could not work today, but as it was her only shift for a few days, did not want to worry her more than that.

The café would be busy with people out and about doing their Christmas shopping, calling in for their festive treats, hot chocolates or even spicy coffees to warm them up. Trudie knew there were others who could help out, people who would probably appreciate the extra hours, let alone the generous tips running up to the holidays. No, she had no need to worry herself about that, and a couple of days resting would not be too bad, surely?

Opening her phone, quickly scanning through her calendar to check there was nothing else she had missed for the coming days, or any messages or emails that needed replying to once she had spoken to Millie and before she closed her eyes again, she discovered a message that had come in overnight. She was astonished to see it had come from Father McNally, the parish priest she had emailed only the previous evening. Suddenly, feeling more awake than she had done just a few minutes earlier, she opened the message and could not believe what she was reading:

> *Dear Ms Lewis,*
> *Thank you for your email.*
> *I do know Connor O'Malley, but as the parish*
> *priest at St Magdalene's for only thirty years, I*

*did not have the pleasure of knowing either of
his parents before their unfortunate accident.
I do however regularly say a mass for them on
their anniversary.*

*If you want to telephone me at your
convenience I will happily speak to you and
see what further help I can provide.*

God bless.

Father Bill

Returning to the bedroom five minutes later, carrying a
cup of tea and two slices of lightly buttered toast,
smothered with raspberry jam, Caroline was surprised
to see her niece sitting up in bed, a broad smile on her
face, her mobile tightly grasped in her hand.

"Whatever's happened?" she asked. "You
look perkier all of a sudden."

"I am, and you wouldn't believe it. I've
managed to track down Betty's uncle in Ireland. I only
wrote last night before I went to bed, and this morning
I've received a response from a priest over there, a
Father Bill. It's amazing. Here, have a read," she said,
excitedly passing the phone to her aunt, whilst
relieving her of the cup of tea and slices of jam on
toast. To think she had struck so lucky on her first
email was incredible, and for Father Bill, as he signed
himself off, to even say he recognised both parents'
names, left her in no doubt she had found the right
person. Of all the Connor O'Malleys in Ireland, what
were the chances or the odds of her being so lucky?
She had heard people talking about the luck of the
Irish, well perhaps she had Irish blood herself. Now
that would be a thought, she smiled to herself.

"Well, that is amazing," Caroline remarked,
after reading the message and passing the phone back

to Trudie, before adding, "that's all well and good, but you're still not leaving that bed today, even if the Pope himself sends you an email! Now, take these tablets and eat your breakfast, and I'll be back to check on you in a couple of hours," shutting the door firmly behind her as she returned to the kitchen, clearly emphasising her point.

Chapter 34

For the next couple of days, although she was confined to her bed, Trudie endeavoured to pursue her mission of finding Betty's family, delving deeper into her ancestry and rummaging through census information for the intervening years, between the late 1960s and the present day. The fact that she had already found Betty's mother's brother was truly amazing, and for the priest to know him, as well as regularly say a mass for his parents, was a good indication that he was still living in the area, which should help to narrow the search. It was starting to get more difficult - not only following the leads, but keeping her concentration levels up when all her body was telling her to do was sleep. Her mind was muddled, the scribbles in her note book now largely illegible.

O'Malley, it would appear from the numerous hits Trudie had received when she originally googled it, was a relatively common Irish name, and without anything to refine her search, she kept hitting a brick wall. It was probable that some of the O'Malleys she was uncovering in and around the Dublin area could be distantly related to Betty, cousins or second cousins perhaps, Trudie thought to herself. Until they had spoken to the priest, she did not want to conjecture too much. She just needed to be patient for a day or so more until she was fully recovered, which was difficult for her to accept. She was normally like a dog with a bone, and once onto the scent of something, there was no holding her back. For now, she simply had to accept she was not operating on full strength and try to relax.

Betty had been excited when Trudie had phoned her the previous afternoon with her news, equally surprised that something had come back so soon, and delighted there was positive news attached to it at least. Trudie had wanted to phone all morning, but the tablets had knocked her out, so she waited until Caroline had watched over her eating a bowl of nutritious home-made soup for her lunch, before arguing she had the strength to make a quick call. Caroline reluctantly agreed, provided Trudie in turn agreed she would go back to sleep for a few more hours once it was done. Trudie smiled kindly at the thought of having to reach a trade-off with her aunt on this point; Caroline, once again failing to recognise Trudie as an adult, not a small child that needed mollycoddling all the time.

"I think we should phone him together," suggested Trudie, when she and Betty had eventually spoken, concentrating hard not to lose her voice. Her symptoms were being managed with the regular painkillers her aunt was administering, although they showed little signs of abating in the next forty-eight hours or so. "After all, it's your search not mine, and whatever information he has, is for you to learn, not me," coughed Trudie when she had finished.

"Yes, I'd like that. Let me know when's convenient and we can phone from here. By the sound of your voice and that nasty cough, I would hazard a guess it won't be before the weekend though," observed Betty. "It will be exciting to learn more I'm sure, but at the same time, I have to admit a part of me does find it all quite daunting. To find out after all these years I may have a blood relative, who's still alive is great news. At the same time, I'm a little nervous at what else I might discover. Growing up believing I had no family was something I've always accepted, perhaps I was naïve never to have questioned it. Now, knowing otherwise, is quite difficult to absorb. It's like your whole life up until this point has been a bit of a lie."

"Yes, I can imagine that." Trudie knew from personal experience the anxiety she had felt when delving into her own background and her parents' past before the accident that had so cruelly taken them away from her. Her nervousness that she would uncover skeletons about them that she would have rather not know, details that would taint her memories.

When they were just memories, albeit in Trudie's case, ones that were fading fast, it was easy to keep them positive. After all, she had only been very young when she had lost them. Growing up and wearing rose-tinted spectacles whenever her aunt and uncle spoke of her mom and dad, it was easy for everyone to focus on the good parts, the happy times. Once the glasses come off, the truth has a habit of introducing darker images; events and situations you'd have been better off not knowing about. No one was spotless, that was for certain, and sometimes the past was best left in the past, hidden.

In this search, Betty would discover what her mother had been like as a young woman, who her grandparents were, and critically why her family had given her away as a new-born baby, sending her thousands of miles overseas to a family they had no obvious connection with, presumably either before or after the adoption had taken place. It would uncover some painful circumstances, Trudie was sure of that; all assuming Connor could still recollect what had happened, which was a big 'if'. With the passage of time, it was possible he had forgotten, or due to ill health, or even dementia given his age, may not be able to recall events nearly sixty years ago.

There was always the chance the news Father Bill had given them may just lead to another black hole. "If you're getting a little apprehensive, or worried, we can stop the search now. After all, other than a quick email to the priest, we've not done anything more serious yet, so there'd be no harm done," offered Trudie, conscious that she did not want to be the one who inadvertently led her friend into getting hurt. Betty had suffered so much over recent months, losing both her husband and her daughter, and now as she was starting to rebuild her life, Trudie was beginning to wonder whether giving her false hope was advisable.

"No, I think I would like to continue. After all, finding an aged uncle in Ireland is unlikely to change my life is it? At least it might shed some light on what happened all those years ago," concluded Betty stoically.

"Well, if you're sure, as soon as I'm feeling a bit brighter, I'll come over and we can make the call. I'll message Father Bill in the meantime and thank him, and I'll suggest a time that might be good. With the time difference, it could get complicated otherwise, and I don't want him calling us in the middle of the night, or vice versa. I guess he's not a spring chicken himself if he's been in the parish for over thirty years, so I don't want to confuse him, do I?" she laughed. "I'll be in touch in a few days. In the meantime, try not to worry."

"Thank you, and you try to get yourself better. Do as your aunt tells you. Let her nurse you back to health. By the sounds of it you haven't got much option otherwise," she laughed as she hung up the phone, feeling lighter than she had in months.

Meeting Trudie had been the start of an unlikely adventure for Betty, and something told her it was not over yet.

Chapter 35

"Well, thank you very much for all your time, Father Bill. It's been lovely to speak to you, and I'm sure we'll be in touch again soon. Good bye for now, and thanks again." Trudie put the phone down and looked across at Betty, who had sat down in the lounge, with a brandy in her hand, unable to fully comprehend what she had just heard. To say she was in shock was perhaps the understatement of the year, leaving Trudie a little concerned for her friend after what the priest had just told them.

"How can that be?" she asked, as soon as Trudie came over to sit next to her, gently taking hold of her hand in an attempt to steady her nerves. "Can he be right in what he says do you think, or is he perhaps a bit confused? After all, it was such a long time ago and he could be getting muddled with other people. O'Malley is a common Irish name, you said so yourself."

"Well, he didn't sound confused to me, or as old as I'd expected, so I tend to believe him," began Trudie. "If I'm honest, I think some of what he said stacked up with a few of the worry beads I've had whilst I've been doing the search for you. Anyway, now we've got Connor's son's mobile number, we can phone him directly. Then perhaps you can speak to him, if you want, and confirm whether what Father Bill said is correct, or not."

"Yes, that would be good. I think I'd like you to do the talking though, if you don't mind?" she asked. "I'm struggling to take all this in, and I wouldn't know what to say."

"Perhaps I should ring Matt and ask him to come over, what do you think?" Trudie asked gently, not wanting to leave Betty on her own to fret.

"Yes, that might be a good idea. Thank you, dear."

It had transpired that Father Bill did indeed know the family, and could talk quite clearly about the tragic events that had led up to the deaths of both Collette and Dominic, Brigid and Connor's parents. He described hearing about the fire that had swept through one of the outbuildings at their dairy farm a mile or so outside the village one autumn afternoon; instantly taking hold, with the abundance of hay newly gathered from that year's harvest. The blaze was further ignited when the flames reached barrels of chemicals being stored on the farm, disinfectants and the like for cleaning the milking sheds out, Father Bill explained. The fire service's investigation concluded it was an electrical fault that initially triggered the blaze; old electric wiring that had not been checked or updated for some time. Sadly, both Dominic and Collette were in one of the outbuildings when the fire struck, soon becoming trapped when an old rafter fell from the ceiling, barring their escape route and rendering them helpless.

It was a mid-week afternoon, and at the time, no one else was at the farm. By the time the alarm was sounded by a passer-by, with the fire service arriving sometime later, they were both badly burned. Although attempts were made to rescue them from where they were trapped, they were sadly unsuccessful. By the time the ambulance arrived, there was nothing left for the emergency services to do, other than pronounce them both dead. The tight knit community was devastated; many fearing similar outcomes for themselves, living so remotely as they did, miles out of the town and much further from any major city or real help.

It had been Connor's afternoon off, so when he returned home later that evening to find the outhouses and milking sheds razed to the ground, their livestock still in the fields desperate for milking, and a crowd of neighbours doing what little they could to save the main farmhouse from a similar fate, he was completely taken aback. He had only left after lunch that day, needing to call into town to do some errands for himself and his parents, before meeting up with some friends for a drink in the local bar.

At the time, Connor was in his mid-thirties. He still lived at home, working the farm with his parents and sharing the heavy load with his father. After the fire and his parents' deaths, his heart was no longer in farming, with the prospect of rebuilding something he did not want to consider. He sold up within two months of the insurance paying up, offloading the cattle to a neighbouring farm, the farmhouse cleared of all that he wanted to keep; little knick-knacks that perhaps had sentimental value, but were otherwise worthless. A young family moved in, with talk of renovation, modernisation and the introduction of new farming methods. Connor had no interest in what their plans were, happy to simply walk away.

He bought a small cottage in the town, furnished it with some of the pieces from the farmhouse and rebuilt his life, eventually marrying one of the local girls, and starting a family of his own. Having farmed all his life, he struggled for employment for a while, until eventually deciding to start up his own business, repairing machinery, servicing cars and generally turning his hand to anything that was broken or unserviceable, converting an old outhouse at the back of his cottage into his workshop.

He had always enjoyed tinkering on the farm, with the tractors and the milking machines, or anything else that needed repairing or had started playing up, so to him this was just an extension of that. He was good with his hands, and people liked him. In the early days, they probably felt sorry for him too, bringing things to keep him busy and feel wanted. Over time, people started bringing no end of items to his workshop for his attention, praying he could work his magic on it, hoping to avoid them having to fork out for something new. Gradually he built up the business, studying to get formal qualifications in electrics and electronics as technology improved, keeping himself ahead of the game, he liked to think. People trusted him, and there was little, if anything he turned away.

Over time Connor made not only a success of it, but a healthy living. He moved to a new industrial site on the outskirts of the town, employed staff and bought a fleet of trucks to enable him to take his business on the road. "After all, he couldn't expect his customers to lug their washing machines to him, could he?" asked Father Bill as he retold the tale. His son, Donal, was apparently now running the business, allowing Connor to enjoy his retirement, although his health was not what it should be, he observed.

Trudie and Betty were fascinated listening to Father Bill as he spoke, rarely interrupting, just allowing him to continue wherever his thoughts or his memories took him. His Irish accent was hypnotic, and his way of telling a story very engaging. Trudie could imagine him in one of the local pubs, a pint of Guinness in hand, gossiping away to the locals and holding court; unlike any clergy she had ever come into contact with before, or likely to meet again, she thought.

"Father, I know you didn't arrive in the parish until sometime in the early 1990's, but do you mind me asking if you know anything of Connor's sister, Brigid, or do you have any records within the parish of her having a baby, sometime around the mid-sixties?" Trudie prompted after a while, in an attempt to bring the conversation back, before waiting for him to continue.

"No, nothing from back then. When she was growing up it was long before my time. But I do recall my predecessor, Father Patrick, God rest his soul, once telling me about the family. I can't recall exactly what prompted it, but he mentioned Connor's sister, in the context of her being a spirited teenager in her day, regularly coming along to the local youth club. The church ran it in the village for the small group of children, in an attempt to keep them out of trouble. I'm not sure how much good it did her though," he laughed to himself. "He said she was a bit of a tomboy in her day, someone with a mind of her own, which working on the farm at the time, and having to stand up for herself was not a bad thing, I imagine," he added.

Betty had smiled when she heard that. It was the first time anyone had spoken about her mother who actually knew of her, and it was wonderful that it was a positive memory. At the same time, she was disappointed there was no record of her own birth. What was more surprising though was the way he continued to speak of her mother, almost in the present tense.

"Can I ask, do you know what happened to Brigid, and more importantly where she's buried? It's just that we've been unable to find any record of her death," enquired Trudie, becoming equally confused by what Father Bill was recounting.

"Buried, Heaven forbid! Whatever made you think that? The woman is still very much alive and kicking, as far as I'm aware," he remarked, the tone of his voice clearly showing how surprised he was at what he had just been asked. "In fact, it was only last Christmas that I saw her over here, visiting her brother if I recall correctly, and she was certainly in good health then, if perhaps a little tipsy I might add!"

Chapter 36

The next few days passed in a bit of a blur, as Betty and Trudie followed up on the conversation they had had with the priest, phoning Donal O'Malley, Connor's youngest son, to find out if what they had heard was in fact true. Matt had come along to sit in on the conversation, eager to hear what was being said and concerned about how Betty might respond to news that could effectively have a huge impact on her life. He had spoken to Trudie, so had a good sense of what may have happened all those years ago, but to have it confirmed was going to come as a huge shock, and Betty's reactions, given her current state of mind, were unpredictable to say the least.

He had dropped Jack off at school, arranging for him to have a play date at his friend Zach's house afterwards, with him collecting Jack some time before dinner. Since his mom's death, Jack had been naturally withdrawn on occasion, with Matt noticing a real anxiety with him whenever he was left at school, or at the swimming baths for his lessons, even at times with his grandmother. However, for some reason there was no evidence of any anxiety whenever he was with his best friend, Zach. He would happily be left there for meals, even sleepovers, never chasing Matt to collect him, and always full of stories whenever he returned. Matt was grateful to Zach's parents for providing the level of support and comfort his son obviously found in their home, a level of normality he assumed he was not getting at his own house.

Matt had purposely avoided having to engage with any of the parents beyond the school gates, comfortable to simply 'drop and run', mindful of the gossip and speculation that would be going on, the sorrowful gazes from the other parents in his direction. So, to find that Zach's parents were so welcoming and obliging, and so 'normal' was something he was pleasantly surprised at. They did not interfere, pry or offer him unsolicited advice. They were simply there to support him, and his son whenever he asked, wanting or needing nothing in return.

He and Jack had bonded more in recent months than they had ever done before, both discovering things about the other that they had never realised, what foods they preferred, common interests they had, even starting to rely on the other emotionally, in a way that had previously never happened. They had both finally accepted that Annie would not be walking back through the front door, shouting "Mommy's home," in her familiar tone as she entered the house, usually with bags of groceries or treats for them.

Jack had taken a long time to process that she would not be coming home, regularly going to the window or the door whenever there was a noise, expecting to see her, looking out for her car on the driveway, listening for the sound of her footsteps up the path. The house had felt so empty without her. He had eventually stopped calling out her name in the house whenever he needed anything, and now spent time seeking his dad out instead; thankfully, nowadays neither too far away nor locked in his study.

Matt knew that although Jack was dealing with it better during the daytime, the evenings presented a different picture, with him regularly crying out for

Annie in his sleep, or waking up fretful and coming in search of her. Matt would rush to comfort his son, trying desperately to settle him back down; always knowing that even when he had succeeded, there was no guarantee that the dream would not reoccur an hour or so later, or that his silent tears would stop. Matt found this hard, because he knew his son's behaviour was simply a mirror of his own.

The child grief therapist assured Matt that Jack's behaviour was perfectly natural. He needed to be patient, and just be there for his son, providing him with whatever reassurance and comfort he needed, in whatever shape or form that took. Every child and situation was different, she regularly reminded him, with no rule book on how to get through it. Children liked stability and routine, and equally they needed a distraction. As such, they developed their own new routines; routines that would not allow them to forget about Annie, but would enable them to get on with their lives. Before bedtime they would cuddle up on the settee in a way they had never done previously, Matt reading the stories that had always been Annie's domain, playing games to keep him distracted, games he had never realised his son enjoyed. It was a learning experience for both of them, each discovering aspects of the other's personality that they had never appreciated before.

The concept of the memory book had helped them both, if he was honest, and at home he had been seeking out things of his own that he could contribute to the collection his mother-in-law was pulling together for Jack. Photos or keepsakes that had meaning, trinkets he and Annie had collected over the years that held a particular story for them as a family. They may all have only represented a brief moment in time, but Matt wanted to ensure the memories they evoked were not lost. The sea shells Annie had collected on the beach the first time they had taken Jack paddling, carefully carrying them home and washing them, before storing them away safely to show him one day; the photo of her when she was eight months pregnant, laughing as she struggled to bend down to tie up her shoe laces, before losing her balance and collapsing on the floor. Matt recalled quickly taking his phone out of his pocket and snapping the image; one that not only captured her fun side, but also reflected the sheer joy she felt at expecting their first child.

It saddened him to recall that after those early days, there were too few precious moments of the three of them together, Matt now regretting how much he had withdrawn from Jack's early development, how much he had missed by leaving the majority of the caring for the baby to Annie. "What I'd give to turn the clock back," he thought to himself ruefully.

Now, having listened in to the conversation Trudie and Betty had had with Donal, he realised that although no one could ever turn back the clock, what Betty had been told had given her a chance to live a life that she had never in her wildest dreams imagined; not only providing her a chance to meet a mother she had believed to be dead all her life, but an extended family, the length of the list of names apparently stretching back over four generations.

After the tragedy of the accident, losing both her husband and only daughter, Betty had truly believed Jack was her only surviving blood relative. She had felt so alone in the world, completely unaware that it was so far from the truth it was laughable. There seemed to be more relatives out there now than seemed imaginable, the product of a good Catholic family, no doubt, as Donal reeled off so many names of aunts, uncles and cousins that Betty soon lost count.

What she would do with this information was perhaps too early to say, or what impact it would have on him or Jack was equally unclear. One thing though that was for certain, was she had no intention, from the way she had spoken after ending the call, of sitting back and doing nothing. No, if the last few months had taught her anything, it was that every day was precious and she needed to live her life. Perhaps not the life she had been born to, or even the life she had expected to live once she and Richard had retired, but a new life. A life full of hope and promise for the future. A life getting to know a family, her family.

"Right, I'll phone you back in a couple of days when I've spoken to the rest of the family about the best way to approach this," said Donal, before adding, "after all, Aunt Brigid is no spring chicken, and she'll have no expectation after all these years of finding you again. So, the last thing we want is for the shock to give her a heart attack, isn't it?" he laughed, in a similar hypnotic Irish accent to Father Bill's; one Trudie was starting to find not only soothing, but strangely attractive.

Chapter 37

By the end of the following week, Trudie was on tenterhooks waiting to hear any news from Betty. They had left it with Donal to speak to the rest of the family, presumably starting with his own father, after which he said he would get back in touch with them. He had both hers and Betty's mobile numbers. He had not committed precisely who he would get back to, which left them both anxious, and at the same time wary of chasing him. Neither Trudie nor Betty knew anything about the family circumstances, other than the little Donal had told them, and if truth be told, he was only a young man by the sound of his voice, so had no real memories or recollections of what had taken place all those years ago. He had just provided them a potted history of what he knew, which had not amounted to anything of real substance, other than the long list of names he had reeled off; admitting that some of them he had not seen in a long time, or in fact had ever met, given they no longer lived in Ireland.

He was Connor's youngest son, and said he had two older half-brothers from his father's first marriage; a marriage that had left him widowed in his early forties. His brothers had long since left the area, moving to the glitz and glamour of Dublin. He had returned to work with his father in the family business after graduating, confirming what Father Bill had said, adding that he was largely running it now that his father was retired.

He had explained that his mam, Ella had worked as a home-help in her mid-twenties, assisting the elderly in the village with any chores, shopping or appointments they needed to attend. As Connor was a recently widowed man with two small boys to raise, the village all chipped in to support him, with Ella apparently turning up one day on his doorstep, advising him that she had been sent to help, gradually taking over the raising of the boys and spending an increasing amount of her free time there.

Over time, they developed feelings for each other, and eventually Connor summoned up the courage to propose, which was a massive relief to the villagers, who had feared he had lost his nerve where relationships were concerned. They were a close-knit community and had watched Ella grow fond of both the boys and Connor, and although none of them felt it was inevitable, there was a feeling of collective celebration when they eventually married. Connor needed support around the house, but he also needed someone to care for him and his sons, and Ella could do both in equal measure. She was an honest, trustworthy and homely girl, who seemed to live her life to serve; her own happiness and wellbeing being derived from the value she added to other people's lives.

Donal told them he had been born just before his father's fiftieth birthday, noting there was almost ten years between him and his half-brothers; at the same admitting they had never been particularly close growing up. They had their own lives, their own families, and although there was the occasional visit home to see their father, those visits were getting less frequent as the years passed, he had noted. It was said in a way that was sad, whilst at the same accepting of the fact that not everyone was suited to a rural life. His voice suggesting that although it was not of his choosing either, he felt more of an obligation to stay closer to home than perhaps his brothers had.

Trudie's phone rang whilst she was sitting in the lounge, watching a television programme her aunt had suggested she might find amusing, although it had failed to hit the mark. As such, she welcomed the excuse to get up and answer it, and sensing it would be Betty, she ran to the kitchen to where her phone had been left plugged in, recharging.

"Hi Josh," she answered, when she saw his name flash up, instantly feeling deflated it was not Betty on the other end of the line. She had not spoken to Josh for at least a week, when he had last phoned to suggest they go out for a drink. She had declined, arguing she was too busy and was starting to hope he had got the message that their relationship was over, but obviously not. "How are you doing? Is everything okay?" she asked politely.

"Yes, I'm fine thanks. I was just wondering what your plans are for over Christmas. It's only a couple of weeks away and we've not discussed it yet. Mom was wondering if you wanted to spend it with us this year. She's arranging a party on Christmas Eve, for a few of their friends, and asked if I wanted to invite some people too. So, I thought you might want to join us, and perhaps stay over for lunch the following day. I can give you your present then."

"I've no plans yet," she replied, desperately trying to think of an excuse on the hoof. "I'm helping Aunt Caroline make Christmas lunch, so I'm planning to eat here with the family. Why don't I phone you in a week or so, and I can let you know about the party then?" hoping that would suffice. "And you shouldn't have got me a present. I'm not expecting anything, given technically we're not together anymore," she added, less subtly, about where she saw their relationship at least.

"Well, I know, but ......" Josh replied, unsure exactly what else to say, sounding like the wind had just been knocked out of his sails. "Why don't you phone me when you know what you're doing and we'll take it from there. I have to go now, Mom's shouting upstairs for me, so I better go to see what she wants. Bye, Trudie."

"Bye, Josh."

After he had hung up, Trudie held the phone to herself for a few minutes, unsure what to do next, her feelings once again confused after having spoken to him. She was desperately trying not to lead him on, or give him false expectations that they were getting back together, or that all was well with the world because they had met up for an occasional coffee together. No, whilst she had no issues with remaining friends, as far as any engagement was concerned, she was certainly no longer on that page, but was Josh? She had stopped wearing her engagement ring, which he had noticed when they met up, but in terms of returning it, well, perhaps that should be her next move. That, if nothing else, would make her intentions clear. It was just the timing was awful. With Thanksgiving over, Christmas a few days away, and New Year around the corner; a time when all the dreams and resolutions for the coming year are expressed, everyone in a hopeful mood for their future, the timing could not have been worse.

And, in terms of Christmas itself, the last thing she wanted to do was return his ring then, just as he presented her with a gift. "Why has life suddenly got so complicated?" she asked herself, at a complete loss how to answer that.

Chapter 38

It was the fifteenth of December, just ten shopping days left until Christmas. Trudie was working in the café, covering another double shift, along with Millie, the café's owner, who had decided it was time to call in the reinforcements and get more staff in.

The lunchtime rush was finally over. The stream of shoppers, coming in for a warm drink and a seasonal snack had made it seem like it would never end. No sooner was one table cleared and it was occupied again; customers almost fighting over tables, so desperate were they to sit down and relieve themselves of the heavy bags of presents they were carrying. Becca, the new young waitress who was helping out today, was completely rushed off her feet. Although, given the number of tips she was receiving, she did not seem to be complaining too much. She kept a welcoming smile on her face, helped carry trays to tables if anyone was struggling, and generally cleared away the dirty cups and plates efficiently, enabling the tables to be wiped and reset quickly for the next occupants. It was good for business, and the customers appreciated the service, as did Millie who kept a watchful eye on her.

Around three o'clock, Trudie saw Betty enter the café, without any bags in her hands, so obviously not on a shopping trip. She approached the counter and smiled at Trudie.

"Hello Betty. How are you today, and what can I get you?" enquired Trudie, pleased to see her friend. They had spoken on the phone over the last couple of days, each anxiously waiting for news, but had not met up since they had spoken to Donal the previous week.

"Nothing, thank you. I was wondering; will you be taking your break any time soon? It's just I'd like a quick word if you've got a minute," she asked, adding, "It shouldn't take too long," smiling in the direction of Millie, who she knew was the café's owner. Trudie had introduced her on a previous visit, and although Betty could not remember her name, she remembered her face.

"Why don't you take your break now, Trudie?" smiled Millie, obviously overhearing the conversation. "The worst of the rush appears to be over, and you haven't stopped all day. I think you're due a sit down for a few minutes. Why don't you go and take that table, and I'll bring you drinks and some cake over?" she offered, seeing a quiet table being vacated and no-one obviously ready to pounce on it.

"Thanks Millie, I won't be long," she replied, wondering once she had sat down and rested, whether she would ever be able to get up again. Her feet and back had started to ache, and she had served enough coffees and hot chocolates today to put her off ever wanting to drink either again. They were due to shut in less than a couple of hours, so she consoled herself, not too long to go. After all, it was good for business.

"So, I had a long call with Donal yesterday. He sounds a lovely young man, and I know what you mean about that accent," Betty said as soon as they sat down, unable to take the smile off her face. "Well, the top and bottom of it is, he's spoken to his cousins, my half-sisters I presume, and the feeling is that they would like to meet me. They've suggested that I might like to go over to meet them, to England, to Liverpool. It's apparently where the majority of that side of the family now lives, and where my mother moved to, back in the late 1960s." She stopped to take a quick drink of her coffee, before continuing. "I'm then going to be reunited with my mother once my sisters have prepared her. They don't want to say too much until I get there for some reason or other. However, they've assured me she's well, so that's something to be thankful for at least. I still can't believe it!"

"That's marvellous news, Betty, I'm so pleased for you," replied Trudie, genuinely delighted for her friend, and hopeful for the family she would find. "When are you planning on travelling?"

"Well, I'm going to book my flights tomorrow, with the intention of going over next week, and then spending Christmas there. I know it sounds sudden. It's just that I've lost so many years, I don't want to miss another minute. Christmas is not going to feel the same here anyway this year with Annie and Richard gone, so I might as well travel and use it as a distraction, if nothing else."

"Yes, I can see the logic in that. Everything has happened so fast. If that's what you want to do, then I agree, go for it. Life's too short after all, we both know that," Trudie added.

"Well, the thing is, what I really want is for you to come with me. I couldn't have done this without you Trudie, and I really don't want to travel all that way by myself. So, I'm planning on booking two tickets, if you would like that; my treat as a small token of my appreciation for what you've done for me. What do you think, do you fancy coming on an adventure, and meeting a few of those relatives you've spent all your time looking for?"

"Wow, I didn't see that coming! And you're going next week, celebrating Christmas away from home, without Jack?" Trudie questioned, surprised at what Betty had just proposed. "Do you not want to take him and Matt with you?"

"No, I've told Matt what I intend doing, and he's not really interested. After all, it's not his family, is it?" she replied, "No, it's you who I'd like to accompany me. If you'd like to come that is?"

"Well, in that case, yes I'd love to come. Thank you so much for asking me. How exciting!" Trudie's smile suddenly lighting up the whole of the café.

All she needed to do now was break it to Aunt Caroline that she would not be home for Christmas, and as a stickler for family traditions, that was no mean feat. At least it got around the problem of what to do about Josh and his mother's blasted cocktail party!

Chapter 39

Their flight into Liverpool's John Lennon Airport eventually landed mid-morning, after a long and uneventful cross-Atlantic flight, followed by a brief stopover in Dublin, Ireland, enabling passengers to clear customs before transitioning to the UK. They then boarded a much smaller aircraft for the short thirty-minutes crossing over the Irish sea. That flight, which only had around twenty passengers onboard, had been relatively bumpy, due to the bad weather, the pilot had advised. They were requested to remain seated with their seat belts fastened for the during of the flight. As neither Betty nor Trudie would profess to be good flyers, or had any intention of moving around the small aircraft, they simply buckled up and sat back, both thankful when the wheels finally touched the tarmac of the runway, and even more so when it skidded to its eventual stop. The rain outside was torrential, and the poor visibility had meant they had not seen much of the skyline on their approach into Liverpool, but the weather had done nothing to dampen their spirits.

Their journey had taken a bit of a convoluted route, as booking at the last minute, and especially over the busy holiday period, it had been all the travel agent, Penny, could arrange for them. Trudie had forgotten Marcus' girlfriend worked at the local travel agents so when she and Betty popped into the office, conveniently situated on the high street opposite the café, she was initially surprised to see her sitting behind the desk.

Penny had sorted the bookings for them, including arranging a small hotel for their first few nights, close to the area Donal suggested, which according to him, was near to where most of Betty's family lived.

Penny had listened patiently as Betty excitedly told her the reason for their journey, emphasising, to Trudie's embarrassment, the role she had played in helping to find Betty's roots, the searches and the digging, the countless hours on the internet.

"Oh, that's wonderful," Penny had said, smiling over at Trudie.

Thankfully, it was a quiet day, everyone was spending their money on presents, not travel. They were her only customers that afternoon, so there was no need to hurry them. Business was notoriously slow this close to the holidays, no doubt it would pick back up again in January, when people started thinking about their next summer holiday and the prospect of sunnier climes. Penny had nothing else that urgently needed her attention that afternoon, so just sat back in her chair and relaxed, accepting she was in for the long haul!

The more Betty spoke, it soon became obvious to Penny that neither woman was an experienced traveller, nor equipped for the adventure they were embarking on at such short notice. Some customers had a clear itinerary of what they wanted when they came into the shop, firm requirements for their time away, whereas these two women not only had no real idea where they were going, or how long they would be away, but had given no thought whatsoever to what accommodation they would need when they got there.

Penny, through gentle probing, eventually managed to decipher what they needed, securing their flights, a small hotel, as well as organising transfers to the airport from home, and ensuring they had all the information and documentation sorted before they left. She had felt, by the time they closed the shop door, nearly two hours later, that she had a real affinity with the older lady. So, wishing them well, she had been determined to make everything as smooth as possible for them. If nothing else, their story had brightened up what would otherwise have been a tedious afternoon, watching the clock tick slowly towards closing time. It would also give her something to tell Marcus about when he next called round to see her, because by the sounds of it, Trudie's family had no idea she was going away.

Trudie was just relieved her passport was still valid, without which the trip would have been a non-starter. She would have been unable to join Betty on this adventure, and perhaps would never have learnt how it would all end. Trudie felt a considerable amount of emotional investment in Betty's story, so from the moment Betty had mentioned it, Trudie had been really excited to be accompanying her, determined she would not let anything, or anyone, stop her from going to England.

Trudie recognised her life had been falling deeper into a rut over recent months; far deeper than she was comfortable with. She had already resolved to sort out her job, her driving lessons and importantly her relationship with Josh, but how that would help, she was still unsure. Although Betty and she made an unlikely friendship, it was the best thing that had happened to her in a long time, and whatever else she did with her life, she did not want to ruin that.

Her aunt had, like Matt, suggested they delay the trip until after the new year at least, using the excuse of waiting for better weather, rather than pulling on the emotional heartstrings about her not being home for Christmas. Trudie could read her aunt like a book. Josh – in true Josh fashion – was more concerned about how he would spend the holidays with her not being around, or who he could take to the party, saying he did not want to be all alone with his mother's cronies! He really did not seem to grasp the concept that they were no longer officially an item. Perhaps the break might emphasise that a little more; if not, she might need to employ a sledge hammer to knock it into him, she thought. No, nothing or no-one was stopping her from travelling.

In terms of all the sorting out that needed to be done, Trudie accepted this was not a conventional holiday, and she would not have known where to start. As such, she had been grateful for all the help Penny had given them. Other than a couple of trips to Canada to visit family there, she had never travelled outside of America, hence going to England was such an exciting prospect. She had dreamed of travelling one day, but life had somehow always got in the way. Now, she finally had the excuse to go, and no reason not to. She had read and heard so much about Ireland during her search, and would eventually like to go there too, whereas England, well, that had always been top of her bucket list.

Betty was a more seasoned traveller, and although it was not that long since she had returned from her European cruise, only a life-changing six months ago, she thought ruefully, she had always left sorting out any travel arrangements to Richard. He had been meticulous in his preparations, with nothing left to chance. Betty, before she retired, had thought nothing of travelling around the state, regularly visiting suppliers or attending various conventions, arranging her hotels on route, confident to travel alone. However, planning a trip like this, at a time when her emotions were all over the place, her mind not always as clear as she would like it; well, that was a different ball game entirely, and even she accepted it was a little much for her to take on. Thankfully, she felt physically fit enough to travel, forever grateful she had continued with all her exercises once the initial therapy sessions had come to an end. No, they were both grateful for all the help they could get.

"I'm so glad Donal offered to meet us here," yawned Trudie, as they waited for their suitcases to emerge onto the carousel at the baggage reclaim area. They were both tired, having not slept much on the flight. They had even managed to upgrade their seats at check-in, giving them extra leg room to stretch out, but they still felt tired and in need of a proper lie down. "It's just a shame he couldn't meet us in Dublin, then we could have all arrived together," she added.

"Yes, that would have been nice. I think he wanted to get here and make sure everything was ready before our arrival. I get the impression, from a comment he made the other evening, that my half-sisters might have mixed emotions about me, a stranger as far as they're concerned, just turning up for Christmas. I haven't spoken to any of them directly as they've always used Donal as a go-between. So, I'm not sure what reception we're likely to get when we finally meet up with them, which I presume will be tomorrow, now," she said. "If it's frosty though, or we're not made to feel welcome, once I've met my mother, we can always fly home early, or do some sightseeing – whatever you fancy. We'll just have to wait and see," Betty observed pragmatically, smiling over at Trudie.

Betty had to admit feeling more than a little concerned about what they might find when they eventually got to wherever it was they were going. "Have I perhaps been a little too hasty flying over?" she questioned herself, or should she have taken Matt's advice and got to know them better before rushing in, perhaps exchanging a few calls and FaceTime chats first to break the ice? Well, it was too late to worry about that now as they were already here. "Time to face the music," as Richard would have said.

Betty had spoken to Donal on a couple of occasions, and in one of those conversations, he had mentioned that Brigid had gone on to have three more children; all daughters, Mary, Ruth and Colleen, with Mary being the eldest. Mary was apparently in her early fifties, based on a vague memory he had of a surprise fiftieth birthday celebration a couple of years previously. He recalled his mam and dad had travelled to Liverpool to attend, with his dad almost kicking and screaming as he boarded the aircraft. He was not one for travelling, or partying, or even visiting family, but Ella, his mam had insisted on them going. She still enjoyed a good knees-up, thinking it was also the perfect excuse for a few days away from small-town life. For her it was a chance to live it up in the city, even the opportunity to visit the Beatles museum, the Cavern Club, or any one of the numerous Beatles haunts Liverpool was famous for. She had been so excited, whereas Connor, her husband, who could not see what the fuss was about, was less so.

Betty was thrilled to learn from Donal that she had three half-sisters. For her though, the real reason for the journey was to meet her mother, and importantly understand why she had been given away all those years ago; a new-born baby, barely days old. The treasured photo she had of that time was safely packed in her suitcase. She wondered whether her mother would even recall it being taken. And above everything else, why had she been led to believe she was dead, when all the time she was living in England, with her new family? A family Betty had never been allowed to be a part of, and until recently was completely unaware even existed.

Betty had to admit, since discovering what she had from Father Bill, her feelings and emotions had vacillated all over the place, tossed around in the proverbial tumble dryer, leaving her above all confused and unsure of herself. One minute she was on a high, ecstatic with the knowledge she had living relatives, no longer alone, as she had feared after the accident. The next, she was angry and saddened at why it had taken her nearly sixty years to discover her heritage. Why had her birth mother not kept her, or at least fought for her, and why had her adoptive parents never told her anything about her background? They had, at best, been economical with the truth; whereas in reality they had lied to her all these years, even going to their graves without ever opening up about the facts of her adoption.

Losing Richard and Annie had made Betty question her life, her values and her place in society. Now, with this added dimension, she began to question her memoires and all the experiences she had ever had growing up. Had she lived a lie all these years?

Eventually, with their luggage safely in their hands, they made their way to the Arrivals Hall, where they had arranged to meet Donal. He had kindly offered to be their guide and chauffeur for the first couple of days, saying he had planned on hiring a car for his stay anyway, so it would be no problem. He was also acting as the interface with the family, smoothing the way; the expectation of problems, or at least difficult questions, never too far from anyone's mind. Betty had no intentions of hiring a car, so was grateful for his offer, and even more grateful for his sensitivity, the way she sensed he was protecting her from what might happen once she arrived. She prayed it was not a bad omen, recognising whatever the truth was, so needed to know. Then she could decide how to deal with it.

As they approached Starbucks, where Donal had suggested he wait for them to come through, assuring them it was so small an airport they could not miss it once they had collected their luggage, Betty saw a young man, anxiously looking around. He was tall, well over six foot she would guess, quite gangly, with a mass of unruly red hair. He was dressed casually in a pair of jeans and a waterproof coat, protected against the weather. As she caught his eye, she was not certain it was Donal, whereas there was no mistaking the woman who was standing next to him, her arms outreached as the gap between them narrowed. Betty had to do a double-take. It was almost as if Annie had come back to life, as the women staring back at her was the image of her beloved daughter.

"Hello, Betty, I presume? I'm Colleen, your sister. Welcome to England," she said, tears in her eyes and her arms outstretched, ready for Betty to walk straight into them. As she dropped her suitcase, and walked towards the younger woman, any qualms she may have had about making the journey disappeared in a puff of smoke. Trudie and Donal were left to stand and watch, as the two women embraced for the first time; strangers, but family.

Chapter 40

Colleen and Betty sat in the back seat of the car, tightly holding hands as if nothing would ever separate them again, leaving Trudie in the front seat next to Donal. Trudie watched as he skilfully nudged the car slowly out of the airport car park, avoiding the puddles and navigating his way carefully around other passengers, who were desperately trying to locate their own vehicles and avoid getting wetter than they needed to be.

Trudie's first experience of Liverpool was seeing a big yellow submarine outside the airport's doors, which felt a little incongruous outside an air terminal, but this was the home of the Beatles, so she supposed anything goes! She was excited what else the city had to offer, and hoped that once Betty felt comfortable with her family, she would have some time to explore. Reading up about the city before she had left home, had left her excited about what lay ahead, and to come at Christmas was even more magical, "if only the rain would hold off," she thought to herself, keeping her fingers crossed.

"I'm going to take you straight to your hotel and let you freshen up after your flight. Then if you'd like, Colleen and I can join you for an early dinner in a couple of hours, or so?" Donal asked Betty, ten minutes or so into the journey. He had not engaged much in small talk with Trudie, choosing instead to remain quiet, unless answering a direct question, allowing her to simply sit back and take in the scenery.

"I think with the jetlag, you're going to feel weary later on, so I'd suggest we wait until tomorrow before you meet up with Mary and Ruth. I'll pick you up and take you over to Mary's house after breakfast, if you'd like?" Donal offered, smiling through the driver's rear-view mirror to Betty in the back seat.

"Yes, that sounds very kind. I think after that flight, both me and Trudie are in need of a short rest and a cup of tea," replied Betty, smiling back. "I hope we've not put any of you to too much trouble by just arriving like this. I'd hate to think we've ruined anyone's Christmas."

"Well, you've not ruined mine, that's for sure." Donal replied, smiling over at Trudie, before adding, "you two have given me the perfect excuse to get out of Ireland for the holidays and have some fun. I've got friends in Liverpool whom I'm hoping to catch-up with between Christmas and New Year, so there's no complaints from me. And with Colleen here offering me a free bed for a few nights, then that's a bonus!" As he spoke, it was the most animated Trudie had seen him since their arrival. He had given her the impression of being a quiet introvert, although something about his recent comment, and the way he had smiled over suggested otherwise. Perhaps one of those 'friends' was someone special, she mused?

"Yes, it's lovely to have you stay over, Donal," Colleen replied, before adding for Betty and Trudie's benefit, "I live by myself and have never married, so I've no one else to spoil. The extra company over Christmas will be lovely, otherwise it would've just been me and the cat, sharing a ready meal, watching Sound of Music for the umpteenth time, before falling asleep in front of the telly. In fact, you two must come over for Christmas lunch. It won't be anything particularly grand, as I'm not the best of cooks. I can always get something in from M&S. They do some great food, and it cuts down on all the hassle of preparation and washing up!"

Neither Betty nor Trudie had any idea what M&S was, or had given any thought to what they would be doing Christmas Day itself, so, they simply thanked Colleen, saying that would be lovely. Silently though, Trudie wondered what Aunt Caroline would think to the concept of a take-away Christmas dinner, without all the trimmings or the traditions that accompanied it. Perhaps she would keep that little nugget of information to herself, she thought, knowing that if she did tell her, Aunt Caroline would insist on her taking the next flight home.

"Right, this is your hotel," Donal announced about ten minutes later, as they pulled into the driveway of a small, three storey red-brick building, with huge bay windows and an imposing doorway, through which a Christmas tree, decked with bright twinkling lights could be seen.

Trudie noticed there were quite a few cars already parked up in the hotel's car park, suggesting it was busy inside; others obviously spending their time away from home like her and Betty. It looked to have a warm, homely feel to it; nothing like some of those impersonal franchise, or group hotels that were common around the globe; providing the same experience wherever you were in the world. No, this one, with only three floors, was small by American standards. Nevertheless, it looked very welcoming.

"It's not a hotel I'm familiar with. I had a quick look at the reviews on TripAdvisor, and it seems fine, if a bit quaint and dated," Donal said reassuringly. "The food sounded okay though, and as I recall you said you had breakfast included, that's a bonus." Switching off the ignition, he added with a smile, "why don't I grab your bags, and we can get you both checked in. You can then get that pot of tea ordered before you both start to wilt."

Chapter 41

Early the following morning, both Trudie and Betty were waiting in the hotel's reception area anxious for Donal's arrival. He had said he would be there by ten o'clock, giving them both plenty of time to get ready and have a hearty breakfast before setting off. He was now ten minutes late, and Betty was starting to get panicky.

"I'm sure he won't be too much longer. It's probably just traffic," offered Trudie, in an attempt to calm her friend down.

Betty felt a little sick. She had not been able to eat anything, her nerves on edge for the day ahead, and her anxiety levels at an all-time high. Any excitement she may have felt the previous day seemed to have disappeared this morning. She had not slept well, tossing and turning, finally getting to sleep around midnight, before waking up around four in the morning, jet lag presumably kicking in.

Over dinner in the hotel's small restaurant the previous evening, she and Colleen had spoken about their lives, Betty telling her about her recent loss, discussing some of the events that had led up to the search they now found themselves on, again emphasising the invaluable role Trudie had played in all of this. She talked about how they had met, her physiotherapy sessions, even the memory book that was designed to not only help her deal with her loss, but provide that valuable keepsake for Jack as he grew older and wanted to know more about his own mom.

As Colleen listened, her eyes misted over, feeling a real sympathy for what she was hearing. She had never experienced the type of love Betty spoke so warmly of. Having never married, or had children of her own, she could not begin to imagine what it must feel like, or how deep that sense of loss must go. To lose one person who is so close to you, is devastating enough, let alone two. And when all that happens at the same time, and under such tragic circumstances, how on earth do you process that, or ever fully get over it?

In return, she told Betty a little of her life, saying she was a researcher at the local university, specialising mainly in the field of engineering. She admitted to leading a quiet life, which at times could be quite lonely she added, with her cat, Twinkle, being her main companion on the cold winter's nights. Although she had dabbled a little with dating over the years, and had even gone on the occasional night out with a colleague, even a blind date with a 'friend of a friend', nothing had ever come of it. Now, in her early forties, and ironically working in a predominantly male environment, she had given up hope. She had resigned herself to becoming a mad cat woman, indulging any maternal instincts she still had on her nieces and nephews.

Trudie would have loved to have asked more about her research work, given as an academic herself it was an area that truly fascinated her, but now was not the time. However, the more she watched Colleen as the evening progressed, she could not understand how someone so kind and caring, and obviously as intelligent as she clearly was, with her pretty face, long russet hair and a not unattractive body, had failed to find a partner. The saddest thing was, the way she

218

spoke so caringly about her nieces and nephews, she imagined motherhood would have come so naturally to her, and something she now felt she had missed out on.

Trudie occasionally glanced over at Donal, noticing him fidgeting with his phone and responding to the odd text message, his expression clearly showing he was nowhere near as enamoured by going down memory lane again as his two cousins were. To be fair, he had heard Betty's story already, during their various conversations over recent days, and if he was anything like Marcus around the family dining table, she sensed by his behaviour that he had somewhere else he would rather be. The speed at which the bill was paid once the desserts had been cleared away, and the swiftness with which he got back into his car, clearly emphasised that point.

Seeing him now as he swaggered into the hotel, wearing the same clothes as the previous day, Trudie sensed she had not been too far off the mark. He had clearly not been home, or if he had, had not bothered changing his shirt, and by the looks of his hair, showering had been the last thing on his mind! His smile, and that voice, no doubt getting him into more trouble than she cared to think about.

"Good morning ladies, are you all set?" he bounded in, full of the joys of spring, despite the light smattering of snow on the ground outside. "Shall we head towards Mary's house and see what she has to say for herself?" he asked. "It's only a couple of miles away, so we'll be there in less than five minutes."

Trudie got the impression from the way he spoke, the tone of his voice and even his body language, that Mary was perhaps not his favourite cousin, or someone, unlike Colleen, he was particularly close to. It was almost as if every time he mentioned the name 'Mary', he checked himself to make sure he did not use the word 'scary' in front of it.

"I'm sorry I'm a few minutes late," he said, as they approached his hire car, parked in exactly the same spot it had been left the previous day. "The traffic was heavier than I expected at this time of the morning, although I suppose two days before Christmas, that's to be expected, with everyone running around doing their last-minute preparations. I'll probably try to call into the shops and pick up a few presents this afternoon, if I get the chance. Otherwise, people will just have to make do with my sparkling wit and personality as their present this year!" he added, laughing to himself.

As he drove the short distance to Mary's house, Trudie, now sitting in the back seat, letting Betty chat away to Donal, reassessed her first impressions of him. He was clearly nowhere near the shy, introvert she had initially presumed, meeting him that first time at the airport. The more she got to know him, the more the different facets of his character became exposed. With his current level of confidence almost as infectious as his smile, he clearly had a lively, if not colourful personality. This was a good thing, as Betty certainly needed any boost she could get today as she potentially came face to face with her past.

To see her now, relaxed and chatting away like old friends with her cousin, she prayed that whatever the next few days had in store, the fates would be kind to her. She wanted nothing to hurt or disillusion her friend, or scar any of the memories she already held, or was likely to make for the future, whatever that future might bring. Today, they would meet Mary, and according to what Donal had implied, the sisters would then discuss how best to approach their mum on the subject.

Donal had mentioned that Brigid had suffered a small fall a month or so previously, so was not as mobile as she had been. It was nothing that was too concerning, just a little inconvenient, but the sisters did not want to worry her until they were sure themselves that Betty was in fact who she said she was. News of her existence had come as a complete shock to all of them, Brigid never having uttered a single word about ever having had another baby. So, until they were convinced themselves, they had no reason to trouble their mum. It was probably just a case of mistaken identity, after all O'Malley was a common name, had been their view.

"Right, we're here. Gird your loins, ladies," Donal announced, pulling up in front of a modest detached house, on the quiet suburban street where Mary lived. "I've just seen the curtains twitch, so I'm sure we're expected," he added, a mischievous glint in his eyes.

Betty got out of the car and made her way nervously up the neat driveway, to the brightly painted front door. She was unsure what the next few hours would hold for her, meeting another of her sisters, revealing another layer of her family to her.

Without needing to ring the bell, Mary appeared and opened the door, ushering them quickly into the warm hallway; the central heating quite stifling inside as they came in from the cold. There were no kind words of welcome, or open-arm gestures as there had been with Colleen, just a terse, "you'd better come through, there's someone here to see you."

Betty nervously entered the small lounge, unsure what to expect, or who would be there to meet her. Perhaps her third sister, Ruth, or maybe one of the many nieces or nephews she had heard spoken about may have called over. No, the sight that met her was one of an elderly lady, sitting with her leg raised on a footrest, a plaster cast around her lower leg and foot, obviously in some pain. By the looks of her, she had either only recently woken, or was on heavy medication, as there was a tired expression on her face. Although on seeing Betty enter, any pain or tiredness was instantly forgotten, replaced by a smile that not only lit up her whole face, but brought a brightness to the tired décor of the lounge.

"Hello Maeve, how lovely to finally meet you again," she said in a quivering voice, whilst at the same time reaching out her arms, tears appearing from nowhere in her eyes. "You don't know how happy this moment has made me. All my Christmases have come at once," she added, falteringly. "Why don't you come over here and give your old mum a hug?"

Chapter 42

Brigid's Story

Brigid O'Malley was like all the other girls in the village, desperate to grow up long before her time. She was anxious to shake off the prim school girl image, those bottle green skirts, knee high socks and a hat that got stuffed in her bag the minute she was out of sight from the ever-watchful eyes of the nuns from the local convent school she attended. The uniform they insisted the girls wear left a lot to be desired when it came to fashion, but what would they know about that, having to wear that drab habit, and hide their hair beneath a wimple day-in, day-out? As far as the sixties were concerned, they still dressed as if they lived in the 1860's not the 1960's.

She consoled herself there was only just over a term left to go. It was mid-February, so in less than four months, she could leave school and get a job, preferably one that allowed her to earn her own living, as well as move away from the farm. She might even try to get into the secretarial college if she got the grades in her exams, provided she could borrow some money from her parents to move to Dublin, because milking cows was just not where she saw her future. The rural life with its early mornings was not for her.

"Brigid, are you nearly ready? Helen's been downstairs waiting for over ten minutes now, and if you don't hurry up, your dad won't be able to give you a lift. I'm too busy, so don't think you can sweet talk me either." Brigid laughed at the idea. Her mammy was certainly not someone anyone could sweet talk into doing anything she did not have a mind to do.

"Okay, Mammy, I'm on my way down," she replied, grabbing her coat and bag, not forgetting to put her bright orange lipstick in her pocket for later. If she put it on now, her mammy would surely send her straight back to her room, yelling "wipe that muck off your face, young lady!"

It was Friday night, and it was the Valentine's Day disco at the church hall. Anyone who was anyone would be there, provided they were below the age of eighteen and could get past Father Patrick on the door, that is. He had only recently moved to the parish, and compared with his ancient predecessor, Father Brendon, was not too bad for a priest. But he still did not allow any messing around, and there was certainly no alcohol or smoking on his watch. As far as fraternising with the opposite sex was concerned, then experience told you to keep a respectable distance whenever he was around, or it would be three Hail Marys and a trip to confession for you.

"Right girls, home no later than ten o'clock. Your dad will be waiting by the post office to bring you back, and Helen, he will drop you off too, so both be there, and don't keep him waiting." At times, Brigid thought her mammy, Collette, would have made a good Gestapo officer; between her and Father Patrick, how was a girl to have any fun? Knowing there was no use whatsoever in arguing, she simply smiled as she walked towards the door, tugging her mini-skirt down a little to make it look more respectable, her mammy tutting in the background.

When they arrived at the church hall, there were already about thirty teenagers milling around inside, huddled in small groups of girls or boys, doing little to attract attention to themselves, and even less to mingle. Brigid recognised some faces, whilst others were new, leaving her to wonder that unless it started to get a little livelier in the next half hour, with perhaps some other people arriving, she had probably wasted her time getting all dolled up.

There was a Catholic boys' college about two miles down the road in the next town, and on occasions such as this, it was usual for several of the older teenagers to be bussed in to swell the numbers. That did not look to have happened so far, and was probably unlikely to now given the time. Their village only had a smattering of teenagers, and not all of those were party animals, Brigid thought regrettably to herself, knowing that having a good time for most of them amounted to kicking a ball around a field, or drinking a bottle of pop sitting on a bench in the village square if the weather was nice.

Helen had her eye on one of the boys who lived in the village, Joseph, whose parents ran the grocer's store. He was nearly eighteen and having recently passed his driving test, it made him a real prospect. He had access to the shop's van if he ever wanted to go to the cinema, or into the next town for a change, or even take a ride into the countryside to impress the girls. He and Helen had gone out a couple of times, but it was all hushed-up, as her parents would not have approved, and although she liked him, it had not progressed very far.

Brigid on the other hand, had her eyes firmly set on the grandson of one of the elderly couples who lived in the village, Declan Murphy. He was tall, dark and handsome, at least compared with some of the local lads. Brigid saw him relatively infrequently, as he lived in England and only came over to Ireland a couple of times a year when his parents were visiting his grandparents. She and Declan had met two years previously, one summer's day whilst messing around on the park with a group of friends. He had come to spend the summer holidays with his grandparents whilst his parents went overseas on business. They had chatted, and over the long summer months had become firm friends. They had fun and shared a similar sense of humour and approach to life.

When Declan returned home, they continued to write to each other, sharing whatever trivial snippets of life they thought the other would find amusing. Things that had happened in the village, or what she had got up to at school were normally the limit of Brigid's news. Declan had more to write about, all of which appeared exciting to Brigid. Declan's cousin was used as their go-between; Brigid knowing that if any letters arrived at her house, her mammy would insist on reading them, and then want to know chapter and verse about what was going on, always assuming the worst, before undoubtedly putting a stop to it. She did not want to risk that with Declan, as she valued his friendship too much. She also devoured the insight he provided to life outside Ireland; real life, beyond their small provincial village.

Declan was fifteen months older than Brigid, so by now had already finished school and had started an apprenticeship, working with a gang of builders learning the house building trade, even going to college once a week to study for his City & Guilds qualifications. He was a strong, well-built young man, who thought nothing of getting his hands dirty, with a solid work ethic that made him a likeable member of the gang. His humour also saw him through some tricky situations, with him being able to laugh off most things, his mentality being not to worry about anything he could not do anything about.

Brigid had last seen him in November, around three months earlier, rushing around to his cousin's house as soon as she became aware he had arrived. When he hugged her, she immediately felt his strength, commenting on the muscles he had developed since his last visit, and the tautness of his stomach as he laughed at something funny she said. The building trade obviously suited him. They both fell back easily into conversation, as if they had never been apart.

By fifteen, she had shed any puppy fat she may have had the previous summer, blossoming into a shapely young woman. Granted it was far from the 'Twiggy' physique some women yearned for, more of an hourglass body that men liked to get hold of, the glossy magazines she occasionally got her hands on assured her. The sight of him all grown up, sporting a narrow moustache, as well as some trendy clothes, sent her heart racing, and by the way he responded to her, she seemed to have a similar effect on him.

By the end of his short visit, they had managed to sneak away on a number of occasions, Helen becoming a willing accomplice, devising a new excuse or ruse each day to keep Brigid's mammy off the scent. Declan would borrow his grandad's car, and they would sneak off to the cinema, or go for something to eat in the next town, anywhere as long as it was far away from prying eyes, or anyone telling tales back to her parents. On each occasion their car would end up parked down some dark lane, providing them with some 'alone time'; time they suddenly realised they needed.

Brigid had never really been kissed before, well not in the way that Declan kissed her, and no one had ever paid any attention to her body, or more precisely her breasts, in the way he did. She knew she was not a traditional beauty, her wavy auburn hair not styled in any particular fashion, her face devoid of any make-up, but Declan saw an attractiveness in her that no-one else had ever brought out. He was sensitive, caring and funny, and whilst she knew she should be careful, the words of the nuns forever ringing in her ears about the dangers of giving into temptation, she could not help herself. She was falling in love with him, and "wasn't that what was important in life?" she asked herself, "to love, and to be loved in return, surely there's nothing wrong with that?"

By ten o'clock, Brigid and Helen were waiting in the lay-by in front of the post office, as instructed, as Dominic, Brigid's dad drove up. He had been to the pub for a swift pint, and was feeling a little jollier that usual, having won the Valentine's Day raffle prize; a meat hamper, donated by the local butcher, that now took pride of place on the back seat of the car. "That bacon and sausage will make a grand fry up in the morning," he thought to himself.

"Hello, you two. Have you had a good time?" enquired Dominic, as they got into the car, being told to be careful not to sit on the hamper.

"Yes, thanks Dad," replied Brigid, politely. In truth it had not developed into a particularly great evening and, if she was honest, she was feeling more tired than she thought possible. She had been watching the clock for the last hour or so, willing it to get to ten o'clock. Helen was happy as her boyfriend, Joseph, was there, so they had chatted together, even having the occasional dance, whilst Brigid had been left to chat to some of her other friends. Without Declan there, she had felt lost. A couple of the lads had asked her for a dance, unaware she was already spoken for, but she had not been interested, so had largely sat by herself, nursing a glass of lemonade. She felt she might be sickening for something. There was a lot of flu going around, so perhaps that accounted for her tiredness, or her loss of appetite. No doubt she would feel better in the morning.

The thought of those sausages for breakfast, or in fact any fried food for that matter, did little if anything to make her feel better.

Chapter 43

Monday morning arrived, and around seven o'clock, as soon as she got out of bed Brigid rushed to the bathroom to throw-up. The aromas of fried food had made their way up the stairs, and rather than the thought of a bacon butty whetting her appetite, it had made her feel nauseous. This was the third morning in a row she had felt this way, and it was beginning to feel like this cold, or flu, or whatever bug she had caught would never go away.

When she got downstairs, dressed in her school uniform, her dad was sitting around the table, a mug of tea in one hand, and a doorstep sandwich in the other. He was reading the newspaper, while her mammy was busying herself around the sink, her apron wrapped snuggly around her ample bosom. Dominic had already been awake for two hours, having got up in the pitch dark around five o'clock to do the milking, and after breakfast he would return to the yard to do whatever else needed tackling. Living on a farm was a tireless and thankless occupation. There was no end to the chores that needed carrying out, with little reward, and even less gratitude for the hours he put in.

Connor, her older brother, usually helped with the cows, but today he had also mucked out the chickens, bringing a fresh batch of eggs back into the kitchen with him. Connor had left school three years previously, and was now working full time at the farm with his parents. As a strapping lad of eighteen, he made himself useful about the place.

"Brigid, you're not looking too good this morning, is everything alright?" her mammy asked as she sat down at the table. "Do you want some sausages frying?"

At the mention of sausages, and before she had time to answer, Brigid flew back upstairs and threw up again.

"Good heavens, whatever's the matter with you girl, are you sickening for something?" her mammy enquired, having run straight upstairs behind her. Her bedside manner never one of her strongest attributes.

"I've just got a bug I think. I keep throwing up in the mornings," she replied. "I'm not sure I want to go to school today, I couldn't face it. I feel so tired and haven't got the energy to run for the bus. Can you phone the teachers for me Mammy? I'm going back to bed."

Rather than phone the school, Collette reluctantly phoned the doctor's surgery. She had seen those symptoms before, and whilst her daughter might believe it was simply a tummy bug, she was left in no doubt what stupid predicament her daughter had got herself into.

That was the last day Brigid ever attended school, too embarrassed was Collette to send her daughter back to the classroom where questions might be asked, or worse still assumptions made about her, or the respectability of their family. They were a good Catholic family, who until that day could hold their heads up high around the village. Never a stain against their name had been mentioned, and as far as Collette was concerned, that would not be changing.

Doctor Nelson, their local GP, had confirmed the inevitable, advising Collette that her daughter was already almost three months pregnant, so the baby would be due sometime in the middle of August. Seeing how distraught Collette was at the prospect of the news getting out, he assured her of his discretion, advising, "there are ways around it, if you need any help." The concept of Brigid having an illegitimate child, and bringing it up in the village, was not only unthinkable, but something neither felt comfortable even voicing, fearful that the walls might have ears, and before long the whole village would be talking about it.

Collette was beside herself, unsure exactly what to do, or where to turn. She was not even sure if she could trust her husband with the news, dreading not only his inevitable disappointment, but the blame he would undoubtedly direct at her for not controlling their daughter's behaviour more. Brigid had always been a free spirit, neither of them perhaps realising how 'free' she had actually been, or with hindsight how much she had managed to get away with, without their knowledge, or even their suspicions being aroused. No, this was something she had to take control of herself, conscious that time was not on her side, and before too long, it would be impossible to disguise her daughter's swollen stomach by a loosely fitting jumper or a smock dress.

Doctor Nelson had practised medicine for over twenty-five years, so was accustomed to situations like this, and although in Brigid's case it did surprise him, he nevertheless knew what needed to be done. He briefly told Collette about a mother and baby home about thirty miles north of Dublin that he had on occasion referred girls in similar situations to, reassuring Collette it was not as uncommon as she might imagine. The home was run by a group of nuns, supported by the appropriate medical professionals, and importantly it was far enough away, for no one local to become suspicious. Equally, it was close enough should they need to deal with an emergency, or anything unforeseen arose during the pregnancy. He had contacts there, and guaranteed Collette that Brigid would be well looked after for the time she would be there, with the baby then being adopted by a respectable Christian family, who could give it a home, raising it as their own. He said it was a homely, clean and comfortable institution, and above all, discreet. No one in the village would be any the wiser.

Collette knew she had little alternative than to go along with Doctor Nelson's suggestion, and without even asking her daughter for her views, or consulting with Dominic, urged the doctor to make the arrangements.

Two weeks later, Brigid was packed off to the home. Doctor Nelson arrived early one dark, wet morning to drive her there, assuring Collette it would be easier for him to do that than for her or Dominic to get involved. Collette certainly had no desire to go to the home, or to get involved in any shape or form whatsoever. As far as she was concerned, the sooner this episode was over, the better, and the least said, the soonest mended was her mentality. She was angry, disappointed, embarrassed – in fact every negative emotion imaginable, and she just wanted it done. And in terms of Dominic, well, what he did not know would not harm him, was her attitude. As far as he and Connor were concerned, or anyone else who enquired about her whereabouts for that matter, Brigid was going to look after a sickly aunt, who had fallen on bad times. Brigid would nurse her and act as a companion during her illness.

Brigid was awaiting his arrival. She was a forlorn figure, wrapped up in her warm coat against the bad weather, standing all alone in the hallway of their farmhouse, a simple brown suitcase by her side, containing the few possessions she would need for the duration. The nuns would provide whatever food and clothing she required, in exchange for her helping around the home for as long as she was able, doing whatever chores were required.

Her mammy had hardly spoken a word to her for the past few days, and the atmosphere around the house had become unbearable. Once the doctor had left, Brigid had been forced to tell her mammy who had done this to her, but as Declan was not a boy she knew, other than by association with his family, she could not go banging on their door demanding he married her daughter, even if she had wanted to. Neither Dominic nor Connor knew what the atmosphere was about between mother and daughter. Both however knew better than to get drawn in, keeping their distance and escaping to the milking shed whenever it became too much.

Even recognising how bad it had become living at home and how she was made to feel like a prisoner in her own home, unable to meet her friends or speak to anyone outside of the house, Brigid still did not want to be sent away for over six months. The place she had overheard her mammy and the doctor talk about was not somewhere she knew anything about, although she feared the welcome would not be as warm as the doctor suggested, or that the nuns would be kind to her, or her baby, regardless of what he had suggested.

At fifteen, Brigid was still a schoolgirl, an immature child not only in the eyes of the law, but in the eyes of the church too. She had no independent means or knight in shining armour charging to her defence. So, even if she had stood up to her mammy, which was something she was ill prepared to do, what other options did she have? No, whilst she was unhappy to be sent away, she reluctantly picked up her case and made her way to the door and to an unknown future.

Chapter 44

The next few months were unbearable for Brigid. The home was far from the homely place the doctor had suggested, and even further from being welcoming and comfortable. Brigid and the other girls, about twelve of them at any one time, all sharing a large dormitory that was housed on the second floor of the convent. They were made to feel dirty, referred to as 'sinners' if ever they stepped out of line, and not only made to work hard for their keep, but feel thankful at the same time.

The girls were forbidden any contact whatsoever with home, or the outside world, and for Brigid that meant letters to Declan were prohibited, her initial request for pen and paper being met with a small smile and an instant refusal by one of the younger nuns. She had been unable to get any word to him, or Helen about her predicament, or the fact she had been sent away. She had no idea what either of them would be thinking if ever they came knocking at her door, or asked around the village, which they undoubtedly would. She imagined neither would buy the ruse of an elderly or sick aunt, someone she had never spoken of, particularly so as time went by. No aunt, no matter how ill she was, would have prevented her from phoning home, or posting the odd letter to a friend, surely?

She felt helpless and trapped, powerless to do anything about it, with the sad knowledge that once this was all over and her baby was born, it would simply be taken from her, without her being able to say, or do anything about it. There would be no one there to support her; her parents, or at least her mammy, effectively having washed their hands of her. Many a night she cried herself to sleep, her emotions and sheer tiredness getting the better of her. Her tears were silent as the nuns did not tolerate them, with any weakness punished the following day by extra chores, as she had learned on a couple of occasions to her cost.

They were not encouraged to make friends with the other girls, or even talk beyond what was strictly necessary. They all seemed to walk around, almost as if zombies had invaded their bodies. Brigid began to notice over time faces changed, as new girls arrived and others vanished. It seemed that no bed was ever left empty for more than a night or two. The girls that had been there longer than her, when their time came to have their babies, were simply spirited off to another place, never to be seen, or heard again. What Brigid also noticed was there was never any sight of babies around the building, no screams in the night for feeding. It was eerily silent once seven o'clock arrived and the dormitory lights were switched off.

By the middle of July, Brigid was the size of a house and getting more uncomfortable with each passing day. The weather was exceptionally warm, with the heat and humidity making it uncomfortable and difficult to move around with any ease. The doctor had examined her a few days earlier, advising her and the nuns that stood by, that the baby was imminent, and she needed to be restricted to light duties whilst she awaited its arrival. The nuns had nodded obediently, but nothing was said directly to Brigid in terms of what that actually meant.

Walking alone along the corridor one lunchtime, after returning from the refectory where she had been unable to eat very much, as her stomach was beginning to cramp, she felt her legs suddenly become wet and sticky under the grey cotton smock she had been given to wear. Looking down, she saw a puddle of water laying around her feet. Crying out to one of the passing nuns for help, she was immediately told it was nothing to worry about, simply her waters had broken.

"Come with me, girl," the nun had said, displaying a complete lack of emotion. "I will arrange for someone to attend to you," before leading her down a passage way into another part of the building, closing the door firmly behind her, to prevent others from witnessing where they were going.

As Brigid followed the nun, the pains in her stomach started to get worse, also coming with more frequency, and by the time she was led into a room about ten minutes later, she was not only uncomfortable, but scared, frightened about what was happening to her. She imagined she was losing her baby. The pain was like nothing she had ever experienced before, leaving her feeling faint and completely disorientated.

Sex education had not been high on the curriculum at the school Brigid had attended, and although she had a vague idea from watching the calves being born on the farm, even helping her dad out on occasion, nothing had ever been explained, or spelt out to her in terms of what childbirth was like, or what would happen next.

The room she had been led to resembled the doctor's surgery she had once visited in the village, a long examination table in the centre of it, and various pieces of stainless-steel equipment scattered around.

"Get on the table, and someone will be with you shortly," said the nun, adding as she opened the door to leave, "and try not to scream too loudly. This is all perfectly natural."

Left in the room by herself, laid on the uncomfortable and sterile table, now in agony, with pains she could not explain, she had never felt more afraid, or abandoned in her life.

Brigid's labour had already been quite advanced, and it was not long after the doctor examined her that she gave birth to a baby; a healthy girl, weighing eight pounds, four ounces the nurse advised. Once the baby had been checked over, she was handed to Brigid for the briefest of moments, before being placed in a small plastic crib and wheeled away to another room.

Brigid watched helplessly as her daughter was spirited away from her by one of the nuns, completely unable to react or do anything about it. Tears fell from her eyes, whilst inside she silently screamed, in the full knowledge that any fuss would have fallen on deaf ears anyway.

After about thirty minutes and having been attended to by the doctor, she was led into an adjacent room. It contained four ancient metal-framed single beds, with the overpowering smell of disinfectant lingering in the air. She was directed by one of the nuns towards the bed in the farthest corner, away from the window or any natural light. Other than the beds and a small chipped wash basin, the room was devoid of any furniture, and had there been bars on the windows, it could easily have been mistaken for a prison cell.

Another young girl, who Brigid thought she recognised from the main dormitory, but did not know the name of, was in the bed opposite. Her head was turned towards the wall, gentle sobs coming from her body. As Brigid got into her bed, neither girl acknowledged the other, and with the exception of the nun telling her to rest, advising that a meal would be brought to her in due course, there was no other conversation. It was perhaps the least cheery place Brigid had ever been in, and before long she was similarly sobbing into her pillow. Homesickness was a feeling that had never been far away for the past few months, and at that moment it was coupled with a feeling of total despair.

The following morning, after a meagre breakfast of porridge, washed down with a cup of lukewarm sugary tea, Brigid was taken to the nursery and asked to breastfeed her baby; the nuns showing her what needed to be done as she had no idea where to start. She gently took the baby, whom she had decided to name Maeve, into her arms and moved to the feeding chair that had been set up for her in the corner of the room.

Once Maeve had latched onto her breast, it aroused a mix of sensations in Brigid that she had never experienced before. The sheer awe at the sight of her baby, gently nestled into her, the warmth of her small body through the plain cotton gown she was dressed in, rubbing against her own flesh, their hearts beating in rhythm, both contented. She watched as the baby's lips hungrily sucked at her nipple, the smells of her newness and the milk she was guzzling filling her nostrils. Brigid laughed at how hungry she was, memories of bottle feeding the calves on the farm coming back to her, increasing her feelings of homesickness even more.

Sitting there for over thirty minutes, Brigid felt a love so strong she could not put it into words, but no sooner had she started to feel relaxed and the baby was fed, Maeve was taken from her. Feeding was over, and it was time for her to go back to her room.

This process continued for several days, Brigid being collected and taken at various intervals, both day and night to the nursery; that routine fast becoming the highlight of her day, and the only thing that kept her going. Gradually she regained her strength and felt able to do more for the child. Although she asked, she was never encouraged to do anything other than her feed.

On the afternoon of the tenth day, a nun arrived with a change of outfit for Brigid, something a little smarter than the gown she had been wearing, instructing her to get changed and make her way to the nursery as soon as she was ready. When she arrived, Brigid proceeded to feed her daughter, as had become the routine, gently picking Maeve from her cot and carrying her to the feeding chair. However, after the feed was over, instead of taking the child from her, one of the nuns produced a camera and took a snapshot of her nursing Maeve, before returning the baby to her cot, and telling Brigid it was time for her to return to her room. That was the last time she ever saw her baby.

The following morning, when Brigid awoke, she recognised the clothes she had arrived in were laid out on a chair next to her bed, in place of the usual gown she had been wearing around the home. She dressed, and instead of being asked to go to the nursery, was taken directly to the front hall where Doctor Nelson from her village was already waiting.

"Good morning Brigid, I've come to take you home," he announced, a gentle, but knowing smile on his lips.

"What about Maeve? I haven't seen her this morning and she'll be hungry. I must at least go and feed her, before saying goodbye to her," she pleaded to both Doctor Nelson and the nun who was standing beside him. Brigid had long since resigned herself to the fact she would have to leave the home without her baby, knowing that putting Maeve up for adoption was something, that although she was unhappy about, she had been offered no alternative to.

"The baby is no longer here. She has already left to be with her adoptive parents," the nun announced, in a manner that was lacking in both compassion and feeling. "Now, come along, and don't keep the doctor waiting. Your bag is by the door."

"Can I at least take the photo you took of Maeve as a small keepsake?" begged Brigid to the nun, desperately trying to hold back the tears from her voice. "It's the only thing I have to remember my baby by."

"I'm sorry that would not be possible. The photo has been sent with the other documents and the baby, so it's no longer in the building," she replied, adding as she opened the door, "thank you, Doctor. Until next time."

And with that they were both dismissed.

Chapter 45

Trudie had watched Betty's face as she had sat opposite her mother, listening for the first time of the account of her birth, and by the look on the faces of both Mary and Donal, this was a story they were hearing for the first time too.

The way Brigid recounted the details, so calmly and clearly, it was almost as if it had happened yesterday, not nearly sixty years ago. The memories were still so raw in her mind, the feelings they evoked obviously still so painful. As she spoke, she kept looking over at Betty, trying to recognise the baby she had been forced to give away, that last image of her having remained imprinted on her mind from all those years ago.

"Is this the photo you referred to?" asked Betty cautiously, retrieving the small black and white snapshot from her handbag and handing it to Brigid.

As Brigid took it from her, and looked at the image of the two of them, sitting in the feeding room, she physically shook. Studying the photo, she recalled wearing that strange dress they had insisted she put on, with Maeve a mere bundle in her arms, wrapped in a pretty shawl, evidently worn for the benefit of the photo. Tears started to fall uncontrollably from her eyes. Memories that had been bottled up for so long, resurfacing in a way she had never imagined they ever would. For a long time, she just sat and stared at the photo, before saying quietly, "I never got to say goodbye to you." Brigid then turned towards Betty and asked, "how long have you had this photo?"

"I found it with my parents' papers when I was sorting their things out after they'd both died. It was in a file, along with my adoption papers, so quite a few years ago, I imagine."

"So, what's made you come looking now?" asked Mary, in a less than welcoming tone. "If you've known for all those years that you were adopted, then what's suddenly changed?" The tone of her voice suggesting Betty was perhaps looking to steal the family silver, rather than reconnect with any long-lost family.

"Well, that's really quite simple, and it's all down to my good friend Trudie here, and particularly her skills on the computer," Betty announced, with a smile on her face. "Although the main reason I've never looked for you before," she said, now directing her gaze at Brigid, rather than face the hostility of Mary, "is that I was always told you had died, due to complications after my birth. And that I had no surviving family left."

"Well, I'm certainly not dead now, although this leg is giving me more gyp than I'd care to admit," she said, smiling over at Betty and Trudie, at the same time disgruntled with what Betty had just said. For the nuns, or whatever authority had taken her baby, to lie to that extent was shocking, and beyond words.

Mary had remained ramrod straight by the door throughout, her arms folded across her chest, the look on her face clearly showing she was struggling to believe any of what was being said. Until the previous week when Donal had contacted her, there had never been any mention of her mother having had another baby, least of all putting one up for adoption. It was all a bit incredulous; to think her mother had been lying to her for the last fifty-two years of her life made her question whether there were any more skeletons lurking in the cupboard.

Her initial thoughts had been to discount it, telling Donal not to engage with the American, and simply ignore her approaches. But there had been something in what had been said that niggled at her, making her curious to meet her. By agreeing to meet Betty, Mary's intention had been to wean out of her sufficient information to decide whether to approach her mother about it, preferably discounting it, and sending the woman off with a flea in her ear. She did not want to upset, or question her mother, without a valid reason to; and until she had cast iron proof, Mary saw no reason to.

The plan had backfired though, when Connor had telephoned his sister directly, breaking the news to her that someone was looking for her, according to what his son, Donal, had told him. He too knew nothing about any adoption, so equally presumed it was untrue, but wanted to hear directly from the horse's mouth, he had said.

Now, standing here, listening to what her mother was saying, she was unable to discount it any longer; her teenage mum, an unmarried mother. Even though it might be true, she was still struggling to comprehend the implications of it. Not only the fact her own mother had given her baby up for adoption, but that there had been someone else in her life before she had married her father. Her mum had always maintained Dad was her first and only love, which was clearly untrue, and although part of her wanted to know the rest of the story, the larger part of her simply wanted to show these Americans the door, and wind back the clocks a couple of weeks before this ghastly business was brought up.

"Mary, will you please straighten your face, then go and fetch us all a brandy. I think we've earned one, don't you?" Brigid announced to no one in particular, making it clear that not only was brandy good for shock, but that they might have something more than Christmas to celebrate. "You might as well make them large ones, if we're to go on with this story, as I'm keen to know how, and where Maeve was brought up. We've got a lot of catching up to do, haven't we love?"

Emotion was something over the years Brigid had trained herself not only to control, but to in fact bury deep in her heart. She was not someone who opened up easily to people, so it was perhaps understandable the look Mary was giving her. Brigid could occasionally be considered cold or bitter in her approach to life, her opinions tinged by the experiences she had gone through, and sadly Mary had inherited that trait. Now, the more she looked across at her eldest daughter, and pondered all those missed years, all those shared experiences they had never had, her normally brittle persona started to fall away, leaving a woman who for the first time in nearly sixty years felt alive again.

"Well, I'm happy to continue," Betty replied, before adding, "I'll tell you a little about my life, and some of my recent problems, which have obviously led us to the events of today, and then perhaps you can continue with your story. I'm fascinated to know why you left Ireland to come over to England."

"That would be lovely," began Brigid, and seeing her husband Mick walking up the path to the house she added, "Mary, you might want to bring an extra glass. It looks like your father has just arrived."

Chapter 46

Brigid found once she was back home, whilst her life had changed drastically over the preceding months, for the remainder of her family, and the people in the village, it appeared to have stood still.

Doctor Nelson had driven her home, saying little in the car to her, other than to remind her that what had happened at the home, and the reason why she had been there, was to be kept in the strictest of confidence; for the sake of hers and the family's reputation, he stressed. Little consideration, if any, was given to the wellbeing of the baby, and any attempts by Brigid to talk to him about Maeve were promptly shut down.

"The sooner you forget about it, and get on with your life the better," Doctor Nelson had advised, when he dropped her off outside the farmhouse, not even taking the time to come in and speak to her mammy. "You're still young and only a child yourself. My strong advice is don't think anything else about the baby. She'll be well cared for by her adoptive parents now. Just get on with your own life, and let this have taught you a lesson."

How he could sit there and say that, all sanctimoniously, when all that was going around her head were thoughts of Maeve, and how she was going to live without her baby; a baby that in the space of a few short days, she had not only bonded with, but grown to love so deeply. She kept remembering that last moment she had touched her, never realising it would be her only chance to say goodbye. She was distraught at the thought that she had no idea where she had been taken, or by whom; just cruelly spirited away without her knowledge, or importantly her consent.

Eventually, getting out of the car with her small suitcase containing her belongings, which amounted to very little, and certainly nothing of any consequence, Brigid felt completely helpless and totally confused. As she waited nervously outside the front door, she knew she would have to go inside eventually to meet her mammy and dad. She had no idea what reception she would receive, or what she should say to them, or her brother Connor. Surely she was not expected to concoct a story of nursing an elderly aunt for months, an aunt that clearly they all knew did not exist? But what could she say, and would her parents dismiss any talk of the baby as summarily, or as heartlessly as Doctor Nelson had done? Surely they would have more compassion for her and Maeve, their granddaughter after all?

It was mid-morning on a beautiful summer's day, with the temperature outside warm, as Brigid walked back into the house, dressed in the same winter's coat and woollen dress she had left wearing that morning several months earlier. As she made her way through to the back kitchen, she began to wonder if the atmosphere would still be as icy inside, as it had been back in February.

Although Collette and Dominic were both pleased to have their daughter home safely, it soon became apparent to Brigid that any discussion of where she had been, or more precisely why she had been away, was not going to happen. The speed with which the conversation was changed whenever she made any attempts of raising the subject was palpable, with Maeve's name never acknowledged by either of her parents.

Collette, once she had reassured herself that her daughter was healthy, spoke no more of it, and Dominic simply gave Brigid a hug and moved on. Dealing with emotional issues, or people in general, was never his forte. Put him in a field with a herd of cattle, and he could happily chatter away endlessly, but try to engage him in general conversation and he soon became very uncomfortable. No, he was more at home with his cows any day. Connor equally never raised the subject of where she had been, choosing to keep his distance from Brigid. He never questioned her, or their parents about her absence.

Brigid soon realised their expectation was simply for her to fall back into her normal routine around the farm and the house, helping both her parents with whatever needed attending to; anything from mucking out the cows to preparing the meals or baking the bread. Now that she had technically finished school, albeit had missed the last few months completely, her parents' assumption was she would become a useful pair of hands that could turn themselves to a wide variety of tasks. After all, she was a farmer's daughter.

For Brigid though, her life had moved on considerably, and whilst she was still only sixteen, she felt more mature than her years suggested. She was no longer the young school girl who had got into trouble, but was now a woman. One who had experienced a side of life, including childbirth, that had altered her perspective. Without qualifications though, what could she do, and where could she go? Because one thing was for sure, she needed to get far away. A life on the farm was not for her.

Brigid contacted her friend Helen as soon as she had got home, discreetly asking the postman to drop a note into her house on his rounds. She wanted to arrange to meet up with her to find out what was going on in the village, but also to understand whether people were talking about her, and if so, what they were saying. Although she was not supposed to tell anyone about her circumstances, not being able to talk about Maeve was tearing her apart, leaving her exhausted and emotionally drained as she cried herself to sleep each evening. She needed someone to confide in, someone who would understand, and importantly, someone who would be there for her.

Helen was her best friend, already proven to be loyal and trustworthy, so who better to turn to? She would have loved to speak to Declan, but as she had not written to him for over six months, or replied to any of the letters he might have sent her, there was no guarantee he would be interested in her anymore. The direction of his life may have changed completely since they had last met. Living in Liverpool, enjoying city life; she could well imagine visiting his grandparents, in a remote part of Ireland, would no longer be high on his list of priorities.

Helen had started a secretarial course in the next town, catching the bus in on a daily basis, returning home around six o'clock most evenings, with the exception of Tuesdays when she finished at two o'clock in the afternoon. Brigid offered to meet her off the bus the following Tuesday, leaving them both plenty of time to catch up, before needing to return home. It was the height of summer, with the long summer's evenings, which meant they could stay out much later than usual, without fear of getting lost in the dark. They arranged to meet in the small café in the village square, where they could grab a drink and a quiet table for their chat.

Brigid had hardly left the house since her return, so was desperate to get out. She was not so much being kept captive, just really had nowhere she needed to be. Now with a purpose, on Tuesday afternoon, after all her chores had been done, she told her parents she was cycling into the village to collect some things she needed from the shops. Had she mentioned to Collette that she was meeting Helen, it would have led to a conversation she was not prepared to have, so a little white lie felt justified. She just needed to remember not to come back empty handed.

Conversation between the two was initially a little stilted, Helen noticeably feeling aggrieved that Brigid had not been in touch for so long, then messaging her out of the blue, expecting her to meet up for a chat, without any explanation. Once they had found a quiet corner, Brigid however opened up to her friend in a way she had been unable to with anyone else, speaking from the heart about the experiences she had faced, trying to put into words what it had done to her emotionally.

As the story unfolded, both girls shed countless tears. Helen was not only surprised by what she was hearing for the first time, but shocked at the way her friend had been treated. She had believed the ruse about the elderly aunt, and had soon become annoyed that Brigid had never written to her, or given her the aunt's address, so they could continue to keep in contact whilst she was away. She had never questioned the story, simply believed her friend had moved on. Now, with hindsight she questioned how good a friend she really was. To learn that Brigid had been aching all this time to get in touch, and had not been able to do so, was heart breaking.

Eventually, Helen asked the question, "and Declan still knows nothing about this, about the fact you've had his baby?"

"No, and he'd probably run a mile if he ever found out! The nuns said that's what boys are like, and we shouldn't trust them at all. Girls are fools to get drawn in by them; being forced to commit sins, losing any respectability we ever had. No one will ever be interested in me now, they said – spoiled, that's what I am apparently!"

"You don't really think that, surely?" asked Helen. "You said you were in love with Declan, and that he felt the same way. Is that not still the case?"

"I've no idea what he feels. I just know I miss him nearly as much as I miss Maeve. Knowing I can't have either is tearing me apart," sobbed Brigid, the coffees they had ordered now completely cold.

"Have you tried to contact him? I presume you still have his address?" enquired Helen.

"I've got an old address, but no. I wouldn't know what to say, or even if he's still living there. And I'm not supposed to tell anyone. I'd get into trouble if they knew I'd told you, so God only knows what would happen if I told him. It would probably be around the village in no time. My parents would never be able to hold their heads up again, they would be disgraced."

"Well, my opinion for what it's worth, is why don't you get in touch with him? That way, you'll at least see how the land lies. If he's moved on, then so be it, and if he's still interested, then what's the harm in talking to him? You don't have to mention the baby until you're sure you want to, or that it's safe to do so," offered Helen. "I've not seen him around here for a few months, so I can't offer any better update. Thinking about it, he might be staying away, believing you've moved on."

"I don't know, but I doubt that," Brigid replied cautiously. "I get the feeling that even if he did come back, my mammy would lock me in my bedroom if she thought I was meeting up with him again. I'm sure Dad would kill him as well if he ever found out he was responsible!"

"Well, have a think about it, and while you're at it, think about what you're going to do in terms of getting a job, because staying on that farm, mucking out cows all day, is clearly not what you're destined to do with your life," she laughed. "There're always places at the college where I'm studying, so you could come along with me if you fancy learning to type and take shorthand. You never know, we could even get a job together in a swanky office, perhaps share a flat in a year or so when we turn eighteen. I don't know about you, but I can't wait to leave this backwater and see the bright lights. Joseph has no intention of ever leaving his parents' grocer's store, so no matter how good a kisser he is for now, I don't imagine it will be too long before he's shown the door!" she said, with a twinkle in her eye.

Chapter 47

By the end of September, Brigid had enrolled at the secretarial college with Helen, the two of them travelling in together each morning on the bus from the village.

Neither Collette nor Dominic had been particularly happy when their daughter announced one evening at the end of August her decision to give up working on the farm. They had noticed how desperately unhappy she was since her return, but hoped that over time she would settle. Although they felt no guilt about their actions, they were not blind to the fact that Brigid held them responsible in some way for what had happened over the preceding months. They had both recognised the polite coolness with which she spoke to them, the distance in her voice, and the faraway look in her eyes, and felt powerless to do anything about it. The closeness they had previously had with their daughter had sadly been lost, with any attempts to reach her constantly being thwarted by the protective wall she had built around her. They knew that keeping her on the farm against her will was not in anyone's interest, least of all their own, with the increased risk to their reputation should the scandal leak out. They reluctantly agreed that if going back to college would make her happy, then so be it. They would just need to find someone else to help around the farm.

What they did not know though, was that Brigid, with Helen's help, had secretly written to

Declan, even receiving a reply to her letter. Helen had subtly enquired after Declan when she had seen his grandparents one afternoon in the village as she got off the bus, using the excuse of a party, and an invitation she was planning on sending him, as a means of establishing he was still at the same address. His grandmother confirmed he was lodging at a boarding house in the city centre, not far from the construction site he was working on. "He's building new houses now," his grandad proudly told Helen, adding "apparently he's not a bad brickie for his age."

Now nineteen, Declan was happily working as a bricklayer on a major housing development project in Liverpool, building homes for the increasing number of families that were moving into the area. With a solid trade behind him, and a constant demand for new houses, he knew he would never be out of work, and with no ties or commitments, could happily move around the country, wherever the gang he was attached to went next.

His parents lived just outside Southport, which was only twenty miles away, so in theory he could still live at home with them and commute into Liverpool on the train each day. Although Southport was not a bad place, and he got on well with his parents, life there was all a bit too sedate for Declan. Living at the boarding house not only gave him independence, but also access to the nightlife the city had to offer, and in the mid-sixties where better to be? No, city living was where his heart lay.

Receiving the initial letter from Brigid though had knocked him sideways. He had presumed, having not heard from her in nearly seven months, that their relationship had ended. It had really saddened him when he had returned to Ireland to see his grandparents over Easter, to find that not only was she not there with her warm arms to greet him, but that no one knew anything about where she had gone. Having been so close only a few months previously, and having developed feelings for her, he had hoped they would pick up where they had left off; so, was upset to discover there was no message for him, and that she had effectively disappeared without trace.

Declan recalled how there had been something particularly appealing about her; an innocence, with a view of life that mirrored his own. She was pretty, with wavy auburn hair falling to her shoulders, a smile permanently on her face, and a body that was shapely, providing plenty for him to get hold of, he recalled, and lips that were made for kissing. The thought of her had kept him going many a time, especially when forced to listen to the other lads telling stories of their adventures with the ladies, bragging about who they had slept with, each trying to outdo the next with tales of their sordid conquests. Declan had only ever slept with Brigid that one time, with the memory of it something he had held onto. Believing her to have gone, he had found other girls to occasionally take out to the cinema or the pub for a drink. None was a patch on Brigid though.

Her first letter had simply enquired after him, offering little by way of explanation for her absence, only sincere apologies for not being in touch. She had said it would be great to meet again if he was ever in Ireland, adding at the same time that she understood if his life had moved on. Declan was quite attuned to nuances, and sensed there was something she was trying to tell him, but could not write; her letter was written in a way that sounded too formal for the girl he thought he knew.

Deciding to pen a reply straightaway, he provided Brigid with a snapshot of his life in Liverpool, describing some of the highs and lows of the building trade, as well as going to some lengths about his landlady. He told her that she treated him like a son, ensuring a hot meal was waiting for him whenever he returned home, even though he was technically only paying for bed and breakfast. He wrote about the fun side of city living, the shops, the fashions, the music scene, even some of the sports he was now enjoying. He made it sound a lot more attractive and exciting than it actually was, deciding not to mention anything about the other girls he had occasionally dated to relieve some of the boredom or homesickness, or to say anything that openly suggested he had missed her.

By the time he had finished, his letter was over three pages long, with anyone reading it being left in no doubt that the feelings he had for Brigid, although not explicitly expressed, were still very much in evidence. He could not hide the sheer happiness he had felt by the fact she had contacted him, ending his response by saying he would love to keep in touch, provided she wanted to, too.

Over the next few months, they continued to correspond, using Helen and her address as their go between, for fear Collette might find out, and try to forbid it. Whilst neither had assumed the other would want to continue a relationship, albeit at a distance, it soon became apparent that was not the case. Even if friendship was all that was on offer, it was better than the alternative they both thought, but never voiced.

Brigid loved to write to Declan, providing him with whatever news she had; delighting at the fact she had finished her typing course, and was progressing well with her shorthand. She had even found a job as an office clerk in a small company that provided building materials to the trade, joking with Declan that she knew nearly as much about bricks and cement as he did. She rarely talked about the farm, her parents or anything else that happened at home; choosing to block the part of her life that made her most unhappy, or stirred up the memories she had yet to express.

She eagerly awaited his replies, and with each response she sensed some of the bravado Declan had originally written about, being peeled away. She recognised a loneliness in him, that mirrored the loneliness in herself; leaving her to wonder whether he suspected there were elements of herself that she was holding back from him.

Their letters got more personal and loving each time, no longer writing as friends or pen pals, but as lovers, eagerly anticipating the time when they could be reunited. They spoke of meeting up, with both Dublin or Liverpool being options. As brave as Brigid was becoming, she had yet to summon up the courage to agree, or to face her parents, on that.

Mid July, and the anniversary of Maeve's birth approached. Her first birthday, and almost a year since she had seen her daughter. Brigid was besides herself with worry about what she would do, or how she would spend the day. The memories were constant, and although writing to Declan and her job provided a welcome distraction, those memories never seemed to be far away. At night she was haunted by what had happened, and still unable to talk about any of it to her parents, became increasingly upset at the unjust way she had been treated. Being forced into giving away her baby against her will had been cruel enough, but now not to receive any compassion from the ones closest to her, the very people that were supposed to love her, was added torture.

Her baby was out there somewhere, and other than the name she had given her, she knew nothing about her life whatsoever. She prayed constantly that whoever had her was treating her well and loving her, but nothing could make her believe that what she had been forced to do was the right thing, for her or her baby. Helen was the only one she could confide in about her feelings, and as appreciated as that was, it was no longer enough.

Brigid decided it was time to talk to Declan, knowing how high the risk was that he might run a mile at the news, whilst at the same time realising that if they were going to be together one day, as they both increasingly talked about, then she could no longer live a lie. She had to be honest and deal with the consequences, however hard or painful that would be. After all, what could be more painful that what she had already gone through?

Brigid wrote to Declan suggesting they meet up one weekend in August. She had some holiday owing, so with the right excuse, she could tell her parents that she and Helen were staying over in town for the weekend, to attend a party with one of her workmates, perhaps? Brigid, now seventeen, had done little to arouse her parents' suspicions over recent months, so they had begun to be more accepting of her movements, rarely questioning her these days, or displaying any real interest in her life beyond the farm.

Within a week of posting her letter, a response was received. Brigid was beside herself with happiness. Declan had agreed to come over to Dublin, even fixing a date and a time to meet up. He appeared as keen as she was, advising that he had already booked the ferry out of Liverpool on the Friday evening, which would arrive early Saturday morning, returning late Sunday afternoon. That would allow them the whole of Saturday and most of Sunday to be together. He even proposed a small boarding house one of his mates knew of, suggesting Brigid book two rooms; one for her and Helen, and one for him.

The arrangements were perfect, with Helen once again happy to be a part of their planning. She had spent the odd day in Dublin before, mooching around the shops and doing some sightseeing with her parents, but to have the full weekend there, with just a friend, made her feel so grown up. It would be a real treat.

"We can catch the bus there straight after work on Friday evening, and you and me can do some exploring on the Friday night, before you go to meet Declan off the ferry on Saturday morning. And then, we can catch the early bus back to work on Monday morning. Just think, three whole nights away from the village," she exclaimed, almost as excited as Brigid at their proposed adventure. "We just need to plan what we're going to need, and then work out how much it's going to cost."

"Yes, and work out what we're going to tell our parents!" Meeting up with Declan, for Brigid, had become so important. The last thing she needed was for her arrangements to be scuppered by a slip-up should either of them say the wrong thing to their parents.

The next ten days, waiting for the day to arrive, would be torture, but at least there was now an end in sight. Brigid resigned herself to having to deal with whatever Declan's response was to her, and her news of their baby. Whichever way he went, at least she would no longer have to keep it all to herself, and if he thought the worst of her because of it, then so be it. It was a risk, though not one she could see any alternative to, other than taking it.

The day eventually arrived, and Brigid stood by the side of the dock, nervously waiting for the ferry to berth. She was wearing a pretty floral summer dress, her hair neatly tied back in a green ribbon, with the slightest touch of lipstick on. She had angst over what to wear, wanting to appear casual, whilst at the same time wanting Declan to feel like she had made an effort. She had not seen him for well over eighteen months, so was unsure whether he would still find her physically attractive or not.

It was only eight o'clock in the morning, and the day was already warm and humid, promising a sunny weekend. She had gone down to the port early, even forgoing breakfast, for fear of missing the ferry's arrival, so was pleased to see she was not the only one waiting for the ship to come in. A small group had gathered, even some people with suitcases, who looked like they were preparing to board the ferry for the reverse crossing back to Liverpool.

Brigid had been unable to sleep the whole of the previous night, her mind going over and over what she was planning to say, whilst Helen had gently snored in the bed next to her, displaying absolutely no problem sleeping. The alcohol had probably helped, thought Brigid, recalling how they had both drunk a couple of pints of Guinness in one of the pubs in

Temple Bar, before staggering back to their boarding house, along the cobbled streets of Dublin. The streets had been crammed with people, groups of girls and lads out partying and enjoying the balmy night. It had all been a bit too rowdy for Brigid. Whilst Helen had loved the atmosphere, and had joined in with the singing when it inevitably began around eight o'clock, Brigid's mind was elsewhere. She felt too tense to relax and enjoy herself.

The anxiety of the previous ten days had weighed heavily on her mind. Now, standing here, watching Declan as he walked towards her, a broad smile on his face, her nerves went into overdrive. He was completely unaware that his words, or actions in the next few moments may very much decide their future, at least as far as their relationship was concerned. Whether he chose to stay, or go was his choice to make, realised Brigid.

"Right, here goes," she said to herself. "It's now or never." Taking a deep breath she ran into his outstretched arms, prepared to take the biggest gamble of her entire life.

Chapter 48

Mick had sat patiently on the settee beside his wife as she told the final part of her story, with one hand gently resting on her leg, as he nursed the glass of brandy his daughter Mary had brought him in the other. He had known Brigid was meeting Maeve that day, and had deliberately kept himself out of the picture, knowing how emotional it would be for his wife to finally come face to face with the baby she had been forced to give away nearly sixty years ago. They had spoken of it often, and although he felt her pain, he could never profess to be able to put himself fully into the position she had found herself in. Many a night he had cradled his wife as she cried herself to sleep, and as each new daughter was born and delivered safely into their arms, he felt the pain, and the loss of her firstborn child being replayed in her mind. That total feeling of helplessness never left him.

He recalled how Mary, Ruth and Colleen had been the prettiest of babies, the most wonderful of daughters, with the love and happiness he and Brigid felt, watching each of them grow and develop into strong and independent women, going on to have families of their own, nothing less than a privilege. Bringing them safely into this world was something he could never have missed out on, counting them among his proudest achievements. However, nothing they ever said or did would ever dilute the memory of Maeve, or the hopes and dreams for her future.

"So, what happened to Declan once you'd told him, Mum?" asked Mary, now fully engrossed in the story, at the same time feeling a little awkward having the conversation in front of her father. "Did he run to the hills as you'd predicted, and did you ever see him again?"

"No, he didn't run to the hills, and yes, we did continue to see each other," began Brigid, for the first time unsure how to resume her story. Taking a steadying drink of brandy, she continued. "After the weekend in Dublin, Declan returned to Liverpool, well to Southport really, where his parents lived at the time."

Although it was clear Brigid was talking to all of them, Trudie had noticed how she had started to direct more of the conversation to Betty. "They had a lovely house in a beautiful part of the countryside. It had plenty of spare rooms, and although Declan wasn't living at home, he still had his own space there. His father ran quite a successful business, making a good name for himself. They were quite well off really.

Declan was their only child, and had always had a great relationship with them, completely unlike mine. He spoke to them, telling them what had happened, explaining a little about me and my circumstances; especially how unhappy I was. He told them he took full responsibility for his actions, and wanted to do what he could to make things better. That weekend, he had told me how much he loved me, and subsequently told me how hard he'd found it going home and leaving me to face my parents and the farm without him by my side. He had wanted to come back with me to have words with my parents, but I fear they would probably have lynched him!"

"So, am I missing something, because if he was so much in love with you, what happened?" pressed Mary, clearly desperate to get to the truth. She had watched her dad throughout, and other than gazing at her mum, he had not uttered a word. She felt his discomfort.

"Well, a week or so after getting home, Helen turned up one morning at the bus stop waving an envelope. A letter from Declan had arrived for me; first class, registered delivery. When I tore it open, intrigued to know what was so important, I couldn't take the smile off my face," the smile returning to her face once again as she recounted the story.

"So, go on." It was Donal who prompted this time, equally keen to know where this was going, but also looking at his watch as he really needed to get going soon. He had thought they would only be at Mary's for about an hour, so had made plans for the afternoon, including doing his Christmas shopping, which, as always, he had left to the last minute.

"Well, it contained a proposal of marriage, with the suggestion of a Christmas wedding in England. His parents had offered to foot the bill. I couldn't believe it. By this time, I'd still not turned eighteen, so marriage was far from my thoughts, but the idea of marrying Declan, and moving to England to live with his parents seemed so appealing and beyond my wildest dreams. I was so excited I could hardly concentrate all day. I kept weighing it up in my mind, including what I'd say to my parents, who I was convinced would say no if I asked them.'

"So, what did you say Mum?" Mary asked.

"She said yes, of course," replied Mick, smiling across at Brigid, now tightly holding her hand too.

"Wind back a bit, I'm confused," said Mary, wondering why her dad had responded in the way he had, the smile so obviously lighting up his face.

"Oh, that's quite simple, did I not say?" replied Brigid, a little mischievously. "Your dad was always known as Mick over here. He'd been given the nickname 'Mick the Brick' by the other builders when he was a young apprentice. There was already another Declan on site, and the lads started getting confused, so Mick was born, and it's kind of stuck. Michael is his given name anyway; Michael Declan Murphy, so he just reverted to using that."

Trudie watched with awe as the realisation finally hit Betty, her initial confusion eventually being replaced by a feeling she could never have imagined. Not only had she found her mother, but here was her dad too, both well and happy, and both evidently still in love after nearly sixty years. Well, this was certainly a Christmas none of them would forget in a hurry, Trudie thought to herself, happy for the small part she had played.

Chapter 49

Trudie yawned as the car pulled into the well-lit hotel car park around ten o'clock the same evening. It had been a long and emotional day for all concerned, and after the two glasses of wine she'd had with her dinner, as well as the brandy earlier at Mary's house, she was in need of her bed.

"Am I boring you?" laughed Donal, in jest, "or have I just walked and talked your legs off?"

"No, I've had a great time, thank you. It's just I think the jetlag you warned me about has finally kicked in; that, or the drink you've plied me with. I'm not usually a big drinker, so should probably have stopped after the first glass of wine, and not allowed you to twist my arm with another one in that bar," she replied, smiling over at him. "I just think I'm ready for my bed."

"Well, it is Christmas, so what's wrong with enjoying yourself and letting your hair down a bit?" he replied, smiling back at her. "But I agree, it's been quite a busy time for both you and Betty. You've hardly been here forty-eight hours, and already look at the mayhem you've caused in the Murphy household," he joked. "I thought the look on Mary's face was priceless when Brigid announced that Mick was Betty's father too. I know it surprised all of us, but you could have knocked her down with a feather, she was so shocked!" he laughed, before adding "she's probably just realising she can't lord it over everyone as the eldest sister anymore. It'll hopefully bring her down a peg or two."

Trudie joined in Donal's laughter at his assessment of his cousin, and although she did not know much about Mary, or her circumstances, tended to agree with it. "Yes, that was a bit of a shock, even for me. I'd always sensed when I was researching Betty's story that something wasn't quite right, but even I'd never considered that possibility. I bet they'll all have a lot to talk about tomorrow, once the immediate shock has worn off."

"Yes, I'm sure they will," he replied, quite sanguine. "What a great conclusion to your search though. You must be feeling very proud of yourself," he added, smiling across at her.

Trudie did not allow herself to feel pride, instead reflected on the events that had led them to this point. Events that perhaps she had still not been perfectly honest about, or faced up to. Had Josh's accident not had the butterfly effect it had, then admittedly hers and Betty's paths would never have crossed, with the events of today probably never unfolding. But was the price her friend had paid, the loss of her beloved husband and daughter, a fair price under the circumstances? Did the end justify the means, Trudie thought to herself, and does the fact everything has turned out well mean that she should no longer feel guilty about not telling Betty that Josh is, or more correctly was, her fiancé when the accident took place?

They had left Mary's house around two-thirty in the afternoon after a small snack, reluctantly prepared by their hostess; her body language clearly showing signs she had much better things to be getting on with in the kitchen, two days before Christmas, than making plates of sandwiches and cups of tea for everyone. She was expecting twelve for lunch on Christmas Day, and there were preparations that needed to be made; once again feeling that Betty could not have chosen a more inopportune time for descending, almost unannounced, on the family if she had tried.

Mary's feelings aside, for the rest of the group it had all got quite emotional as they had continued to talk. Especially for Betty, as she relived her recent accident, leading to the tragic loss of both Richard and Annie. She touched briefly on the physiotherapy she had needed afterwards, and the support she had received from both Matt, her son-in-law and Trudie to get her emotionally and physically back to a place where she wanted to live again; survivor's guilt being one of the keenest emotions she had felt at the time.

She smiled as she outlined the concept of the memory book they were preparing for Jack, delighting at how that had led her onto unearthing the photo they had all just been looking at, and the subsequent search to find some distant family, touching briefly on the invaluable role Trudie had played in that process. Nothing was mentioned about her early life, her adoptive parents or her upbringing, Betty sensing, quite rightly, that perhaps the time was not right for that part of the story to be relived just yet.

Trudie, who prided herself on reading situations, began to notice both Betty and Brigid were getting tired. Mary was clearly distracted and not at all comfortable with what was being discussed, and Donal was feeling fidgety, constantly looking at his watch and needing to be somewhere else. So, she suggested, as subtly as she could, without wanting to break the mood, that perhaps it would be a good time to call it a day.

Mick, equally concerned about his and his wife's emotional welfare, suggested he and Brigid meet with Betty the following morning, even offering to collect her from the hotel and take her to their house for the day. That way they would have time to not only talk, but show her around their home. He mentioned that he and Brigid were lunching at Mary's house on Christmas Day, so neither of them had any pulls on their time, and even if they had, what could have been more important than catching up with their long-lost daughter?

As Donal had driven away from Mary's house, he had glanced back to Trudie, sitting behind him, and suggested that unless she had anything better to do with her afternoon, she might fancy a bit of sightseeing, with some Christmas shopping thrown in, whilst Betty had a well-deserved rest.

"Oh, that sounds like a nice idea, Trudie," Betty had said.

Initially taken aback, believing he had somewhere better to be rushing off to, she felt like declining and spending the afternoon in her room too, catching up with a good book. But sensing the invitation was in fact genuine, she had thanked him and agreed.

After the fastest trip imaginable around the shops, Donal obviously being a typical male when it came to Christmas shopping, leaving it all to the last minute and then buying the first thing he could lay his hands on, they made their way to a small Italian restaurant, where, Trudie was assured, the pizzas were the best on the planet.

She simply followed in his wake, offering to carry the increasing number of bags and parcels as they went from shop to shop, gazing in awe at the city, with all its bright lights and decorations festooning the shops. She marvelled at the huge Christmas tree, proudly standing in the centre of the pedestrian shopping arcade, with brightly wrapped presents at its base, nestled among the artificial snow, with musical penguins and an oversized reindeer standing guard over them.

There was a crisp nip in the air, although nothing to discourage the countless buskers and entertainers lining the streets, the constant sound of music, or laughter wherever they walked. Having never been to Liverpool before, Trudie had no idea what to expect. She was amazed at what the city had to offer, and with the warmth of the welcome they received from the locals wherever they went, although she did have to concentrate hard to pick up on their accents.

Over pizza, Donal had chatted quite openly about his home and his family back in Ireland, describing the small town he lived in as a 'bit of a backwater', and the maintenance business he was running for his father now that he was effectively retired, as something he was committed to and building up, but not a real passion for him. He talked warmly of his mam, Ella, who he was especially close to, admitting that with such a massive age difference between him and his dad, as much as he loved him, they were not as close as he would have liked.

"By the time I came along, Dad was already in his fifties. His days of kicking a ball around the field were long behind him, and his grasp of computer games, or anything 'new-fangled' as he would term it, was non-existent. So, I suppose I grew up quite quickly, and became relatively independent early on, spending more of my time helping them out, rather than the other way around. After coming over here to Liverpool for university, I probably shouldn't have moved back home when I graduated, but by then Dad wasn't too well, so he'd asked me to step in to run things. Like Colleen, I'd studied engineering, and I'd always been quite hands-on and practically minded, so it was no big deal."

"What about your brothers - did they not want to help out?" asked Trudie.

"No, neither of my brothers showed any interest. They had their own lives and families, so it was left to me. Otherwise, the business would have collapsed, and the staff would have lost their jobs. Frankly, I'm not sure how Mam or Dad would have coped with that, or if in fact they would have survived it. In such a small town, quite a few families rely on them for their livelihood." Listening to him, Trudie realised how much older and more mature he sounded than Josh, their completely different lifestyles and upbringings obviously having a huge bearing on their approach to life and responsibility.

After their meal, they had gone a few doors down the road to a traditional British pub, where the bar was crowded with revellers, mainly dressed in fancy dress and Santa outfits, intent on enjoying their night out. The noise level was making it difficult to hear themselves speak, let alone hold any meaningful conversation. They were so tightly crammed in, that Trudie was unsure whether it was the warmth of the fire, the emotions of the day, or the pure hypnotic tones of Donal's voice, as he stood so close to her, that was giving her such a feeling of peace and contentment.

"So, what are your plans for tomorrow? It's Christmas Eve after all," Donal almost shouted in her ear to make himself heard.

"I'm not sure," she replied honestly, after realising she had given it no consideration whatsoever. "I'll probably just mooch around during the day, possibly have a swim in the hotel's pool, then see what Betty wants to do when she gets back from Brigid and Mick's," she replied, standing on her tiptoes to reach up to his ear. "It'll probably just be an early night, with a good book for me, after we've had dinner that is," she added, unsure what, if any of that he had actually heard.

It was certainly like no other Christmas she could ever recall. Other than feeling a little guilty about not being at home with her family, helping Aunt Caroline to peel the potatoes or getting the house ready with Uncle Scott, the rest was not bothering her too much. After all, she was on an adventure. She was experiencing a whole new world, meeting some great new characters, so what did it matter if the usual traditions were not being observed in their time-honoured way?

Josh had messaged her yesterday to let her know he had eventually found someone to go to his mother's party with him, so that was a relief – for him at least. He had not thought to ask if her journey had gone well, or if she was enjoying herself. As usual, he was only thinking about himself. So, all in all, if you added in having dodged the bullet of the cocktail party, then if nothing else, that had to be a bonus.

"Thanks for a great afternoon Donal, and for the pizza. It was as good as you promised it would be. I owe you," said Trudie, as she prepared to get out of the car once it had stopped in the car park.

"How about I pick you up around eleven o'clock, after your swim, and we spend the day together tomorrow? I'm meeting some friends for lunch, with a few drinks afterwards. What do you say? It's got to beat sitting alone in your room, reading a book on Christmas Eve, no matter how good a bestseller it might be!"

"No, I wouldn't want to intrude with you and your mates," she replied, reluctantly.

"Nonsense, I think you'll love them, and I'm sure they'll love you," Donal insisted.

"If you're sure, then that sounds like a great idea," Trudie said, quite taken aback, struggling to hide the joy from her voice. "How about I message you in the morning to confirm, once I've spoken to Betty? Just in case she's no other plans for me," she said, her fingers crossed praying that would not be the case.

Walking back into the hotel, Trudie turned around and waved to Donal as he drove off, a broad smile on her face. He had obviously heard every word she had said over the noise of the bar, and other than just thinking about himself, in true Josh fashion, he had thought about it, and then taken the trouble to include her in his plans, even to introduce her to some of his friends.

This Christmas was shaping up to be a lot better than even she had imagined.

Chapter 50

A week later and Betty and Trudie were on their flight home, exhausted after their brief stay in Liverpool, but each delighted at how things had turned out, both commenting on how remarkable a trip they'd had as they had sat, waiting to board the aircraft.

Betty felt a little sad to be going home with her promises to return soon welcomed, especially by her parents, who felt they had so much catching-up to do. She had spent a marvellous Christmas period, getting to know not just Brigid and Mick, but her three sisters and their families, her two nieces and two nephews.

She and Trudie had spent Christmas Day with Colleen and Donal as previously agreed, enjoying a relaxed meal, pulled together from an assortment of ready-made or pre-prepared food. It was clear Colleen was not a cook. Even so, she was great company and a generous hostess; providing a constant flow of drink throughout the day, before collapsing in front of the television to watch the King's speech. Betty, although American, was a true royalist and had been greatly saddened by the death of Queen Elizabeth earlier that year. Listening to King Charles as he spoke, his words displaying early indications of the type of monarch he would become had, she exclaimed, been one of the highlights of her day.

They had then visited Ruth and her family for a Boxing Day brunch, meeting Bobby, Ruth's husband, and Jamie and Ruby, their delightful fifteen-year-old twins. They lived in a large detached house on a new housing development, a few miles outside the city, one of which Bobby proudly advised Trudie, he had overseen the construction.

Mary, and her husband Dave, had turned up mid-afternoon, with their two children, Alex, nineteen and Elliott, seventeen, both in tow and both looking like they would rather have stayed at home, if that had been an option. Although Trudie sensed a slight change in the atmosphere when Mary entered the room, after a couple of drinks she seemed to loosen up a little, even reluctantly taking part in the game of charades the twins had arranged, making everyone roar with laughter each time it was her turn as she struggled to get to grips with the rules. It was clear she was still not warming to the idea of another sister, but as the rest of the family had made Betty more than welcome, and the children particularly were keen to find out about their American aunt, even angling after a trip to the States to visit her the following summer, she was at least making an effort.

Mick had paid to have both their seats upgraded for the return flight back to John F Kennedy airport, arguing it was the least he could do after missing so many years of birthday and Christmas presents, assuring them at the same time it was no big deal financially, so nothing for them to worry about.

It transpired that in the property boom of the 1960s and 1970s, Mick had branched out on his own, and with a little investment and support from his father, he and Brigid had started a small building company. He and his father had a lot of contacts, through both his father's business and himself having worked as a bricklayer for other builders over the years, and Brigid knew how to run an office. Her time spent working as a clerk in Ireland had not been wasted, she often quipped, when anyone asked her what she did.

Mick had gradually brought in a variety of different trades; qualified plumbers, electricians, and plasterers to work alongside him. Over the years, the business had not only grown, but had become very successful, establishing a good reputation in the industry for affordable and quality workmanship. Murphy's Construction was now responsible for a significant number of major infrastructure contracts across the north west of England.

Bobby had joined the business some years previously, starting off as a plumber. His eye was soon caught by the fiery redhead, who occasionally worked in the office; her bright smile and infectious laughter being a real tonic in the builder's yard. Ruth, his boss' daughter, worked alongside her mother in the office whenever she was on holiday from college, earning extra pocket money to fund her passion for fashion, always wanting to be seen in whatever were the latest trends. They started dating, and two years later Bobby plucked up the courage to propose, nervously asking Mick for his daughter's hand. He was from a very traditional family, and prided himself on doing things properly. When they married the following summer, Mick proudly escorting his daughter down the aisle, Bobby often joked he had joined the family firm in more ways than one; wedding him to the business, as well as his beautiful bride.

Now, twenty years later, he and Ruth had taken on the day-to-day control of the company, allowing Mick and Brigid the freedom to retire and enjoy the fruits of their labours.

Trudie had delighted at Betty's good fortune, finding such a normal and welcoming family. The sisters seemed like real characters; Mary, the conventional stay-at-home housewife, who was perhaps a little too domineering for Trudie's liking, but deep down appeared to have a heart of gold; Ruth the fashion crazy kid of the seventies, who had matured into a very beautiful and accomplished business woman; and Colleen, the baby of the family, a mad cat woman by her own admission, and someone who despite her quirkiness, was obviously highly intelligent and successful in her own field.

Trudie had enjoyed getting to know a little about each of them, fascinated to understand how their stories had developed, as well as intrigued to see how their lives would be impacted by this recent news. Most of all, she had loved getting to know Donal, realising how easily they had gravitated towards each other, and how comfortable he had made her feel during what could have been a very awkward situation for her. She was in the midst of a family in which she played no part, listening to their most intimate stories; stories that had previously gone unheard, and for whatever reason, it had felt right.

After dropping her off at the hotel the night before Christmas Eve, they had barely spent a day apart. He had shown her the sites of Liverpool, taking her to some of his old student haunts, or to visit bands that were playing in the area, as well as introducing her to his wide group of friends over a beer or two; a grouping that could best and most politely be described as eclectic. She had laughed and relaxed in their company, eventually growing to enjoy the banter, and their British sense of humour, once her mind had started to distinguish and understand the competing accents over the noise of the pubs. The Irish accent was one thing, but the Scouse accent was a whole new ball game, with following some of their in-jokes proving a little tricky for her at times!

It was obvious that Donal was letting his hair down whilst he was in Liverpool for a few days, simply enjoying the Christmas festivities, without feeling any of the pressures of being at home. His personality as 'one of the lads', Trudie imagined, was the complete opposite to the man he identified himself as, at home in Ireland. Here, there were no cares, whilst at home he not only felt a responsibility for his parents, but as a trusted and respected employer, was mindful of what he said and did around the town. It was almost a fear of what effect any negative behaviour could have, in terms of impacting his family's reputation, and hence their livelihoods.

One evening, in a roundabout sort of way, over a glass of particularly good red wine, they had touched on relationships. Trudie discovered that Donal had a girlfriend at home, a local girl called Shauna. "Nothing too serious for the time being," he had said – well, not as far as he was concerned, at least. Although he admitted that she might argue differently. Given they had been going out together for nearly three years, he sensed there was certainly an air of expectation, from both his and her family, that he would be popping the question at some stage.

Trudie laughed to herself at the comparison with Josh; the obvious failure to commit by either of them possibly the only similarity she had seen between them so far. Why was that, she wondered, when on every other level, physically, culturally and emotionally they were so different?

She told Donal a little about Josh, elaborating on some of her annoyances about his selfish and entitled behaviour, even his failure to see their relationship as over, although she drew the line at mentioning anything about the role he had played in Betty's accident. That was something she was still torturing herself about, and feared the day it would ever come out, or what impact it could have on hers and Betty's friendship.   Donal listened, without offering an opinion either way.   It was none of his business.

Josh had continued to message Trudie over the week she had been away, providing snippets of what he was up to, including telling her about the cocktail party she had missed, even joking about the girl his mom had so obviously been trying to matchmake him with. Trudie at that stage had felt sorry for Marcia, wishing her better luck next time. Clearly, she had got the message, so perhaps she could explain it to her son in capital letters, because Trudie's approach was clearly not working.

No, she would miss Donal, but life needed to go on and get back to normal as soon as she got home. Glancing over, she noticed Betty had drifted off to sleep, hopefully with happy dreams floating around in her head, thought Trudie, realising how life-changing their journey really had been for her friend. How the despair she had felt, only a few short months ago, was now replaced by a hope and an expectation that she could never have imagined. A family, with proper blood ties, of which she and Jack now had the chance to be part.

But where did it leave Trudie, she thought as she sat back and relaxed into the flight? She cradled the chilled champagne the stewardess had brought her earlier, allowing her mind to wander towards what was awaiting her when she eventually got back home. Tomorrow was New Year's Eve, and all those resolutions she had been parking about her job, her living arrangements, learning to drive, even her relationship would inevitably come back into sharp focus as soon as she walked through the door and into her aunt's welcoming embrace.

The brief sojourn she had enjoyed had come to its inevitable end, meaning now it was time to get on with her life, whatever that life involved.

Chapter 51

Rather than New Year sparking the wave of enthusiasm for all the resolutions Trudie had promised herself, January proved to be a bit of a damp squib, leaving her feeling unusually miserable. Her normal joie de vivre had abandoned her, with whatever she turned her mind to, failing to capture her interest for any length of time. She felt like she was simply going through the motions, her heart was not in it, and the reason for her depressed mood not at all evident to her.

Although she had returned home in time for the new year celebrations, instead of heading out to party with either Josh or any of her friends, Trudie found herself staying in at home with her aunt and uncle, watching the celebrations in Times Square on the television; the crowds partying as they brought in the new year, watching the famous ball drop from the top of One Times Square. There would undoubtably be champagne corks popping all over the country as the clock struck the hour, but she was happy nursing a small glass of wine that Caroline had bought in especially for the occasion. Marcus had gone away for a few days with Penny, staying with some of her friends in a log cabin they had rented, so the house was quieter than normal; and with the mood she found herself in, that suited her perfectly.

Her rotas for both the hospital and the café had arrived whilst she had been away, and Trudie dutifully turned up for each of her shifts, working as hard as ever, just without her usual enthusiasm. Cynthia, like

Caroline had been eager to hear all about the trip and about Betty's long-lost family, as had Millie at the café, but with each it was conveyed in a way that felt mechanical, rather than emotional. Trudie had simply answered their questions, "Yes, everything had been fine; Yes, her family was lovely and welcoming; Yes, Liverpool was a fantastic city," without adding any more than was strictly necessary.

It was not that she did not want to talk about it, or that anything had gone wrong. It was actually quite the opposite. She would happily have spoken about the fun she'd had, the people she'd met, the sites she'd visited. All that would have done though was trigger thoughts that she was not yet able to process, or words she felt difficult to articulate. Getting on the plane and leaving everything and everybody behind had left her feeling flat.

By the end of the month, Caroline had started to worry, as not only was Trudie quiet and introvert, but she had started picking at her food, even missing the occasional meal, declaring she was either not hungry, or she was too busy to eat – when in fact Caroline knew both to be untrue. Trudie had a healthy appetite, and as far as being too busy was concerned, well, when had that ever stopped her eating before? She could normally juggle so many things at the same time, the words 'too busy' had never previously been part of her vocabulary.

It was so unlike her niece to be down, or to turn her nose up at food, and whatever Caroline tried to tempt her appetite with, or say to bring a sparkle back into her conversation, failed miserably.

Scott had noticed it too, and he could not shed any light on it either. The one positive was that at least she had started to learn to drive, booking lessons as soon as she got home, and throwing herself into learning both the practical and theoretical elements of the process with equal vigour, even asking him to start looking out for the perfect car for her.

It was Marcus who pinpointed the problem one evening as he was rushing off to meet Penny, after he had crossed with Trudie in the hallway on his way down the stairs, nearly bumping into her, as she failed to get out of his way in time.

"Well, it's obvious, isn't it? She's pining for Josh," he declared, when Caroline asked him what he thought, adding "I know she took him his engagement ring back a few weeks ago. There was a bit of a showdown between them in the café, which didn't exactly turn nasty, but wasn't pleasant, from what she said. My guess is she's regretting it now. That's all it'll be. She'll be fine in a month or so, when she's met someone better," he said, with a confidence that suggested he had solved the world's greatest mystery, without breaking sweat.

"I'm not saying I disagree with you about Josh, and I'm glad she's finally drawn a line under that too, though I'm not convinced that's the problem here. No, there's something she's not telling us, and I suspect whatever it is, has to do with Betty and their recent trip to England. Trudie's not been herself since she came home. I don't think she's been round to visit Betty at all in the last few weeks. Before they went away, they were almost inseparable. I'm not sure if they've even spoken recently."

"I don't know anything about that, but he's a real loser, so she's better off without him in my view.

In fact, I might introduce her to one of my mates to avoid her thinking she needs to go crawling back to him. I'll just need to think carefully about which one first."

"Oh, I'm not sure about that, Marcus!" Caroline said, directing a horrified smile at her son. "I don't think Trudie's done anything so bad to warrant one of your mates, has she?"

"Well, mark my words. There's a bloke involved somewhere. I'll guarantee you that."

Then picking his bag and jacket up from where it was slung over the back of the chair, he kissed his mom goodbye, and headed to the front door, advising her not to wait up, as he would probably not be home for a day or so. Penny had plans for them over the weekend, apparently, but he had no idea what.

Caroline reflected on what her son had just said. It was the most she had ever heard him say against Josh, and it was evident Marcus was not one of his greatest fans. His parting shot though had certainly given her something to mull over.

Chapter 52

By the end of February, Trudie's mood had lifted a little. However, at the same time she appeared to be in a real quandary, which from what little Caroline could ascertain, seemed to be linked to her niece receiving a message from Donal, Betty's cousin. She had not heard Trudie speak anything about him in recent weeks. She recalled he was the young man they had originally spoken to when the search had initially begun, and even recalled that he lived in Ireland, but that was the extent of her knowledge.

"So, are you going to tell me what the message says, or am I to get my crystal ball out and use my psychic powers?" asked Caroline, when Trudie had entered the kitchen, cradling her phone in her hand, declaring she had a bit of a problem and needed some advice.

"Well, Donal, Betty's cousin, has just invited me over to Dublin. Apparently, his Aunt Brigid is seventy-five later this year, and the family is throwing a surprise party for her at some glitzy hotel. He thought that as I've met the family, I might like to go over and meet them all again. He said they had all spoken well of me when we left, and were appreciative of the way I had tracked them down and reunited them with Betty."

"Oh, that sounds nice dear. Isn't it a long way to go just for a party though, saying nothing about how much it's going to cost you on flights and accommodation?" she questioned. Money was not an issue to Trudie. Financially, she had no worries on that score, not after her parents had died, leaving her the sole beneficiary to their estates. Even so, she knew her niece was careful with money, and not one to squander it, always happy to muddle through on what she earned from the café, never dipping into her savings unless it was essential.

"Apart from which," Caroline added, "I thought it was Liverpool where she lived. Isn't Brigid Betty's mother – or have I got that confused? There seemed to be so many sisters, I do remember that, but I don't recall all their names."

"Yes, you're right, she is. It's Mick, her husband who's planning the party. I think the sisters, Mary, Ruth and Colleen are all helping out, although it's his idea, from what I understand."

"So, why is he inviting you to Dublin? Am I missing something, or did I mishear you?" she questioned, still not fully sure what either the issue, or the problem was.

"Well, no, not really. It's just Donal lives in Ireland with his parents. He thought that if I was flying in via Dublin, like we did last time, that I could perhaps stop off there, and spend a few days sightseeing, before flying over to Liverpool. He only lives about forty minutes outside the city, so he's offered to meet me and show me around, and then fly over to Liverpool at the same time."

"I see," replied Caroline. "And what about Betty? I presume she's been invited too, given it's her mother's party. What does she think about going to Dublin for a few days beforehand?"

"Well, I'm not sure, and to be honest, that's where the problem lies," began Trudie, unsure now exactly how much she wanted to say to her aunt, or frankly where to begin. "It's just that I've not spoken to Betty for a few weeks, and whilst I presume she's been invited, I've no idea what her plans are, or in fact if she intends going. And I couldn't go without her, could I?"

"For the last few months, you two have been as thick as thieves, and I thought had become really good friends, so there's obviously something going on that I'm missing. Because otherwise, you'd know exactly what her plans were. In fact, you'd be making your plans together," observed Caroline. "Are you going to tell me what's been going on, or just leave me to wonder?" an element of frustration now evident in her voice.

Sitting herself down at the table, Trudie let out a massive sigh. "I think I've messed everything up, and it's all my fault!" she cried, tears now flowing freely from her eyes, all the weeks of emotion that had been bottled up, suddenly finding their release.

"There, there dear, whatever do you mean?" said Caroline, offering Trudie the box of tissues. "Surely, nothing can be so bad that you need to cry over it. Come on, I'll make us both a strong cup of tea, and you can tell me all about it. A problem shared they say, is a problem halved."

As they sat, their drinks abandoned on the table between them, Trudie explained what had happened back in the first week of January, when she had gone round to Josh's house on her way to the café to return his engagement ring, determined as she was that the time had finally come to end their pseudo-relationship. She had resolved to do it in the new year, and after her time away in Liverpool, this had only strengthened her resolve.

Josh had not been at home though, with his mother reluctantly taking the message that Trudie needed to speak to him in person. Josh, believing it to be positive news, had rushed straight round to the café, no doubt with the intention of claiming his fiancée back.

At the time, the café had not been too busy. Business was generally slow those first few weeks of the year, when people had no desire, or need to hit the stores in the bad weather. Although Trudie had never planned to announce it so publicly, at the same time she could no longer pretend, or worse still give him false hope. When she saw his optimism, so evident on his face as he walked into the café, it was clear his expectation was that they were getting back together. Unfortunately, as she handed him his ring back, with the banal words that it was 'her' not 'him' that had changed, it just so happened to be the exact moment Betty walked into the café, hoping for a drink and a catch up with her friend. She had errands in town, with half an hour to kill before her next appointment, so what better way to while away the time, than a drink and a piece of cake, had been her view.

Josh's manner and attitude, and the few choice words he decided to utter, would have left no-one with any question as to what had just happened, and as he stormed out of the café, slamming the door behind him for good measure, Betty had looked directly at Trudie, the unspoken question in her eyes.

"That was the young man who caused the accident, wasn't it? Josh, I seem to recall is his name," she eventually asked, quietly so as not to cause a further scene in front of the remaining customers, some of whom were still looking over at the counter, wondering presumably what all the kafuffle had been about.

"Yes," Trudie replied, quite sheepishly, unsure what else she could say.

"And am I to take it he's your fiancé?" questioned Betty.

"Well, he was, but not anymore. I've just returned his ring to him."

"I see." And with that, Betty simply turned and walked out of the door, leaving Trudie at a loss as to whether to run after her or let her go. If she had, what could she have said to repair the damage? Whilst she had never directly lied to her friend about Josh, it was evident that at best she had deceived her by not coming clean on their relationship, or even mentioning the fact that she knew him.

"So, are you saying you've not seen Betty since then, and you've not discussed what happened with her? Surely, you've tried to explain, haven't you? At the end of the day, the accident had nothing to do with you. As I recall it, if you hadn't said anything to Josh, Betty would never have had the closure she had when he wrote that letter, and didn't you say that had made her feel better, and that the two of them had even met up before Christmas?" argued Caroline.

"I know all that, but I still feel like I've deceived her, and worse still I probably used confidential information in a way that I shouldn't. Without me coming into contact with her at the hospital, no one would ever have put two and two together, or made the connection, so in a way I am responsible."

"Well, whatever the wrongs or rights of the situation are, I think this has gone on far too long. In my view that poor woman has suffered enough, without losing you as a friend as well. She's bound to feel hurt and betrayed, and you need to stand up to that and, if necessary, eat a bit of humble pie in the process. I suggest you go round and make your peace, without any further delay or harm being done."

"I know you're right. It's going to be hard to know where to start, or what to say though," sighed Trudie, at a complete loss of how to proceed.

"Well, I'm sure you'll find a way, particularly if this trip to Dublin, or Liverpool is important to you, which I sense by the way you're reacting, and the way your face lights up whenever you mentioned this Donal's name, it is," said Caroline, to an astounded Trudie. "Oh Trudie, don't look at me like that. I've seen the way you've been moping around the house for the last few weeks - Marcus said there was a lad involved somewhere, and I'm starting to see now exactly what he meant."

And with that, she moved back to the sink to continue peeling the vegetables for dinner, leaving Trudie to stew on her aunt's words, and ponder whether Marcus was more perceptive than even she had given him credit for. Surely, she did not have any real feelings for Donal, did she?

Chapter 53

The following morning Trudie arrived unannounced at Betty's house around eleven o'clock, carrying a cake box she had asked Millie to make up for her, with a selection of the cakes they had seen Betty enjoy over the months she had been a customer at the café. Trudie was not stupid enough to think she could buy her friend's affection back so easily, but who could stay angry when faced with a huge slice of lemon meringue pie, or a piece of carrot cake when it was presented to them, accompanied by the slice of humble pie Caroline had said she needed to eat herself?

"Oh, Trudie it's you," exclaimed Betty, a surprised look on her face as she opened the door. "I wasn't expecting to see you today. Is there something you need?" she added, her manner and tone of voice a little dismissive.

"Do you mind if I come in, please? There's something I'd like to explain to you." Trudie simply smiled in return, and proffering the box towards Betty adding, "I've brought you some of your favourites from the café, if you've time for a drink."

"Well, you'd better come in then, no use standing on the doorstep," suggested Betty, taking the box of cakes and standing back to allow Trudie in.

Although Trudie had been in Betty's house on many an occasion, always being invited to make herself at home, feeling both comfortable and welcomed, today's atmosphere created a tension that had never existed between the two women before.

"I'm in the kitchen preparing dinner for Matt and Jack this evening, so you had better come through," she said, leading the way through to the back of the house and placing the box of cakes, unopened on the Welsh dresser, where Betty's cook books and photo frames were proudly displayed. The modern kitchen was normally so pristine, but today there were pots and pans everywhere; ingredients strewn all over the work surfaces, with some interesting aromas emanating from the stove. "You'll have to excuse the mess. As you can see, I'm very busy," the dismissive tone still lingering in the air.

"I won't stay long, it's just I feel I need to explain about the day in the café, and perhaps clear the air between us," Trudie began quite hesitantly.

"I'm sure there's no need for that," replied Betty, making it difficult for Trudie to know where to start, or how to move forward.

"Well, I would like to try, because I know I've hurt you, and that was the last thing I ever intended," Trudie said, falteringly. "Your friendship these last few months has been so valuable, and these last few weeks have been a nightmare for me; unsure what you're thinking, or how you must feel towards me." As Betty did not respond, Trudie continued, "I would like the opportunity to explain, and hopefully make amends, if at all possible."

"Sit down then, and I'll make us both a drink. I suppose I could spare a few minutes." Whilst Betty clearly had no intention of making it easy, at least she was prepared to listen, which was better than nothing, thought Trudie to herself.

The conversation began slowly. The more Trudie opened up, explaining how she had inadvertently pieced together Josh's involvement in the accident some weeks after the event, it began to get easier. She told Betty she had been furious with him – not because of the trip, that was a genuine accident, but for his complete self-centredness after the event, caring only for himself, even expecting her to wait on him hand and foot as he recovered from a sprained ankle. She explained how she had confronted him about it once she had made the connection after the police report; realising how typical his behaviour had been, and how for her it was the final straw for their relationship.

"When he wrote to you though, I saw a different side to him, a humbler side and I felt there was an element of remorse in his actions, possibly even hope for our relationship. I saw that it had given you some closure, and I was happy for that at least. But I was a fool. In the long run, I know Josh cares about Josh, period."

"Why did you never tell me that you knew him, or that he was your fiancé, when I told you I'd received the letter, or even later after I'd met him?"

"I honestly don't know. I keep asking myself that, and I can assure you I have felt guilty hiding it from you. I just didn't know what to say. I think I felt that if I said something, it would harm our friendship, which clearly it has done anyway. I'd grown very fond of you, and that was the last thing I wanted to do. The closer we got, the harder it became. I'd resolved to end it all before Christmas, then we went away at short notice, so it got parked. As soon as I got back home, it was the first thing I did. Being away with you and your family in England had made me realise that Josh and his egotism, was not what I wanted to spend my life on."

"So, what's made you wait nearly two months to come round to tell me all this? If our friendship was so valuable to you, then what's prompted you today?" Betty asked.

"Donal messaged me out of the blue yesterday, inviting me over to the surprise party for your mother's seventy-fifth birthday. I'm sure it was only him being kind, and I realise I can't accept, but it was the prompt I needed to come round – well that, and my aunt giving me a good talking to, telling me it was time for me to eat humble pie," she replied honestly, as she stood up, ready to make her way to the door. Having done what she had intended doing, and having now said her piece, it was time to leave Betty to return to her preparations. She could sense by the look on her friend's face, that her speech had not made a great impression on her mood, so it was better to go before she upset her further.

"Before you rush off," Betty started, as Trudie moved to the door, "I hope that box doesn't contain any of that "humble pie", because it's not my favourite. I thought you knew me better than that," she smiled, as she lifted the box's lid. "Ah good, there's enough for both of us, so unless you need to hurry off somewhere, why don't you sit back down while I make us another drink, and we can start planning our next trip. I was starting to worry that I might have to go without you. One thing's for sure though, if Donal's invited you, it must be because he wants you there. He doesn't strike me as a young man who doesn't know his own mind, does he you?" remarked Betty. "And, what's more, if what Colleen said, when she spoke to me last week, is correct I believe he's currently a free agent. The girl he was seeing is apparently no more."

The smile on Trudie's face seemed to appear from nowhere. She was unsure whether it was due to the way Betty was looking at her, their friendship obviously back on track, or the fact she was sharing her cakes with her, although possibly not the carrot cake. What other reason could there be? It could not be the news about Donal and his break-up with his girlfriend, could it? That had nothing to do with her. She had certainly got on with him very well, and admittedly had thought about him every single day since she had last seen him, looking forward to those quirky texts he kept sending, but they were just friends, right? They had enjoyed each other's company, had a good laugh. That had been all, not a touch or a glance that could have been construed any other way.

Surely, it was nothing more than friendship that was behind his invitation to spend a few days in Ireland with him, was it, she wondered to herself, as Betty placed the cakes on the table, a knowing smile on her face.

Chapter 54

By the end of March, their flights had been booked and the trip was all planned.

Penny, at the travel agents, had been surprised to see them both again, so soon after their original trip, and was interested to learn how everything had worked out with their Christmas adventure. Betty delighted at telling her the news, how she had not only discovered a family, but connected with them on a level she could never have imagined possible. She had felt particularly close to her sisters, Ruth and Colleen, with them messaging and phoning frequently since her return home, and she had even introduced them to Jack, their great-nephew, the youngest member of the family it would appear, and to Matt, his daddy. Penny listened with a smile on her face, as Betty recounted details of their trip; thankful it was a quiet Wednesday afternoon and they were not expecting to get too busy.

Whilst Matt was happy for Betty to have found her family, it did nothing to help him deal with his own grief, or the loneliness for the family he had lost. He wondered whether he would get the same reception if he turned up unannounced on his own brother's doorstep after all these years, realising not for the first time, that other than Jack, Simon was all the family he now had left it the world. He recalled sadly, how it was over five years since they had last seen each other, Simon and Sara having called in and spent the night with them when Jack was just a baby. They had been taking a road trip though the States, and as Annie and

Matt's house was not far off their route, they had arranged to call in for a couple of days.

The visit had not ended well, with Annie so stressed with their new-born that her visitors had been left far from feeling welcomed. Simon and Sara had packed up the following morning, and simply driven off, without even stopping for breakfast. That had been the last time they had met, and other than the occasional Christmas card, there had been no contact. Matt knew that they had never been particularly close, but was that sufficient reason not to try again he wondered to himself, as Betty told him all about another trip she was making to see her new found family.

Betty, as well as getting close to her sisters, had spoken often to her parents over recent weeks, pleased to learn that Brigid was now out of the plaster cast, and back on her feet, and from what Mick had said in a light-hearted way, back to issuing out the orders. It was so obvious from the tone of his voice how much love he felt for his wife. Betty was reminded of the spirited teenager Father Bill had told her about, what seemed like a lifetime ago, and was pleased her mother had not lost her zest for life.

Betty had opened up a little about her adoptive parents, careful in the way she described them, whilst at the same time not prepared to gilt over her childhood. Brigid had asked her to sort out photos, and anything else she could find, to help them understand the childhood she'd had; baby photos, school certificates, wedding photos – in fact anything they could use to help bridge the years, and the memories they had missed out on. Betty laughed when she had told Trudie, realising she was now creating two memory books, for two worthwhile, but completely different reasons.

"Well, I think we have everything sorted," said Penny, as she finalised the booking and handed Betty a piece of paper with all the details printed out. "I have you booked onto flights, into Liverpool, John Lennon Airport, via Dublin, returning to JFK. The outbound flights are confirmed, and the return flights are both open-ended. You'll just have to confirm the details as soon as you know when you'll be travelling home and will probably need to do that online, or call into a local travel agent in Liverpool if there's any problem, or to enquire when they have availability. I've also included transport to JFK, and as you don't need any accommodation booking this time, I think that's everything sorted," she said, with a smile on her face. "Have a lovely time, ladies, and enjoy the party. It sounds like another great adventure for you both. I almost wish I was coming with you."

"Thank you for doing all that for us," replied Betty, smiling back at Penny. "At least this time around we've got some idea of what's awaiting us, unlike last time when it was a real test of faith; a journey into the unknown in more ways than one, wasn't it Trudie?"

Trudie smiled. She was not as convinced as Betty about what would await her, or more precisely what Donal's reaction would be when he met them at the airport in Liverpool, as he had offered to do. If anything, it just added to her anxiety, as she started to imagine different scenarios that may or may not play out, and feeling stupid for even thinking that way.

All of his messages were purely platonic, so why was she reading into everything, trying to find a deeper meaning, and with an expectation that had no right to be there? He was a good friend, so what was she concerned about, and why was she wanting to consider anything that would compromise that? The fact he had recently split from his long-term girlfriend did not mean anything, and certainly did not mean he was now pursuing her, so why was she worried? It was just a few days holiday, checking out Dublin and enjoying the craic, as Donal kept saying. Just two mates, enjoying life and having a laugh.

So, why had both Betty and Caroline intimated it was more than that, making her question her own feelings in the process? Okay, the more she thought about it, the more she realised she did find him attractive, albeit in a quirky sort of way, and she acknowledged she had missed seeing him since coming back to the States. However, having just broken off her engagement with Josh, the idea that she was looking to jump into another relationship, something on the rebound, was laughable. No, friendship was what she should be looking for, with any other feelings she might be experiencing, packed safely away.

The more she told herself that, the more her mind wandered back to Donal. He was definitely not Josh in the looks department or the glamour stakes. With his ginger hair, tall-lanky frame and the casual way he dressed, displaying a complete indifference to what he looked like, he would certainly not have won any prizes in the 'Mister World' competition, if that was such a thing. But there was something magical about his eyes, that dreamy Irish accent, his genteel manner, and above all else, the way he made her laugh and put her completely at ease whenever they were together. He included her, even when he was amongst his friends, unconcerned about what they may think; constantly considering her feelings above all else, regardless of what they were doing, or who they were with. No, other than that 'failure to commit' gene, which seemed to be more common than she had realised in men of his generation, that was where their similarities ended.

After initially speaking to Betty about the trip, Trudie began to rethink the whole plan. She had been careful not to mention Donal's suggestion of her flying over to Dublin a few days before the party for a spot of sightseeing, once she realised the invite had not been extended to Betty too. She had also sensed Betty still had some anxiety about flying alone, happily assuming Trudie would be sitting next to her on the flight to keep her company.

She was also considering the ideas Caroline and Betty had seeded in her mind about her potential feelings for Donal, or more specifically their conjecture about his feelings for her. She was worried about what she may be getting herself into. What if they did meet and it was a total disaster; both with their own expectations, just not aligned? Although that did not help, given that Trudie, until that point, had never had any expectations, or for that matter imagined Donal would have either.

What if there had been a massive misunderstanding, or embarrassment during their stay in Dublin, would she then have wanted to go onto the party, her tail between her legs, or make her way straight home? Realising it would undoubtedly be the latter, where would that leave her, or more importantly would she ever be able to face Betty again, knowing that Donal may have gone to the party, talking about his disastrous time in Dublin, laughing about her behind his back or to his friends? No, it would be a much better idea if they put off visiting Dublin until after the party. That way, she could test the waters first, and then only if she felt comfortable to arrange the finer details of their trip, then do so. It would also give her a clearer idea of the status of their relationship; whether it was friendship or something else that was on the agenda.

Trudie could not mention any of that to Donal, or risk scaring him off with her romantic notions. No, she would simply argue that with open ended flight tickets, she had more flexibility, adding that if Betty wanted to stay on with her family for a few days more than she had planned, she could easily hang around in Dublin until her friend was ready to fly back across the Atlantic.

Donal responded by saying that was a grand idea, adding he was flexible either way. One of the lads was going to manage the business whilst he and his parents were over in Liverpool, so there was no need for him to hurry back. In fact, he could help his mam with the mammoth task of getting his dad to the airport, and onto the flight if he travelled with his parents, because once again his dad could see no sense in coming all that way just for a party. After all, he told Trudie, "he didn't have one when he was seventy-five, so what was all the fuss about anyway?"

Connor sounded a real character, and if he was anything like his son, she was sure she would love him.

Chapter 55

Throughout April and May, as spring slowly turned into summer, Trudie managed to keep herself both busy and distracted, counting the weeks down until the date arrived for her trip to England. The fog she had been under during the early months of the year was now fully lifted and she felt on top of the world, happier than she had felt in years, both personally and professionally.

Josh had finally gone from her life, and other than the odd occasion when he had dropped some things off at her house, or bumped into her in the town, they had not spoken. He had eventually stopped messaging, and although there was an element of Trudie that missed him, her overall feeling was one of relief. Now, as she looked back, she realised that their time together had been lived on his terms for too long, and Trudie was under no illusion that life was too short to let that continue. No, she had her own life to lead, her own adventures to be had.

On the work front, she had continued to manage her shifts at the café alongside Millie, with her shifts at the hospital for Sister Cynthia. Her volunteering work at the hospital had become almost second nature to her by now, with her confidently dealing with patients and demonstrating all the right skills for her profession. So, as far as getting the experience for her CV that she had been looking for, taking the role had worked out well, leaving her assured that when the right job did come along, she would no longer have any qualms about applying for it.

The role Cynthia had mentioned at the end of the previous year, as a potential opportunity for Trudie, had sadly not materialised. The lady who had been planning on leaving the hospital and moving to another area of the country, had been forced to change her mind at the last minute, due to personal circumstances, Cynthia had told her, without breaking any confidences. Although Trudie had been a little disappointed, in the scheme of things, it was not a major concern for her. She was a firm believer in fate, so in her mind knew there was a reason she had not got it. The right role would come up eventually, she just had to be patient.

She had also focussed on learning to drive, completing a course of driving lessons, twice a week with a professional instructor. Uncle Scott had originally taken her out for an occasional drive in his car, confident he could at least teach her the basics, but once it was determined that he was perhaps not the most patient, or relaxed of teachers, his foot perpetually on the non-existent brake pedal, Trudie knew it was time to seek professional help. His nerves made Trudie nervous, and that was generally even before they had left the driveway, where Caroline insisted on watching over them as they drove away from the house, before she returned inside to anxiously await their homecoming.

With the right instruction, Trudie had taken to driving like a natural, wondering to herself why she had left it so long before taking lessons, especially as most of her friends had learnt before going to university. Having taken her test at the beginning of May, and passing first time, she was now enjoying the independence it gave her, to come and go as she pleased, no longer having to rely on asking Uncle Scott or Marcus for lifts, or cycling around on her aunt's trusty bike, always worrying whether the next storm cloud was heading in her direction.

She had treated herself to a sporty little red convertible, second-hand from the showroom where her uncle worked, and longed for the summer days, and the warm evenings when the roof would be off, and she could drive around the surrounding countryside, the wind rushing through her hair, and the freedom to go wherever she pleased. The only problem was, other than driving to work or visiting Betty, she did not have many places to go, or friends that lived locally to visit. Now that she and Josh were over, she really needed to work on her social life again, hopefully reconnecting with some of those school or university friends she had foolishly let drift, the more she had allowed herself to get absorbed into Josh's world.

"So, are you all ready for your holiday, have you got everything you need?" asked Caroline, late one afternoon, as Trudie sat in the kitchen checking her messages, whilst having a much-appreciated cup of tea and a slice of freshly baked banana loaf. She had been at the café all morning, and although her phone had buzzed several times with incoming messages, it had been too busy for her to read them. Other than a quick glance at the senders' names to ensure it was nothing urgent, she had decided to wait until she got home to go through them. Whittling them down now, and after deleting the spam and the adverts, it left four messages that were of interest.

The first, was from a hospital she had recently applied to. She had seen a vacancy advertised for a junior physiotherapist to join the hospital's busy physiotherapy department. It was looking for someone with Trudie's qualifications, adding some relevant experience would be beneficial. It sounded ideal, and mentally Trudie ticked all the boxes they were looking for. The downside was that the hospital was located roughly two hundred miles away from home, in the southern part of the state, around two to three hours' drive away. Cynthia had looked over the job specification with her, agreeing it sounded like the perfect role, adding it was also a great place to live. She knew the hospital personally, she advised Trudie, having lived and worked in the area herself, before moving north when her husband's role was relocated seven years previously; even offering to put a good word in for her if she was interested.

The idea of moving away from home had been something Trudie had been toying with for some time now, even the possibility of buying her own flat, but this was the first real opportunity that she had been excited enough to think seriously about. So, although she had been a little apprehensive, she had applied, keeping the news to herself for fear of getting either her aunt or uncle worried a moment earlier than was necessary. As with the previous role, if it was the one for her, then there would be no risks with her moving; it would clearly be meant to be. Now, opening up the email, and delighted to see an invitation to attend for interview the following week, just two days before she was due to travel to England, she realised she could not delay breaking the news to her aunt any longer.

The second message was from Hannah, an old friend from high school, who she had not seen in a couple of years. She had messaged to say she was in the area visiting her parents, and would love to meet up, if Trudie was not too busy that weekend. She and Hannah had remained friends, emailing regularly to each other, even after Hannah had moved to live in California with her husband and their three-year-old son. It would be good to catch up and share their news.

The third message was from Betty. She was excited to say that Matt and Jack were planning on coming over to Liverpool to meet the family, giving her an opportunity to introduce Brigid and Mick to their great-grandson. Matt had been in touch with his brother, Simon suggesting they could meet up, and hopefully rebuild some of the bridges they had allowed to crumble over the years. They were flying over the day after Betty's flight, directly into Heathrow, planning on visiting Simon first, then driving up to Liverpool later that week. Trudie had sensed Matt was a little unnerved after Betty had discovered her family, obviously wondering where that left him, so was glad he had taken the initiative to do something about it. Losing contact with family was often inevitable when life happened, but it was never too late to try to reconnect, as Betty would no doubt attest.

The final message was from Donal, who was now apparently counting down the days until the party, and her arrival into Liverpool. The message was quite chatty, without saying anything specific at the same time and it made her laugh. He recalled an incident with one of his customers, that had resulted in him ending up flat on his backside in a puddle of mud after he had responded to call-out at a farm, where some of their machinery was playing up. He had managed the repairs, but in the process of squeezing out of a tight gap, had tripped, ripped his jeans, ruined his boots and lost his dignity into the bargain. The farmer's wife had tried to assist him, although she ended up laughing too much to be of any use, he recounted.

Although they swapped news on a wide variety of issues, he had still not officially told her about his split from his girlfriend, and Trudie had been too polite to mention it, partly for fear that Betty might have got it wrong and raised her hopes unnecessarily. At the same time, she recognised she had not told him about her split from Josh either, so he probably thought she was still engaged. Oh well, too late to mention it now. At least it will give them both something to laugh about, or cry over when they finally got back together.

"Sorry, what did you say?" asked Trudie, realising that her aunt had spoken to her some moments ago when she had been distracted going through her emails and messages.

"I said, have you got everything ready for your holiday, or is there anything else you need to do? It's only ten days off now, isn't it?" repeated Caroline, aware her niece had been lost in her thoughts for some time.

"Yes, I think I've got everything, although I might need some help finding another outfit," she replied.

"I thought you'd already bought a nice dress for the party, and that the rest of your clothes were all sorted. So, what do you need to find another outfit for?" her aunt enquired, a little confused.

"Well, I've just received an invitation to attend a job interview next week, and I'll need to look my best..." she began, before taking a deep breath and explaining to Caroline what the interview might mean, and importantly where she would be moving to, assuming she was successful and offered the position.

Chapter 56

The day of the flight to Liverpool arrived, and both Betty and Trudie were excited at the prospect of the next few days, neither sure exactly what they would find on their arrival or when they would be returning home. Either way, they were relaxed at the prospect and looking forward to their trip. Betty was also pleased that Jack was coming over too, and had spoken to Matt the previous evening to ensure all their arrangements were now in place, giving him the address of where she was staying, so that he could get in touch when he drove up north.

Donal had arranged to pick them up from the airport, and then take Trudie to Colleen's house, where she would be staying, before driving Betty to her parents' house, where she had been offered a room, along with Donal and his parents, Connor and Ella, who were flying over for a few days. Betty had told Trudie that her parents lived in a big detached house on the outskirts of the city, an impressive property set in its own grounds, with an indoor swimming pool. "I've packed my bathing suit, just in case, and suggested Jack bring his trunks!" she had said when they had spoken a few days earlier about what they were taking and planning on wearing for the party.

Trudie had not wanted to be any trouble, and had offered to book herself a room in the hotel they had previously stayed at, even suggesting she would hire a car now that she had her licence and was able to drive herself around. Colleen would hear nothing of it.

"There's a spare bed at mine, so provided you don't mind sharing it with the cats, then why fork out for a hotel?" she had said, adding "apart from which, having some company around the house will be good, and as far as driving goes – this city is manic with all the traffic and roadworks going on, so I'd suggest you give that a miss, unless you're really desperate or mad!"

Brigid was now fully aware of the party, and was actively taking a role in planning it, Mick being unable to keep the secret from her for more than forty-eight hours, it had turned out. Knowing her husband so well, she had suspected there was something afoot, and with the right amount of pressure, had easily teased it out of him. Although Brigid had said she did not want any fuss, and regretted the expense of people having to travel, deep down she was really looking forward to getting everyone together again, and as far as her own expense was concerned, she was throwing everything at the party. Around seventy people had been invited, an eclectic mix of family and friends, old and new gathered over the years, including Helen, who she had stayed in contact with all these years.

There was a champagne reception planned at seven o'clock in the hotel's grounds - weather permitting, followed by a three-course dinner in one of their private ballrooms, with a band booked to play until midnight. It had been instructed by Brigid to mix the music up, asking for "enough of the classics for us 'oldies' to smooch along to, as well as some of 'that new stuff' for the youngsters to boogie to," adding that under no circumstances were they to play the music so loud that the guests could not hear themselves speak!

At seventy-five, she was pragmatic enough to know that putting things off was not the best plan, so if they were going to do anything, then they just needed to get on with it and do it right. "After all, what's the point of having all that money, and not being able to enjoy it with those you love?" she had asked Mick, when he saw the invoice for the cake she had ordered.

For Trudie, who had spent a chaotic few days before the flight, not only getting all her things in order for the holiday, but preparing for her job interview, her nerves not helped by the idea of the long drive to get to the hospital, the eventual flight over to England finally gave her some time to relax.

The thought of the interview itself had been quite unnerving. It was her first formal interview for some time, and the closer it got, the more she feared she would just freeze under the scrutiny, as she had with the previous roles she had applied for. She had no real understanding of what they would ask her, or what she would need to provide, so had turned to Cynthia for advice. Cynthia had not only helped prepare her for the types of questions she might receive, plus taught her some useful tips on technique, but had settled her nerves, reassuring her that she could easily do the role, so not to feel overawed by it. She just needed to relax; her qualifications were unquestionable, and her natural personality would speak for itself. "Any hospital would be lucky to have you on its staff," she had said, wishing her good luck, instinctively knowing her loss would be their gain.

The thought of the drive down was also something that had worried her. Two hundred miles of new roads to navigate. Until now, the extent of her driving had been quite restrained; pootling around town or meandering through the quiet country lanes, in her small convertible with the roof off, keeping well below the speed limit, just in case she needed to do an emergency stop. When she contemplated the journey to the interview, the traffic, as well as the busy roads, it suddenly felt daunting and too much for her.

"Why don't you book a small hotel close by the hospital, and stay over the night before?" suggested Caroline, now resigned to the fact that one day, sooner or later her niece would be leaving home, so she had better be supportive and not worry about it. "That way, you can break your journey up, as well as have a good breakfast before you set out for the hospital. It will be less stressful, and you won't have to worry about the time, or the traffic."   As the interview was at eleven o'clock, Trudie had been planning to leave home early, between six or seven in the morning, thereby ensuring she not only got there safely, but had time for a quick drink, or something to eat before the interview began. The last thing she wanted, was to pass out because she had not eaten, or worse still, have her stomach rumbling all through the interview, because she knew how off-putting that would be, for both her and the interviewer!

No, her aunt's suggestion was perfect, and had removed all that angst, and with Cynthia's help with her preparations, Trudie had entered the interview room as ready as she could be, her nerves managed and under control, and her tummy full.

The interview had gone well, and when she had got back to her car two hours later, Trudie felt pleased with herself, knowing she could not have done any better. It was now in the lap of the gods. She had surprised herself, answered all the questions with confidence and ease, and demonstrated all her practical skills when presented with a couple of scenarios by the practice nurse, whilst talking openly about the work she had done during her volunteering work, touching on the wide variety of cases she had been exposed to. The nurse, along with one of the hospital's business managers, who was supporting the interview, appeared to be impressed, frequently nodding and smiling at Trudie as she spoke.

As Trudie listened, the role they outlined sounded perfect, and the package they were offering was just what she was looking for. The hospital was not the newest of buildings, but it was centrally located, and the physiotherapy unit was modern and well equipped. The town even looked a nice place to live, and from the little she had seen of it the previous evening when she had arrived in time to do a recce and go out for a meal, there seemed to be a good mix of stores, bars and a lively social life on offer, if the groups of people wandering around was anything to go by. No, if she was lucky enough to be offered it, then she would bite their hands off.

"Ladies and Gentlemen, the captain has just switched on the seat-belts sign. We will shortly be arriving into Liverpool. Can I please ask you all to return to your seats, whilst we prepare the cabin for landing," the stewardess could be heard saying over the tannoy.

"Oh, that was a very short flight," said Betty, opening her eyes all of a sudden, the announcement appearing to wake her. "Are we there, already?" she asked, looking out of the window and seeing the cloudless skies beyond and the sea below.

"Yes, it's been a very smooth flight so far. I think you've managed to sleep through most of it, Betty," laughed Trudie, not sure that she needed to mention the gentle snoring that had been coming from her friend for the last fifteen minutes, or the strange looks from a few of the other passengers who were sitting nearby, and who had obviously been disturbed by the noise, unsure perhaps whether there was some technical problem with the small aircraft's mechanics. "And I think we've made good time. By my reckoning, we're probably about ten minutes ahead of schedule." The connection in Dublin Airport had gone smoothly, with their flight to Liverpool departing on time, thankfully, Trudie thought to herself, not wanting anything to mar their journey.

"Well, if we're early, we'll just have to get a coffee or something until Donal arrives. If I recall, there's a café, isn't there, where we met him and Colleen last time? We could always go there and wait."

"Yes, we can wait in Starbucks if he's not there," replied Trudie, although something in her water told her that he would be there and already waiting, possibly as anxious as she was about their meeting.

"Gosh, that's six months ago, where does time go?" added Betty, her mind wandering back to that first meeting with a member of her family; a family she had, over such a short period of time, not only come to know, but come to love.

Yes, six months, thought Trudie to herself, thinking how much had happened in both hers and Donal's lives since they had last met up too. Although they had messaged each other often and occasionally spoken on the phone, sharing their news and banter, who knew what meeting face-to-face again would feel like for either of them, or what the next few days would bring, in terms of how they would take their friendship forward?

With a smooth landing now behind them, all that was left to hope for was that the next few days would go as smoothly, with any clouds staying well and truly off the horizon.

Chapter 57

"Oh my, don't you look as pretty as a picture?" remarked Colleen as Trudie came down the stairs, wearing an evening gown, her hair styled in what Colleen's hairdresser had termed an up-do.

"Do you not think it's a bit over the top?" replied Trudie, feeling a little self-conscious with both her outfit and her hair, styled in a way that even she thought was a little too glamourous for a family party.

"No, I think it looks perfect, and you look absolutely stunning. I'm just glad Julie had time to do your hair, as I hadn't thought to mention it when I'd asked her to do mine. That style is very sophisticated, and certainly finishes off the outfit nicely," she smiled.

Brigid and Mick had decided that they would theme the party as a midsummer ball, inviting everyone to dress up and come in formal wear. For Trudie, who was more used to wearing jeans and a sweater, it had posed a bit of a challenge. In fact, the last time she had dressed up in a ballgown was for the function she had met Josh at all those years ago, and look where that had got her! On that occasion, she had worn taffeta, and recalled looking and feeling like a meringue.

This time, with the help of a very patient store assistant, she had found a full-length, midnight blue chiffon dress. It was worn off-the shoulder, and fitted in a way that accentuated her figure, but was not too tight. "It won't make you feel uncomfortable, or look like you've been squeezed into it," Caroline had commented encouragingly, when Trudie had tried on the dress. It was also lightweight, so practical for travelling, fitting easily into her suitcase, along with the diamante shoes and clutch bag the assistant had assured her were a must with 'that dress'.

"Thank you. And, you look lovely too, Colleen. I think your trouser suit is very stylish, and if I might say, very flattering on you."

"Why thank you. Yes, the thought of wearing a ballgown was too much for me. This seems to fit the bill, don't you think? I've decided that if they throw me out because I'm not wearing a frock, then I'll simply pinch a bottle of Prosecco, and grab a taxi home," she replied in a jovial manner. Colleen had a great sense of fun, and of the sisters, with the exception of Betty of course, Trudie found her the easiest to get along with. She did not take herself, or her surroundings too seriously, just enjoyed life and whatever it threw at her. And at only forty-eight, her view was that she had a lot of living still to do.

Hearing a car pull up outside, Colleen said, "Right, that sounds like our taxi. Shall we head on out, and see what the night brings?" grabbing her bag and wrap for her shoulders from the hall table. "You're sure you've got that spare key I gave you? Just in case we decide to come home at different times, or if I'm lucky, not at all," she asked Trudie. "You never know, tonight might be my lucky night, and the night I meet my handsome prince," she laughed, as she pulled the front door firmly behind her.

Twenty minutes later the two women were walking into the hotel where the party was being held, being directed towards a ballroom at the rear of the building.

On entering, they could see through the room to the double set of patio doors, where people were gathered outside, chatting and sipping champagne. Trudie could hear the gentle sound of a pianist playing somewhere, but where the sound was coming from was a mystery.

The room looked stunning and was beautifully laid out, with nine or ten round tables, each seating eight, a bar at one end of the room, and a dance floor at the other, where, by the looks of it, the band was setting up ready to play later in the evening. Donal had mentioned there would be dancing, even joking that if she did not mind him standing on her toes occasionally, he would be pleased to lead her around the floor for a quick foxtrot. It was said in a way that left Trudie questioning whether it was in jest or not, given she had no idea whether he could dance; she certainly had two left feet.

Since Donal had met them at the airport the day before, dropping her off at Colleen's house shortly afterwards, they had not really spoken, other than a quick text before bed to say good night, with the comment that for once it was nice that they were in the same time zone. It had become a bit of a standing joke between the two of them over the last few months that, whenever Donal texted, he needed to question the time, with him never mastering whether he was five hours ahead or behind.

At the airport, he had given both her and Betty a quick hug, nothing more than that, before leading them to the car and driving off. They had chatted on the journey, discussing the weather, the flight and the plans for the party, which he assured them everyone was excited about – well, perhaps not his dad, but everyone else at least.

Trudie had been completely unsure, and a little nervous if she was totally honest, about how Donal would react when they met again, conscious of perhaps reading too much into why he had invited her over, and mindful of what Betty and Caroline had said, building up her expectations that there was more going on than she imagined. But her mind was put at ease almost immediately, Donal's behaviour clearly indicating that there was nothing on his mind other than friendship. There was no edge to him or shyness, in fact nothing that was any different than the friend she had last said goodbye to six months earlier, and in a funny sort of way Trudie was fine with that.

"Hello, you two," said Mick, seeing them both standing in the doorway, simply looking around and taking everything in. Kissing Colleen on the cheek, he added, "Colleen, your mum's over there, talking with Helen and, Trudie, I believe Maeve, sorry Betty, is over there talking to the twins. I think Jamie and Ruby are desperate for a trip to New York next summer after they've finished their GCSEs, and I fear they're badgering her already," he laughed, completely relaxed.

"Thanks, Mick. I'm sure Betty would have no problem putting them up for a while, and they'd love it where we live, although it's not that close to Manhattan if that's what they're thinking. Thanks again for the invite, by the way, it's lovely to have been included."

"You're very welcome, young lady. Brigid and I can never repay you for the part you've played in reuniting us with Maeve, sorry, Betty. I really need to get used to her name now, don't I? If you only knew how many tears we've shed over the years at the loss we suffered. So, now to be brought back together again after all this time, well, it's simply amazing; and it's all down to you." At that he raised his glass and proposed a toast, "to you, Trudie Lewis, with our sincerest thanks. Enjoy your night," before kissing her and walking off to re-join his wife.

Trudie felt a little embarrassed at the attention his little speech had drawn, with a few onlookers now smiling in her direction, obviously making the connection as to who this beautiful young woman was, and therefore her link to the family. She thanked Mick anyway; it was lovely to feel included, but tonight was not her night, and she certainly did not want to do anything that would draw attention to herself.

"I think you've got a fan there," whispered Donal in her ear, appearing from nowhere and suddenly standing next to her. He was impeccably dressed in a dinner suit, wearing a black and silver dickie bow tie that didn't appear to sit too comfortably at his neck. "You look absolutely stunning by the way, if I'm allowed to say that?"

"You've not brushed up too badly yourself, although, here, let me straighten your tie. It looks like it's got a bit twisted." Trudie reached up to Donal's neck, feeling a strange fluttering sensation deep in the pit of her stomach as she touched his skin to release the collar.

"Is that better?" she asked, a little embarrassed at the reaction the touch had had, fearing her cheeks would probably be bright red by now.

"Perfect, now let's go and get you a drink, and find somewhere quiet to talk. We've not had a moment together since you arrived, and it will be good to have a catch up before we go into dinner. We need to start planning what we're going to do in Dublin," he said smiling at her, taking her hand without thinking. Donal skilfully led the way through the crowds, careful not to catch anyone's eye for fear of being stopped, over towards a waiter, who was expertly carrying a silver tray, laden with flutes of champagne. Relieving him of two glasses, he then guided her to a small table and sat down. They were both completely oblivious to the looks of some of the family who had watched them, or the smiles on the faces of both Colleen and Betty, who nodded sagely to each other with a knowing smile.

The gardens of the hotel were immaculate, and on this beautiful summer's evening, with the sun gradually setting, and the fairy lights twinkling in the trees, it felt truly magical. Trudie felt like a glamorous princess straight off a movie set; dressed in a gown fit to die for, her hair sophistically styled, a pair of sparkly shoes peeping out from under her dress, and as she looked round, everything felt so unreal she almost needed to pinch herself.

She also had a nervous excitement about the man sitting beside her; her mind vacillating between whether he would turn out to be her own Prince Charming, or just her new best friend.

Chapter 58

The following morning as Trudie woke around ten o'clock in the spare room of Colleen's house, a tabby cat curled at her feet, and the chiffon gown flung over the chair beside her, she began to re-live the previous evening, a smile not far from her lips. Was she imagining it, or had Donal kissed her as the clock struck midnight, whilst they were smooching to the final song of the evening, the floor still packed with a mix of family and friends who had managed to pace themselves and survive until the end?

It was not a passionate embrace, nor an out-and-out show of affection, simply a gentle, sensitive kiss on her neck that had sent her body into overdrive. She had not known how to react or respond, so had simply moved closer, tightened her grip around him and hoped her body told him what she wanted him to know. At the end of the dance, he had walked her to the taxi that she and Colleen had booked earlier, kissing them both on the cheek and simply saying to Trudie that he would see her tomorrow. It had all been very low key, very discreet, but 'nice'.

The whole evening had been like a fairy tale. The food had been excellent, the wine had flowed and the band had been outstanding, playing songs that had everyone on their feet from the outset. There had been a few tears along the way, particularly as the speeches were made and Brigid's cake was cut, Mick giving thanks for her life well lived, believing him and Brigid to have been blessed by the family and friendships they had made over the years.

Bobby had spoken on behalf of the family, wishing Brigid the happiest of birthdays ever, and telling her how beloved she was among them. Even Mary had a tear in her eyes, her normal reserve falling away as she and Dave danced along with the rest of the family, her usual indifference towards Betty parked for the evening as they chatted together like old friends.

From the moment they had sat down in the garden, to the point Trudie had climbed into the taxi, Donal had rarely left her side. He had been attentive to her throughout, ensuring she was introduced to his parents and other friends when the opportunity arose, otherwise steeling her away for himself, finding a quiet place to chat about their trip to Dublin or dragging her onto the dance floor, where to Trudie's amazement he turned out to be surprising light on his feet. He had made her laugh, never taking himself or his family too seriously, and had listened attentively when she had told him about her interview, and what a great prospect it was, even adding the fact that moving home was not a big issue, now that she was footloose and fancy free again.

He had gently taken her hand whenever he guided her around, and been courteous throughout, but the kiss had not happened until it was nearly time to go home, the dying moments of the last dance. It was almost as if he had built himself up for it; holding back throughout the evening, scared to go too soon, or risk what they had. Unsure perhaps until that point whether it was friendship or something stronger that he was feeling too.

"Good morning," Colleen smiled, as she opened the door and brought Trudie a strong mug of tea in. "I thought you might appreciate this, and there're some painkillers there if you need them. I've already taken mine, and am heading back to bed for an hour to sleep this headache off! You on the other hand, probably need to get up, as Donal is waiting for you downstairs in the kitchen. He turned up about ten minutes ago, and apparently wants to talk to you," she added, a knowing smile on her face.

"Oh, right," Trudie replied in a blind panic. "Can you please tell him I'll be down in five minutes." She looked in the dressing table mirror and almost screamed at the mess that reflected back at her. Her hair was still in the up-do, but now with strands escaping all over the place, part of it flattened from where she had been sleeping on it. Her face, still with last night's make up on, now well and truly smudged, with her eyes still puffy from the lack of sleep. And her head! OMG, now she moved it, she knew that perhaps the painkillers Colleen had left were not a bad idea, noticing after tasting the cup of builder's tea, her mouth felt like the proverbial 'bottom of a budgie's cage', her breath perhaps not the freshest it had ever been. "Perhaps you'd better make that ten!" she suggested to Colleen as she watched her exit the room, a wry smile on her face.

"Don't worry. I get the impression he'll wait," she replied, putting two and two together, and feeling quite smug that she had seen this coming.

Chapter 59

Three days later, on a bright Thursday morning, Donal and Trudie arrived at Liverpool's John Lennon Airport, ready to check in for their short flight over to Dublin, and their sightseeing trip. As they walked hand-in-hand to the check-in desk, Donal dragging Trudie's suitcase, whilst she carried their hand luggage, she could not believe her luck. The speed with which their friendship had developed into something a little more intense, was simply incredible. It was less than a week since she had landed in Liverpool, uncertain what those next few days would bring, and now, here she was, ready to jet off into the unknown with a man, who on paper was not her type at all. Simply incredible.

After Donal had arrived at Colleen's house, the morning after the night before, they had become almost inseparable. Donal arriving every morning around nine o'clock, to collect Trudie and take her out for breakfast, returning her safely to Colleen's before midnight each evening, after dinner and a few drinks. They had spent their days wandering around Liverpool, revisiting some of the friends and old haunts Donal had introduced her to over Christmas, as well as discovering new places to drive out to, now that the weather was warmer and the days longer.

Donal had hired a car, and they had driven along the coast to the seaside town of Southport, where he reminded her Mick had been born. Another day, they had driven further inland to Chester, a beautiful city, where they strolled through the streets, marvelling at the Tudor architecture, and climbing the medieval city walls. Wherever they went, they simply walked around aimlessly, happy to just be in each other's company, chatting away, holding hands and stealing the occasional kiss, whenever they felt that no-one was looking. Donal was the archetypal gentleman; unwilling to rush anything that might jeopardise their burgeoning relationship.

On one of their walks, Donal had admitted to Trudie how distraught he had felt after he had left her at the airport the previous Christmas. He knew she was returning to her life in the States, which clearly involved her fiancé Josh; with him going back home to Ireland, where his long-term girlfriend Shauna would be waiting, still full of the expectations she had for them, no doubt expecting that New Year proposal she had hinted at.

Those few days in Liverpool had really disorientated him. Not only discovering more about his family, and the newest members of it, but meeting Trudie and making a connection with her that he had simply not expected. His plans, once he had deposited Betty and Trudie at his cousin's house, had been simply to spend a few days boozing with his mates; a bit of male bonding.

Trudie had brought out a side of him that had long since been buried. A younger, more adventurous side, one that wanted to have some fun, not just get bogged down by running the family business, being the dutiful son. He knew he had no right to feel ungrateful for his life, but something about Trudie had sparked a reaction in him, that once he was back home had become impossible to dismiss. The result was it made him uncomfortable and awkward around people, his behaviour becoming uncharacteristically short and less tolerant; especially towards Shauna, who soon noticed the change in him.

Ella, his mam had also noticed the change in her son, wondering why he was 'mooning about' so much, unable to settle into doing anything, and looking like he had the weight of the world on his shoulders. One day when they were alone, she had questioned him about it, assuming incorrectly that he had got Shauna pregnant, and was worried about telling them, perhaps having to face a shotgun wedding, as some still believed was expected in the more rural areas of the country.

He had always been able to talk to his mam, and if he was honest welcomed the opportunity to open up about how he was feeling, particularly as it meant correcting her on something that could not be further from the truth! He knew his mam was the one person who would not judge him, and after discussing his feelings with her, he realised something needed to change in his life. Shauna was not necessarily holding him back, it was just her expectations were certainly not aligned to his, and the longer he allowed their relationship to continue, the more guilty he would be of leading her on.

In terms of anything else, or what other changes would need to be made, he had no clear idea what he wanted. He admitted that his feelings for Trudie at that stage were largely platonic, although tinged with a smattering of jealousy, if he was honest, at the thought of her going back to Josh and making up. She might have been the catalyst for him ending it with Shauna, but he had certainly not done so with any romantic notions of a rebound relationship, with Trudie as her replacement. No, his feelings for Trudie developed much more slowly; gradually becoming more real with each email they exchanged, each text they sent, each conversation late into the night. She was funny, independent, intelligent and had something about her that was attractive. Even then, Donal had no expectation that it would ever go any further than friendship.

It was only when the party was mooted, that the idea struck to invite her, coupled with the bold move on his part to suggest a few days in Dublin together. He was astounded when she agreed to it, and the knowledge that by then Josh was out of the picture, gave him the slightest glimmer of hope that their friendship could develop. The reality of it was only a pipe dream though, given she was not only beautiful, but so clearly out of his league! He knew he could make her laugh, whereas the thought that he could make her love him, in the way that he was starting to feel for her, well, that was almost laughable.

He managed to keep his feelings hidden, at the risk of scaring her off too soon, until the night of the party made it impossible for him anymore. To see her walk into the room, looking like a movie star, had been too much for him; and when he had got to hold her as they danced, his arms gently caressing her, he had been unable to contain himself. The kiss had not been planned, or the reaction to it expected, but it had triggered in them both something he could not have believed possible.

The following morning, he had gone round to Colleen's, with the intention of apologising and blaming it on the champagne if things got awkward. However, from the moment Trudie walked into the room, looking perhaps less glamorous than the night before, but even more beautiful, he knew there was no need to apologise. Her kiss told him everything he needed to know.

As they got out of the taxi, about to enter the hotel they had booked for their four-day break, Donal turned to Trudie, a concerned look on his face.

"Are you sure about the double room I've booked, because I can always ask them to make it two singles if it's too soon for you? I certainly don't want to put any pressure on you."

Taking him into her arms and kissing him passionately on the roadside, oblivious to all the stares from the passers-by, she simply answered, "what do you think?" as she bounded up the stairs to the hotel's lobby, a broad smile on her face, leaving Donal to worry about her luggage.

Sex had certainly not played any part in their relationship up until that date, but Trudie had a funny feeling that over the next four days, they would more than make up for their omission.

Chapter 60

"Now are you sure you'll be alright?" asked Trudie, sitting on the bed when she spoke to Betty the night before her flight home. She and Donal had spent four fantastic days and nights in Dublin, with heavy emphasis on the nights, Trudie smiled to herself, recalling how it was not just the weather that had got them both steamy. Now it was time to head home, and tonight was their last evening out, before she headed to the airport in time for her lunchtime flight, and Donal went back home, and to his business that had been put on the backburner for too long.

"Yes, I'll be fine dear. Matt and Jack are here with me now, and they're due to fly back in a couple of days. Matt's going to try to change my ticket, so that I can fly back with them, or find a date we can all travel back together if there's no seat available on their flight. So don't worry about me, just enjoy your last night with Donal, then get yourself home and concentrate on getting yourself ready for your new job."

"Thank you. Well, I'll ring you when I get settled and let you know how I get on."

"You'll be fine. Good luck anyway. I'm very proud of you," added Betty, realising how close she had become to Trudie over the last few months, almost in a maternal sort of way. "Right, I should go dear, because I can hear Jack calling. It's way past his bedtime, and I've got the strangest feeling he's not going to go up without a struggle. Mick has been really spoiling him these last few days, and Jack is lapping it up!"

"Okay. Well, take care." Trudie said, hanging up the phone.

"Is she alright?" Donal asked, emerging from the bathroom after his shower, wearing nothing more than a towel and a smile.

"Yes, she's fine. Matt's there and is sorting everything out regarding her flight, so there's nothing for me to worry about," before adding with a mischievous smile, "other than perhaps how late we're going to be for that table you've reserved," as she whipped the towel from him, and pulled him down onto the bed next to her.

Betty put down her phone and smiled to herself. It was funny how life turned out, she thought quite ruefully, and how things that you were so certain of at one stage, could change almost overnight.

It was now twelve months since she had lost Richard and Annie, and not a day went by when she did not think about either of them, or the lives they had so sadly missed out on. She thought about the plans she and Richard had made for their retirement, as well as the dreams Matt and Annie had shared for their son, and perhaps the other children that might have come along over time, God willing. All those dreams and aspirations simply changed on the flip of a coin, or as it turned out the careless trip on a wet sidewalk.

But for all the heartache that accident had involved, who could ever have imagined the direction her life, and the lives of so many other people, would have taken had that incident never occurred? How would fate have played out if that day they had driven home a different route, or if the rain had not been so bad, or they had left the station five minutes earlier, or even booked a taxi rather than arranging for their daughter to collect them? So many what ifs.

For certain, Richard and Annie would still be here, laughing and joking as usual. She would have her husband, her daughter and Jack would have his mom, Matt his wife. Life would surely have gone on, just with different adventures and experiences for all.

Instead, Betty was now enjoying a family she had never known existed; two loving parents, who wanted to make up for lost time, and cherish her in a way they were never allowed to as a baby. She had sisters, nieces, nephews, an uncle, even cousins – some of whom she still had to meet. Relationships now being built that would remain with her for the rest of her life.

Even after all her suffering, and there were certainly many dark moments in those early days when she did not want to go on, she had pulled through, or more precisely had been pulled through by two exceptional people, giving her the strength to carry on.

Matt, her son-in-law, despite his own suffering had been there for her; gently coaxing her back into life, supporting her in whatever way he could. He'd had his own grief to contend with, his own demons to fight; including having to bond with a son he had never felt particularly close to, but watching them over the last few days, happily playing together and relaxed in each other's company, she sensed that battle at least had been won. She also knew how vulnerable he had felt without his family around him; compounding his loneliness and sense of isolation. The fact he had reached out to his brother, Simon and his wife, Sara had been a massive step forward, ending a period of estrangement; and from the early positive signs, rebuilding their relationship. Matt had talked warmly about the welcome he had received from his brother and sister-in-law, pleased he had made the first step, and hopeful for their future. "Baby steps," he reminded Betty, was what he needed to take.

And Trudie. Well, where did she start regarding that remarkable young woman? She had not only helped her to walk again, and get her strength back, going well beyond her job description, but had provided emotional support, knowing her recovery was dependent on something much deeper than healing the physical injury itself. Above anything else, Trudie had been the catalyst for where she was today. Without her suggestion of creating a memory book for Jack, or her skills and tenacity when delving into Betty's history, where would any of them be? She was truly a remarkable woman; someone she was proud to call her friend, and whoever knows, if she and Donal got their act together, maybe one day even family?

She smiled at the small role she had played in bringing them together, recalling Donal's reaction the first time he had seen Trudie, in the airport all those months ago. Although he was meeting his cousin for the first time, his eyes had never left Trudie, and whilst she and Colleen had embraced, he had stood nervously by. Betty did not profess to know her cousin especially well in those early days, but equally she was not too old to see the signs of attraction, and the vibes, from what she could feel, were certainly positive. The way Donal behaved whenever Trudie was in the room, the way he created situations for them to be together, and the way she reacted to his attentions, all spoke volumes. Even if neither of them had cottoned on in those early days, she and Colleen were not stupid! No, they had just needed a gentle push, and the right circumstances for the magic to happen. All it took was a gentle word to her sister; leaving Colleen the task of suggesting to Donal that he might like to think about inviting her to the party, and then sit back and enjoy the fireworks!

Chapter 61

Five Months Later

It was the week before Christmas, and as Trudie took her afternoon break, sitting alone in the canteen, nursing a hot chocolate and gazing out of the hospital window, she was starting to feel homesick. The scene outside was truly magical, the perfect Christmas setting, with the pine trees still laden from the heavy overnight snowfall, and the bright winter sun just starting to set on the horizon; twinkly lights of the stores in the distance, and the car's headlights as they drove past all adding to the festive feel. But she was not feeling it at all.

Trudie was now almost five months into her new role at the hospital, having started the second week in July, a matter of only days after she had returned home from her trip to Dublin. She had received the email from the hospital when she was in Dublin with Donal, formally offering her the role, and proposing an earlier start date due to some staffing issues the hospital had. They assured her that they would provide whatever assistance she would need with any relocation, including finding a place to live, and asked for her to advise by return whether she would be taking up the position.

Trudie had been delighted with the offer, although anxious when she thought through all the organisation that would need to be done in such a short time. If she was honest, she had all but forgotten about the interview since leaving home, and now the email was forcing her into making a decision about her future. And that was making her nervous. On paper it sounded amazing, faced with the reality of it, it had become quite daunting.

Donal had been supportive, advising her to reach for her dreams, and not hold back on such a great opportunity, adding, from personal experience how she could live to regret it if she did not push herself. He still rued the day he had decided to return home after university; taking on the family business, instead of having the confidence to follow his own dreams. No, it was time to follow her own path, and to do the job she had trained so hard to do.

His advice had been sound, and although she was loving the role, recently she had started to miss her family and friends. She got on well with her colleagues, but there was no one she had really gelled with outside of work, meaning her evenings and weekends were a little flat. If she was truthful, she was lonely.

Today was not a good day as far as her mood was concerned. She had been planning on going home to see her aunt and uncle for the holidays, driving the following morning for a long-overdue two-week break, returning in the New Year. At the last minute, her holidays had been cancelled due to a virus that was spreading around the hospital, resulting in severe staff shortages, with people being called back in to fill the gaps.

She had phoned home to let them know about the change to her plans, and although Caroline had been understanding, it was obvious she was upset. Having not seen her niece for over two months, she was longing for a catch up, and the chance to spoil her again. Scott knew how much his wife found the house empty without Trudie around, and he too was upset with the change. It had not helped when Caroline had tried to lighten the mood, joking that it would be the second Christmas in a row Trudie had avoided helping to peel the vegetables, but rather than making her laugh, it had the opposite effect. Memories of the previous Christmas in Liverpool, and with that, memories of Donal immediately became reopened.

She had not seen him since he had dropped her off at the airport, recalling how they had clung to each other that one last time, before she had run to catch her flight; both promising that it was the start of their relationship, not the end. Neither had known what the future would hold, let alone how any relationship could stand a chance of survival with thousands of miles between them.

Sadly though, fate was to play its cruel part. Just two weeks after Donal returned home, his father, Connor had a serious fall down a steep flight of stairs, not only breaking several bones, but sustaining injuries from which he was unable to survive. He died five days later, the doctors being unable to do anything to save him. They advised Donal that there may have been some underlying condition that had gone unnoticed, and as Connor had not visited a doctor's surgery in over ten years, that was not surprising. For his age, he had felt fit, and although he had slowed down in recent years that was just due to his age, he had always assured anyone who asked after his health.

The shock had left the whole family reeling. Betty had taken it especially hard, having not really had the chance to get to know her uncle particularly well over the short time they had been together. She had said to Trudie, "to think, only two weeks before, we had danced at Brigid's party; all of us unaware of what lay around the corner. How cruel could life be?" the irony not being lost on her about the reflection on her own life.

Donal had rung to let Trudie know what had happened, and although she had offered to fly over for the funeral, he had insisted with her new job that she needed to stay and concentrate on that. He assured her he would be in touch as soon as he could, although with the funeral to arrange, the business to manage and the support his mother would need to sort out his father's estate, he did not know when that would be.

"I love you, and I wish I could be there for you," she had said, as she had listened to him sobbing on the other end of the line, helpless to do anything to console him. "I love you too," he had replied.

That had been nearly five months ago, and other than the occasional message, or late-night call, they had not managed to speak much. The time difference did not help, and neither did her shift pattern, or the fact Donal needed to put more hours in to the business to keep everything afloat. It seemed that the gods were definitely against their relationship going any further than it had. In fact, the last time she had properly spoken to him was two weeks ago, and other than a quick message to tell him about the prospect of her miserable Christmas now she was on call, there had been nothing.

"Oh well, break time over," Trudie said to herself as she picked up her cup and returned it to the tray of dirty crockery that stood in the corner or the canteen. "Let's go and see what delights this afternoon has left to offer." She smiled to herself, remembering as she made her way back to the ward, ready for her three o'clock appointment, that Mr Elmwood was her next client. He, with his dodgy hip and his even dodgier sense of humour, was certainly a character who could be relied upon to brighten up her day.

Chapter 62

At six o'clock, just as her shift had ended and Trudie was making her way along the corridor to the staff room to change out of her uniform, back into her jeans and woolly jumper, ready to brave the short walk home to her apartment, to enjoy the microwave meal for one she had planned, she felt her mobile vibrate in her pocket. They were not supposed to take private calls during their shifts, so Trudie switched her phone onto silent during the day to avoid any embarrassment.

Surprised to see it was Donal, she answered straight away. "Hello, there. It's lovely to hear from you. It's a bit late for calling, is everything okay?" she asked, concerned by the hour, although at the same time, knowing he had never mastered the five-hour time difference, not completely surprised.

"Yes, I'm fine. I'm just a bit cold sitting in the car outside the hospital," he replied, Trudie almost hearing his teeth chattering as he spoke.

"The hospital, why? What's the matter. Is your mam okay?" Trudie knew Ella had not taken her husband's death well, but she could not imagine what must have happened for Donal to be phoning her so late, and from the hospital's car park.

"Well, she was alright when I left home yesterday. So, as I've not heard from her since, I presume she's okay. Thanks for asking though," he replied, quite mischievously.

The penny had still not dropped for Trudie.

"I've just finished my shift, so shall I phone you when I get home, if you're still going to be up, that is?" she asked.

"Well, you could – or you could just hurry up and get changed. I've been waiting for at least the last hour, and I'm getting a little impatient now to see you, as well as fearing my extremities might be getting frost bitten," he laughed, unable to string her along any longer. "I'm outside now, staring at that ridiculous Christmas tree in the foyer, and watching everyone go by in case I missed you. So, please just hurry up and put me out of my misery," he pleaded.

Trudie almost sprinted to the staffroom, managing to get changed in record time and dashing out of the building in less than five minutes from putting the phone down. She could hardly believe that Donal was here, at her hospital, and not in Ireland as she had imagined!

Donal was standing by the car as she hurried towards him, conscious that running might see her flat on her back with the snow and ice that had settled throughout the day, and that would not be a pretty sight. As soon as she reached him, he scooped her up into his arms, saying "good surprise?" searching her eyes for her response.

"The best surprise ever. Why didn't you let me know you were coming?"

"I only decided a couple of days ago, after you'd messaged to say your holidays had been cancelled. You sounded so down, that I couldn't do anything other than jump on a plane." He smiled at her, pleased with the response his arrival had created.

"The ticket cost me an absolute fortune at the last minute," he joked, "but I think you're worth it!"

"Well, why don't we go back to my apartment and get you warmed up. If we stay out here much longer, you're going to get hypothermia," the grin on Trudie's face now so broad she could hardly speak.

Once they were in the car, Donal reached over into the back seat to retrieve a Dunkin Donuts bag, passing it directly to Trudie. "Here, I've brought you this," he said.

"Oh brilliant, I could do with a coffee and donut. I'm starved," she replied, opening the bag, surprised to find that rather than the warm drink she had expected, or even the sugary snack, in its place was a small red velvet box, with an ornate clasp on the top.

"What's this?" she asked, almost scared to open it.

"Well, it's something my mam mentioned I might want to bring along as a little Christmas gift," he replied quite sheepishly. "Apparently it's a family heirloom, handed down through her side of the family, and I'm supposed to give it to the woman I intend to marry, so I just wondered if you wanted to try it on for size."

"Is that what I think it is?" asked Trudie, amazed to see an antique solitaire diamond ring staring back at her when she had opened the box. "It's beautiful," she added taking the ring out of the box and holding it between her fingers.

"Here, let me," said Donal, taking the ring from her. "Do you want me to see if it fits?" the unspoken question in his eyes, as he took Trudie's left hand in his, and moved the ring slowly towards her third finger.

"If that's your way of proposing, then I suppose the answer is yes," she laughed, as the ring was slipped comfortably onto her finger, her grin stretching from ear to ear, as he reached over to kiss her. "I do love you," he said, before adding "now, we just need to figure out what to do next, don't we?"

"What do you mean?" asked Trudie, unsure precisely where his question was leading.

"Well, there's the small matter of where we're going to live, how I'm going to earn a living to support you, or how soon we can make this official, because I for one can't wait for the day when I can call you Mrs O'Malley."

"Oh, I'm sure they're only minor details, and we'll work them out in due course" Trudie laughed, reaching over to kiss him again. "For now, though, let's get you back to my apartment, and I'll see if that microwave meal I'd planned for my dinner can stretch for two."

As Donal put the car into drive, she smiled to herself. Rather than being the miserable Christmas she had anticipated, she now thought that perhaps this could even turn out to be the best one ever.

The End

Finding Home

When Amanda's father Ken dies suddenly, she is not only devastated, but is faced with a secret that he has kept to himself for over 25 years. Is she prepared to bury the secret with him, or should she follow his final wishes and see where it takes her?

Amanda has to decide whether to follow her head or her heart, knowing that neither way will be an easy journey nor without major consequences for herself and her family.

As the stakes get higher and the repercussions of her actions begin to impact those around her, not only does Amanda get in much deeper, but second chances begin to present themselves.

Is Amanda brave enough to embrace these chances, knowing the impact they could have, not only on her life but on those around her, will be significant? Do the difficult compromises and the risks involved justify her finding the happiness she seeks?

Finding Home is a heart-warming story spanning two continents of a family coming to terms with loss and of a woman facing life-changing decisions that question the fundamentals of her life, her family, her loves and above all where she calls home.

Angela Hartley

Forever Home

WHERE FAMILY
COMES FIRST

Forever Home is the sequel to Finding Home and picks up the story of Amanda Reynolds two years on. The intervening years have not been without their troubles for Amanda, leaving her fighting to keep her relationship alive and her family together; whilst at the same time focussing on building up the career she has grown to love.

When events from the past conspire to upset the delicate balance of her life, and tragedy strikes, Amanda must once again find a way to navigate her way through, calling on all the resources and support of her family and friends along the way.

But will it be enough to keep her family together, and where do you draw the line of what family really means? Can Amanda find the compassion she needs to open up her heart and her home, knowing the risks she must take in the process?

Forever Home is another heart-warming story from the author of Finding Home. It's full of all the characters you grew to love in the first novel, plus some newcomers.

Its fast-moving pace will mean this novel is as compelling as the first.

Download or order via Amazon.co.uk

Printed in Great Britain
by Amazon